Satyagraha

Story: Carl Bowen   Art: Melissa Uran   Lettering: Aileen E. Miles

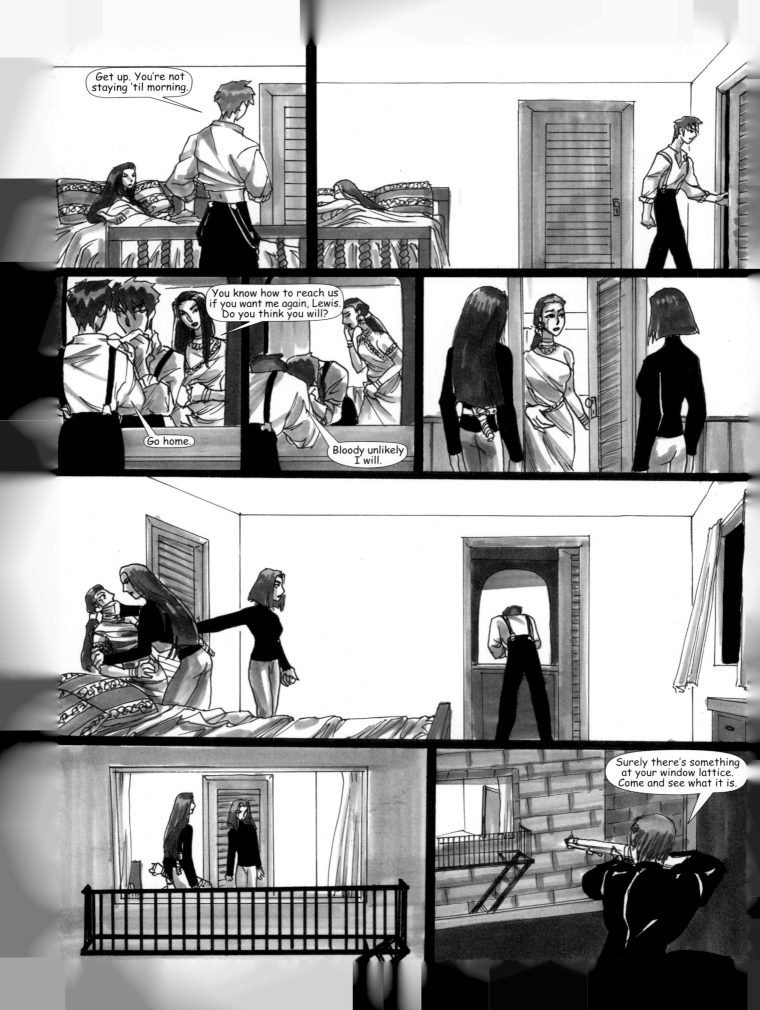

3

8

NAGAH™

The Kings Under the River

BY KRAIG BLACKWELDER, CARL BOWEN AND ETHAN SKEMP
WEREWOLF CREATED BY MARK REIN•HAGEN

Credits

Authors: Kraig Blackwelder, Carl Bowen and Ethan Skemp

Additional Herpetological Material: Nick Esposito

Werewolf and the **World of Darkness** created by Mark Rein•Hagen

Storyteller game system designed by Mark Rein•Hagen

Editor: Aileen E. Miles

Art Director: Aileen E. Miles

Art: Jeff Holt, Leif Jones, Steve Prescott, Alex Sheikman, Ron Spencer, Melissa Uran

Layout, Typesetting & Cover Design: Aileen E. Miles

Back Cover Art: Steve Prescott

Coming Soon for Werewolf...

BLACK FURIES

WHITE WOLF
GAME STUDIO

735 PARK NORTH BLVD.
SUITE 128
CLARKSTON, GA 30021
USA

NAGAH™

Contents

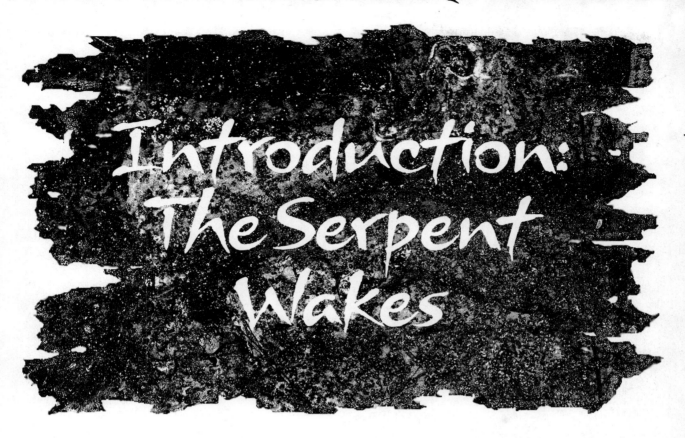

Introduction: The Serpent Wakes

"Who is Nag?" said he. "I am Nag. The great god Brahm
put his mark upon all our people when the first cobra spread his
hood to keep the sun off Brahm as he slept. Look, and be afraid!"
— Rudyard Kipling, "Rikki-Tikki-Tavi"

It would have been the most beautiful garden ever to grace the face of the Earth, if it were indeed on Earth. But it was not. It was perfection of the sort that no living garden with insects and worms could match, a home for brilliant rainbow-colored birds that fluttered from emerald tree to emerald tree. If one walked far enough, one would come to the great walls made of spirit stone, which stood like marble mountains against the shifting tides of the spirit world without. A visitor might even have come across the vast golden gates set about with carved dragons — but only if the lords beyond those gates wished it. It was Paradise, hemmed by monstrous walls and guarded by great spirit dragons.

And every visitor to come to this wondrous garden within the last year had always left with the same fear — the fear that they would live to see the walls tumble down.

Three Nagah sat by a fountain near the center of the garden, reclining on the pillowed benches and soft lawns shaded by a great palm tree. At first glance, an observer might presume that they were quite relaxed, even sleepy, from their casual posture and the quiet tones of their conversation — but the faint tension in their eyes and the slight edge to their voices gave a different impression.

One was a woman who wore her hair long and affected the casual dress of a traveler. Her smile was soft and gentle-seeming, although she was not smiling at the moment. The second was Chinese, or at least partially so; there was an indefinable cast to his features that hinted at some other heritage. He toyed with the jewel set upon his brow as he sat, staring past his colleagues into the garden. The last was lean and hard-eyed, and he wore his silken robe as if it were gang colors. And despite the tension that hung in the air between the three, it would be all but impossible to find three people closer to one another than the Nest of Night's Passage.

"We're the only ones in the garden," mused the woman. "It feels strange. Can we really be the only Nagah in all the world to call on the Sesha these past few days?"

The man with the jeweled brow dipped a hand into the fountain, sipped from his cupped hand, then wiped his hand on his breast. "I dare not think that we're really so few," he sighed, "but who can say? I hope it's not a poor omen."

"I hope so, too," she replied. "But the Sesha must sleep sometime, so perhaps it's not all that unusual." The third member of the nest simply grunted dismissively.

The woman gazed solemnly at the large velvet bag that lay on the ground between the three. "At least the old one's sleeping soundly. He deserves that much."

"Let it be, Sajita." This came from the steel-eyed third, who stared coolly at the sack as if it were full of manure. "You haven't convinced us that he deserves anything more than a swift bite and a swifter pulse of venom."

"May I remind you, Indra's Dart," said the other man, sitting up a little straighter, "that neither have you convinced us that we have seen enough evidence to merit a kill. That's why we're here a season ahead of our time."

"Even though it shames us," added Sajita softly.

"Yes." The Nagah called Indra's Dart shifted his position ever so slightly. "For once in our lives, we are deadlocked — a sorry state for us to be in, my nest. I argue for prudence. You argue for compassion. And Dragon Boat won't side with either of us."

"No, I won't." The Chinese Nagah didn't sound embarrassed. "You know me, Ind. If it were any other observer, any target, things would be different. But such a thing — we would be remiss not to bring a case such as this before the Sesha before closing it entirely."

"And I think that we are acting poorly by involving the Sesha at all. We are judges. We are executioners. We punish; we do not pardon unless the circumstances are unquestionably extraordinary."

"And these circumstances are not?" Sajita left off playing with her long hair, straightened and gazed back at Indra's Dart. "From all we can tell, he's no ordinary Khurah. He has lived over a century and a half — incredible, for his kind. His wisdom must be profound. He deserves a chance to live."

"You give the coyote far too much credit," replied Indra's Dart in a cooling tone. "His jaw hangs loose. Sooner or later, the wrong words are sure to roll off his tongue onto the floor, for anyone to find."

Somewhere above the tops of the trees, near the garden's vaulted ceiling, a chime softly rang. The three reflexively looked up, then met one another's gaze and rose as one. Indra's Dart lifted the velvet bag and hoisted it gently over one shoulder.

"Well, my nest," Dragon Boat said softly, "now we shall see."

And, that said, the three walked wordlessly into the Hall of the Sesha.

The Serpent People

Humanity has always had a particular dreadful fascination with the snake. Snakes are so unlike everything that a person might consider "normal" — they slither on their bellies rather than walking on legs, they're covered with smooth scales rather than fur or feathers, and they're eerily silent save for the occasional low hiss. They never blink; they taste the air with their tongues. They shed their skins regularly, seeming almost to gain new youth — and of course, some of them can kill just by biting a person once. To many cultures, they are either the most mystical creature in existence — or a personification of everything humans fear.

And in the World of Darkness, humanity has particular reason to fear or venerate the serpent (or both). For the World of Darkness has its own race of serpents that can shed their skins to take on human guise, creatures of great wisdom that can kill almost impossibly quickly and effortlessly.

The World of Darkness has the Nagah.

Who Are the Nagah?

Although serpent-shifters appear here and there in tales and legends around the world — particularly in India — to the rest of the Changing Breeds, the Nagah are nothing more than a historical footnote. As the tales have it, the wereserpents were hunted to extinction during the War of Rage, and few shapeshifters miss them. The few tales of the Nagah that survive paint them as cold, aloof creatures that had no discernable purpose in Gaia's plan — perhaps the most expendable casualty among the shapeshifter races.

But the tales are wrong on both counts. The Nagah were indeed given a purpose — and they are not extinct. And the children of Snake will do all in their power to make certain that the Garou Nation and the other Changing Breeds never discover otherwise.

When the world was young, the Nagah were given the task of watching the other Changing Breeds, to make certain that their cousins performed their jobs fairly and well. They had no need to reward those faithful to Gaia and their duties — those that did well found reward enough. But those who betrayed their duties, who abused the trust given them — these shapeshifters were the true targets of the Nagah. For the Nagah had been given venom — and their job was to punish.

Unfortunately, even the Nagah were not immune to corruption, and one of them fell to temptation at perhaps the worst possible time. As a result, the Nagah were unable to perform their duty sufficiently to prevent the War of Rage — and during the War of Rage, so many Nagah died that when the rest went into hiding, the other Changing Breeds were all too willing to believe the Nagah extinct.

However, the Nagah refused to let such a setback hinder the performance of their duty. They continued to silently monitor their shapeshifter cousins, marking those who betrayed their duties. Many of these criminals eventually met with a well-deserved fate at the claws of their own kind — but for those who seemed likely to escape justice, the Nagah were there.

The Nagah are not perfect. Even when they were at the height of their strength, they couldn't punish every lawbreaker or traitor. Many a shapeshifter has betrayed his ideals over the millennia and managed to live to laugh about it. In the World of Darkness, justice is not absolute. But the Nagah refuse to give up their duty; though it may seem hopeless, they will continue to avenge the most terrible sins until Apocalypse comes.

Cold and Warm Blood

The feel of a story focusing on Nagah is going to be quite different than one that focuses on werewolves. A pure **Werewolf** story contains a mix of explosive, frenzied violence and boundless spiritual variety. On the other hand, a Nagah story features violence of an entirely different sort — the coldly premeditated variety — and a limited supporting cast of spirits bound by a common theme.

The Nagah are consummate professionals — or, at least, that's the ideal they aspire to. A wise Nagah never allows his personal feelings to interfere with a mission; they are trained to make as few mistakes as possible, and to strike with superhuman speed and stealth.

But although the Nagah have trained themselves never to question the necessity of their deeds, they are not as cold as one might think. The wereserpents are well capable of joy and sorrow, anger and regret. From their constant association with death, the Nagah have learned to appreciate the immeasurable joys of life itself.

In this way, the Nagah are as flawed as any of the shapeshifters they have set themselves to police. They don't let their tempers get the better of them as often as do the Garou — but they also lack the werewolves' more beneficial passions and close relations with their Kin. Conversely, they aren't as cold and unemotional as the Ananasi — but this can cause difficulties in performing the task that defines their lives. The Nagah are compelled to strive for a perfection that is forever beyond their reach — and so they become a fascinating subject to explore in a roleplaying game.

Playing the Assassins

The demands of a Nagah character are relatively obvious, and certainly not to be ignored. First and foremost, Nagah are about the worst of all possible shapeshifter characters to try playing in mixed-group chronicles. If a Nagah joins a pack of Garou or other shapeshifters, that Nagah can expect hit squads of wereserpents several ranks above him and the rest of his pack coming to kill him and his friends as quickly as possible. As a race, they deliberately do not associate with any other supernaturals — at least, if there's any chance at all that their true identity might be revealed. This isn't as much of a problem in hengeyokai chronicles, but any Nagah in a hengeyokai sentai must still be as secretive as possible when dealing with anyone not directly of their court.

Another trait of the wereserpents that might put off some players is the Nagah's generally dispassionate air. Nagah burn with Rage, but it affects them differently. A Nagah doesn't have temper tantrums or histrionic crying jags; they don't wax poetic about their undying love for their mates or swear oaths of terrible vengeance. Playing a Nagah is an exercise in subtlety, which isn't for everyone.

So then, if some of the more elaborate pleasures of roleplaying are denied the wereserpents, why play a Nagah — or more to the point, a nest of Nagah — at all? The answer is

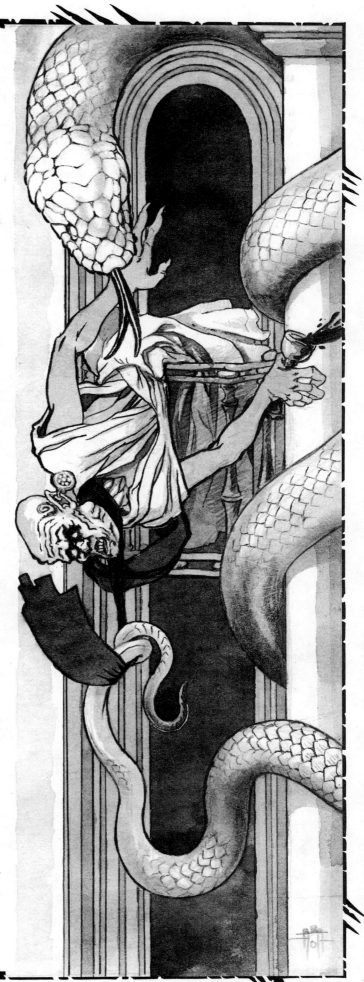

mystique. The same rules that forbid Nagah from indulging in casual associations and melodramatic soliloquies give the wereserpents an exotic, mysterious feel. "Cool" is an entirely subjective thing, but the Nagah certainly seem to fit the "playing by their own rules" tenet well enough for the label to fit.

What's more, because the Nagah don't associate with the other Changing Breeds, everything old can become new again. A group of Nagah players can enjoy the opportunity to look on the Garou Nation and all other shapeshifter races with a dispassionate, neutral eye. Because they are charged to *fairly* judge their targets, the Nagah can sometimes see the virtues (or sins) that others miss. Players who are used to the old stereotypes like "The Shadow Lords are all treacherous and untrustworthy" might see things in a totally new light as their Nagah characters are compelled to acknowledge a Shadow Lord target's devotion to the ideal of justice or passion for a wiser, stronger Garou Nation. Similarly, players who are used to the Corax being uniformly benevolent and cheery might find a new perspective as they judge a Corax whose muckraking and incendiary tactics have destroyed the lives of numerous innocents.

Finally, playing a Nagah can be a fascinating intellectual — and even emotional — exercise in balance. The Nagah champion balance as an ideal, which is excessively hard to do in the days since the Balance Wyrm's devolution into the Corrupter Wyrm. Excess in any one thing is something to be avoided, a tenet that can require constant discipline. The Nagah must balance bloodshed with preservation, the human world with the wilderness. This is a fairly philosophical approach to a roleplaying game, but that's not without its merits. In exploring the Nagah ideals, one even has the potential to learn something new about the way one sees the world.

How to Use This Book

Like the other books in the Changing Breed series, **Nagah** is aimed at both player and Storyteller. It's important to remember that, *particularly* in the case of Nagah, the mere existence of rules enabling one to create a character of a particular type is not the same thing as the inalienable right to play such a character in any chronicle one chooses. Nagah do not play well with others, and a Storyteller is more than within his rights to forbid Nagah characters in anything other than an all-Nagah chronicle if he so chooses. After all, the Nagah can make a game distinctly less than enjoyable for the players of non-Nagah characters.

But, that said, it's our hope that this book goes a long way to convince even the most recalcitrant players that an all-Nagah game is certainly worth the extra effort. The wereserpents may not be that suited for crossover chronicles, but a chronicle focusing on the assassins of the Changing Breeds can be about as intense and rewarding as you could ask.

Chapter One: The Great Epic details the history of the Nagah from their perspective, including their unique insight into the War of Rage and its beginnings.

Chapter Two: Coils Within Coils concerns itself with Nagah society, from their organization to their global distribution and opinions on other shapeshifters and even other supernatural groups. Although the Nagah don't organize themselves into septs, tribes or even any groups larger than three (save the Sesha), their cultural traditions are as rich as those of any other shapeshifter race, and they can be found wherever there's a need for them.

Chapter Three: The First Skin goes into the nitty-gritty of character creation and all the rules essential to crafting well-rounded Nagah personae. It contains details on all the traits peculiar to the wereserpents, as well as the game effects of their auspices, breeds, Gifts, rites and other tools of the trade.

Chapter Four: Songs of the Executioners is aimed squarely at the Storyteller. It deals with advice for meeting the challenges of running an all-Nagah game, or using Nagah in other sorts of chronicles.

Appendix One: Judges contains four Nagah templates (one of each auspice) suitable for immediate insertion into a chronicle, as well as a few legends of the greatest and most infamous Nagah ever to pass judgement.

Finally, **Appendix Two: Snakeskin** presents useful information on real-world snakes (particularly the venomous sort), all the better to accurately portray the other half of the Nagah's world.

Lexicon

Age of Kings: The legendary period of time during which the Nagah lived alongside humans more openly than any other shapeshifter since.

Ahi: Metis Nagah.

Ananta: The Umbral "den-realms" that the Nagah use; they are, unlike other den-realms, portable.

Apsa: A powerful Incarna of fresh running water such as rivers and streams. Equated by many Nagah with the Hindu "Ganga."

Azhi Dahaka: The "war form" form of the Nagah.

Balaram: "Homid"; balaram, lower-case, refers to the human-born breed, while Balaram, upper-case, refers to the human form.

Crown: One of the regional councils of Nagah.

Devi: Gaia; the Emerald Mother. In particular, refers to the "knowable" aspects of Gaia that can be expressed to others, rather than Gaia as a whole.

Jeweled Pools: Young Nagah argot for the Serpent Waters.

Jurlungur: The Crown that watches over Australia and the South Pacific.

Kali: The winter auspice, given to direct and efficient action.

Kali Dahaka: The "great serpent" of the Nagah.

Kamakshi: The spring auspice, inclined toward actions of renewal and healing.

Kamsa: The autumn auspice; prone to endeavors of a psychological bent.

Kartikeya: The summer auspice, Nagah of which tend to be the most outgoing of the race.

Khurah: Non-Nagah shapeshifters. The term has a connotation of "our charges" or "our wards."

Naginah: An archaic term for female Nagah. More common among Kinfolk "in the know" than among the Nagah themselves.

Nandana: The Ananta of the Sesha; the "divine garden" and first among Ananta that bears the gate to Xi Wang Chi.

Nemontana: The Crown of Nagah who have taken up the duties of judging Europe's shifter population.

Nest: The most basic social unit of the Nagah; a nomadic "pack" of two or three.

Samskara: Nagah rites.

Sannyasin: A Nagah renunciate.

Sayidi: The Crown overseeing sub-Saharan Africa's Nagah.

Serpent Waters: Aquatic Glens sanctified and claimed by the Nagah.

Sesha: The ruling council and highest body of government of the Nagah race.

Silkaram: The mostly human, partly reptile form of the Nagah; roughly equivalent to the Garou's Glabro.

Three Mothers, the: The spirits of Earth, Moon and River; more properly Gaia, Luna and Apsa.

Vasuki: The "cobra" form of the Nagah, although it may be that of any poisonous snake species.

Vritra: The Crown of Nagah that metes out judgement on India and Asia's shapeshifters.

Wani: The great dragon-spirits that serve as ultimate patrons to the Nagah, protecting their secrecy and teaching them Gifts. Also called "the Dragon Kings" and "Lu Long."

Xi Wang Chi: The Umbral realm of the Wani.

Yamilka: Serpent-folk of Arabian myth; a name assumed by the Nagah Crown who have taken it upon themselves to hold judgement over the Middle East and North Africa.

Zuzeka: The Crown that polices the Americas.

Recommended Inspiration

Films

Movies about assassins and hitmen are relatively easy to come by. The trick is finding the particularly worthwhile ones. A James Bond movie might serve as decent inspiration for a Nagah chronicle, but Bond's a little flippant and his villains usually fairly cartoony. *Pulp Fiction* is also an influential movie, but not that serpentine in mood.

The main difference between most of these movies and the Nagah way of doing things is that human assassins operate alone, and wereserpents don't have that luxury. Even so, they're still worth a look.

Ghost Dog: The Way of the Samurai — Although the title character doesn't really have the "Nagah look," this is nonetheless a great look at the life of a hitman who's very concerned with his personal code of honor. Also worth it for a couple of the more clever assassination techniques on display.

The Killer — Although there's plenty of dramatic license taken in this film, it's the John Woo/Chow Yun Fat collaboration that really started the Hong Kong action movie craze over here. A seminal movie that wound up influencing a lot of filmmakers.

La Femme Nikita — This film is a classic look at why a person can't treat assassination like a day job. The original film is recommended over the American version (*Point of No Return*) and the American TV series.

The Professional — This story of an immigrant hitman is particularly significant for its focus on the relationship between the title character and a young girl who winds up as his charge.

The Punisher — Just kidding.

Books & Comics

Ennis, Garth & John McCrea, *Hitman* — Although this DC comic series has come to an end, try to track down some of the compilations. The sense of humor may be more Ratkin than Nagah, but a number of ruminations on the assassin's code, sliding scales of morality and the value of real friends are buried under the whacked-out underworld figures and outrageous death scenes.

Koike, Kazuo & Goseki Kojima, *Lone Wolf and Cub* — These classic Japanese comics have thankfully been recently re-released in compilations. They follow the story of a ronin-turned-assassin and his child, and are a neat departure into historical settings. The glossary describing segments of feudal Japanese culture is an additional bonus.

Samura, Hiroaki, *Blade of the Immortal* — Like *Lone Wolf and Cub*, this is another samurai manga (also with compilations available), but one that delves into the fantastic — immortal assassins, freakish swordsmen and a recurring theme of justice versus revenge. Beautifully illustrated, and excellent characterization.

The *Ramayana* and *Mahabharata* — The biggest epics of Hindu culture, these are also incredibly ornate and a wonderful inspiration for Age of Kings chronicles. The William Buck adaptations (which aren't literal translations at all) quoted in this book are not as scholarly, but are much easier going for the Western reader.

Chapter One: The Great Epic

> *From underground rose four tall Nagas, like great cobras,*
> *the treasure guardians of Earth's riches; their hoods were flat out;*
> *they were hissing and weaving, swaying and spitting fire, turning*
> *their red eyes at the people; they were all dressed in jewels and*
> *rippling silver scales like moonlight on the ocean's waves at night.*
> *That opening widened, the serpents were one at each corner, and*
> *from below rose up a throne carved of stones, and wrought of*
> *roots and set with diamonds.*
>
> *On that throne sat Mother Earth.*
> — the *Ramayana* (William Buck retelling)

The Trial

The Nest of Night's Passage had stood in the Sesha's tribunal hall several times before, and each time the hall had changed slightly. This time, the hall was not unlike that of an ancient Chinese district magistrate — it was spacious, with a high ceiling, with a floor, walls and thick pillars all of polished wood. Very few decorations hung in the hall, apart from several inscriptions on the walls, quotations from the volumes of Nagah law.

The three Nagah, still carrying their burden, walked the length of the hall and finally knelt before a wide dais at the far wall. Upon the dais was a wide bench, a desk covered with scarlet brocade upon which rested a few writing implements and official seals. Behind the bench were the Sesha.

There were nine of them. Three sat on benches in human form; three, wearing their cobra skins, coiled in cushioned baskets hanging from the ceiling; the final three reared high in the massive coils of the Azhi Dahaka. Some wore modern clothes; others were draped in the finery of the courts of kings long dust. But above the head of each one of the nine, hanging in the soft air, shone a golden crown.

The nest knelt down on the hard floor, bowing their heads deeply before the nine before Indra's Dart set their captive before them. Then the three lifted their eyes again to the nine great Nagah before them. At a gesture from one of the three wearing the Balaram, the nest stood once more. Another of the nine, a long cobra with a wide hood, looked directly into the eyes of Sajita, who stood between her nestmates. A voice sounded in her head:

"Speak."

She bowed.

"Sesha, you have our deepest gratitude for granting this audience on such short notice.

"My nest and I will be brief. The concern we have brought to you may be found in the large velvet bag you see before you.

It contains an old and quite accomplished Nuwisha named Manyskins. My nest and I discovered him following us. We immediately attempted to capture him and discovered him to be a most clever opponent. After much effort, my nest and I succeeded in temporarily neutralizing him. Before resorting to the use of venom, we were able to determine that Manyskins had long been looking for evidence of the Nagah. It appears to be little more than intuition that led him to my nest and me, but once he began his investigation, our stealth tactics were not equal to his skills, a failure we shall strive never to replicate.

"Under most circumstances, assuming we were dealing with an honorable individual, we would simply congratulate him on his fine observations and draw the Veil of the Wani across his eyes and leave it at that. However, our repeated efforts to do so met with no success. In such an unusual case, we would be inclined to apologize to the worthy tracker for our own incompetence at redacting his memories and, sadly, kill him to maintain our secrecy. In this case, however, my nest and I have determined that it is not our place to judge this honorable Nuwisha man. Not only has he not transgressed against Devi, but his accomplishments are greater in Her eyes than are our own. He is a noble instance of an honorable people, favored both by his kind and by Devi. We are not the ones to determine his fate, and we feel that attempting to do so would be both unjust and incompetent. Therefore, we have brought him before you and — through you — the great Wani.

"As we are revealing our failings by asking for this formal intervention, my nest and I have prepared for our own hearing and judgment by you, Sesha."

She paused, bowed again. The nine Nagah of the Sesha made no reply, but Sajita thought she felt the silent pulsing of their thoughts brushing against one another. Several long seconds passed before one of the Nagah in the center uncoiled his massive form a little further, flared his hood as a human might clear his throat, and leveled his huge cobra head at the nest. His voice rumbled in the minds of the three like far-off thunder.

"It is rare that a nest as accomplished as your own must come to us to seek ruling." His coils shifted, almost restlessly. "It… distresses us, for we feel that you should have received such an education that a situation such as this would not arise. If you know our songs and our laws as you should, there should be no hesitation."

Dragon Boat bowed deeply. "My Sesha," he replied, "we do not believe our education to be at fault. It is our judgement that this instance is truly unique."

As Dragon Boat left off, Indra's Dart picked up almost instantly, as if speaking with the same breath. "If you would do us the honor of testing our education, Sesha, then you may determine where our failings lie and instruct us."

The three felt a rumble of satisfaction emanate from the great Azhi Dahaka. Dragon Boat almost smiled; they had answered correctly. It was rare that the Sesha called for such a test, but no Nagah was permitted to remain ignorant of the law; if the Sesha felt it was important to test a nest's knowledge from time to time, it was all the more incentive for each Nagah to learn the lore required of him.

One of the Balaram-form, a man in a neat suit, steepled his fingers and leaned forward ever so slightly.

"Begin, then."
Sajita took a step forward.
"At the beginning," she said.

• • •

My name is Sajita Jadavi. My father is of Indian blood and from the Kshatriya caste. My mother is British — Kinfolk, child of a Nagah who serves under the Nemontana. I was born Kali, and I serve my nest as a scholar.

This is what I know.

The First Times
Birth of the World

Listen —

There was a time when there was a Nothing that cannot be imagined. It was less than chill, less than darkness, less than void.

Into this primordial Nothing crept chaos, the Creator. Chaos was not Nothing — which made her Something, Anything and Everything — but beyond that, she was unbound by definition. For eons, all noise, all matter, all energy, all form swirled together in the first great storm, and everything arose a hundred thousand times, but nothing lasted for more than a moment because Chaos creates, but does not sustain or preserve.

After Time, Chaos spat forth a piece a part of Herself that had become self-aware. This part quickly learned to value pattern and form. For eons, it refined itself until it became he, until he became nothing *but* pattern and form. He could not create, but he could spin the stuff of Chaos into the smooth silk of Order. Where he moved through Chaos, he carved a swath of logic behind him, and the Preserver pulled solid ground from out of the storm of the Creator. For eons, the Preserver pulled potential from the storm-jammed belly of the Creator and created and refined his relentlessly orderly kingdoms.

This became a problem.

Space, while vast, has its limits. So long as the Creator created only ephemeral objects, there was no danger of running out of space. After eons of pure Order weaving pure Chaos into solid form, however, all space was full. There was not room for more to be created or formatted. The Preserver's loom itself was in danger of being crowded out by the excess.

Chaos, blissfully unburdened by any concern, continued churning out her ephemeral creations, and it happened that, for the first time, the creation of something caused something solid to cease being. The dance of Entropy began and the destroying talons of Time sank deeply into all that existed. By that act was the Destroyer born and it began moving in time to the rhythms, the patterned sounds, of the Preserver's mighty loom.

The Destroyer's dance negated all that it touched and caused even the simple passage of time to take a toll on all things. The Creator never particularly noticed, since her infinite forms faded within the tiniest fractions of a second anyway. The Preserver, on the other hand, being self-aware, was delighted. And horrified. His delight came from the vast open spaces that had been opened up for him to fill again; the horror arose at seeing the end of patterns he had created that had lasted for eons.

The Preserver was too busy creating Order from the Creator's Chaos to give the matter any more consideration. The Preserver was curious to see if he could shape patterns that the Destroyer's dance could not destroy, or, if not, if he could shape patterns that *could* shape patterns that the Destroyer could not destroy. In that moment was born innovation, and the world became much more interesting.

Over time, the Destroyer discovered another way of acting on the Preserver's creations: through random minute acts of destruction throughout a pattern, it could render the Preserver's creations imperfect, thereby bringing new randomness to the Preserver's work. While this shocked the Preserver and delighted the Destroyer, it was neither a good thing nor a bad thing. It just was.

The universe worked this way for eons, and during that time, the stability of the patterns established by the Preserver allowed life to flourish.

Devi, the Emerald Mother, wove Her tapestry of life in this sector of the Preserver's complex loom, and thereby established the world that we know.

Were it left at that, the world would be fine. It was not.

There were forms that the Preserver had made that it favored over others. Fancying himself quite clever, he made these more durable, in hopes that the Destroyer would not be able to harm them. That was folly. The Destroyer's ability to destroy is absolute. His dance brings an end to all things. It is his essence.

When the Destroyer had delivered even the Preserver's most durable artifacts into the well of oblivion, the Preserver fashioned a new thing called an emotion. That emotion was frustration. Frustration quickly degraded into yet another emotion — anger — and spurred the Preserver to generate an entirely new class of actions: revenge.

For eons, the Preserver had formatted Chaos, and by so doing, He had been able to control *everything that was*. The Creator could have done the same thing had she been less capricious, but she had not. Now, his absolute control had been challenged in a way that he found unacceptable. He was the Preserver. Control was his essence. If he wanted something to remain the same, it *must* remain the same. And thus he formed an optimistic suspicion: If he could shape and control the Creator's Chaos then there was no reason that he should not be able to control the Destroyer's Destruction....

...

It *could* have been right, Sesha. Had the universe been just slightly different. Had the Preserver not already collapsed possibility around that fundamental point, who's to say that Order could *not* harness Destruction to his will?

But he was not right.

When the Preserver attempted to format the Destroyer in his attempt to inflict Order on the Destroyer's dance, he performed an invalid act. Negative one has no square root; even the finest computer cannot divide by zero. It cannot be done. Just as the Preserver attempted to control the Destroyer, the Destroyer lashed out to destroy the Preserver's control over it. The two embraced for a millennial moment in a fundamental conflict too abstract for a sane mind to fathom.

What happens when an irresistible force meets an immovable object? In the world we've come to know, we say that such a thing can't happen, that something has to give.

That was not the case when the Preserver and Destroyer locked together. Neither could win, lose or freely disengage. The horror and cataclysmic upheaval that comes with that kind of struggle ultimately serves the Destroyer far more than it serves the Preserver. Not just kingdoms, Sesha, but worlds, whole galaxies collapsed in that conflict.

In the end, both the Preserver and the Destroyer were forced to rip themselves apart in order to be free of the other, thereby begetting two new, if slightly redundant forces.

The Destroyer gave rise to a stunted second self. Its dark reflection, the Corrupter, was incapable of properly destroying things, only twisting and corroding them. While the Destroyer could destroy the Corrupter, it suffered while it was joined with the Preserver; It now fears conflict with another fundamental principle. Together, the Destroyer and the Corrupter make up the entity known as the Wyrm. While the Destroyer attends to its work and clears away the old to make way for the new, the Corrupter twists and distorts, its goal being none other than to bring the whole of the universe to the point of its greatest degradation, death-in-life. Until the Destroyer develops the courage to destroy Its own foul reflection, the Kali Yuga, the age of destruction, can only grow worse.

The Preserver, on the other hand, was ripped into *at least* two reflections, some ancient cosmological treatises suggest three. The only two we have been able to discern are the Preserver and his dark reflection, the Trapper. The Preserver shapes and sustains the stuff of chaos, granting it duration. The Trapper, on the other hand — in his paranoid fear that the things he shapes will be destroyed — attempts to inflict absolute stasis on the things he touches, preventing them from growing or changing even in healthy, organic ways.

The Preserver and the Trapper, when taken together, form the force that most of the Khurah call the Weaver.

All of these forces have many faces, of course, and many legions of spirit servitors, but ultimately they are so far removed from us that we have no comprehension of them. Even talking about "the Preserver" or "the Wyrm" while trying to imagine their true immensity, we can only envision a fourteenth generation ramification of the true force.

That said, Sesha, unless I have said something that should be challenged, perhaps it's time to reduce our scope a bit and look at something a little more personal, like...

The Origins of the Nagah

When the Emerald Mother, sometimes called Devi, sometimes Gaia, formed the interconnected pattern of life, she created stewards to nurture those life forms with the greatest potential. She created her first Changing Children, the Mokolé, to keep track of the memory of those species she had created before — in part to see what worked and what didn't.

The surface of the Earth was verdant and teeming with life. The physical world and the ideal world of spirit were barely separated, if at all. The great ancestors of the Scaled Courts ruled the world and the great thundering Mokolé remembered all that had come before.

At this time, the greatest of the spirits were the Dragon Kings. In them was embodied the junction of phenomenal and animal spirits. Theirs was the fury of the great primal forces: volcanoes, earthquakes and, mostly, storms; theirs also were the ideals of the great lizards. When the titanic Dragon Kings visited the physical world, the ground shook with even their softest step. Those who pleased them were rewarded with great knowledge. Those who angered them were reduced to ash by their fiery breath or flattened with a casual flick of a tail. The world was orderly.

And then the conflict between the Preserver and Destroyer shook the universe to its foundation. Many worlds were destroyed outright. While the Earth was not destroyed, it was — to understate the point — catastrophically depopulated.

The dinosaur kings, whether through malice or by sheer karmic caprice, were gone. Some few members of the Scaled Courts remained, but the Furred Courts and the Feathered Courts arose and grew strong.

In time, the physical world found a new equilibrium.

Years later, Devi realized that the new face of the world required new Changing Breeds.

To maintain a natural order, and to keep subsequent children from misbehaving, Devi's first new children would be enforcers, stern older brothers to shepherd those races that would come after. Sun wanted to assign that task as well to his well-favored Mokolé — who better to oversee the young but the larger, older cousin? — but the Mokolé already felt burdened by the weight of Memory as it was. So Sun, protecting his only remaining child, determined that it absolutely must not be Mokolé after all.

The choices were limited. At that time, species were still recovering from the conflict between Preserver and Destroyer and there were not many suitably imposing animals to choose from.

Devi presented Sun with a great lizard with six legs for his blessings, but instead he said, "That's just a Mokolé with six legs."

Devi presented him with the giant Turtle and he said, "That's just a swimming Mokolé with a shell."

Then Devi presented them with Snake and he said, "Absolutely not. That's the most ludicrous animal I've ever seen. It's just a Mokolé without legs."

Devi was through asking Sun for his blessings. "My bringer of punishment will be the child of the serpent," she said. "Though it is not a Mokolé, it is like one, and it must be like the Mokolé, because the Mokolé are my memory.

Without memory, there is no knowledge of wrongs; with no knowledge of wrongs, there can be no proper judgment; without proper judgment, wrongs cannot be punished, and wrongs *must* be punished lest the entire world go awry. If you will not give your blessings to the Nagah, someone else will."

Sun was insulted. He looked at Snake again and remained nonplused. This small creature had no legs; it could be no farther from him without being underground. Without legs, it stood no chance of making any sort of decent enforcer of Devi's laws, and any blessings he gave it would be wasted. Sun left, and it was night.

In the deep shadows cast by Moon, who had appeared as soon as Sun departed, Snake quietly glided through the river looking for prey. Moon watched in delight as the stealthy legless one ate and then took shelter at the bottom of the river.

Devi saw Moon watching Snake and asked, "Will you bless the Nagah?"

Moon, more aware of her station than the Sun, nodded respectfully. While the Mokolé had enjoyed the blessings of both Sun and Moon, the Nagah would receive the blessings of only the night mother.

Moon had only seen Snake in the water, however and did not realize that Snake was a land creature as well. The Nagah's ability to enter the world of spirits only worked when the creature was in its water realm, or Ananta.

When Devi asked the other animal spirits to bless her new children, they beheld the humble snake and, following Sun's lead, withheld their blessings.

There was one other who offered blessings to the Nagah. River spoke to Devi saying, "I will grant the serpents succor and swear that they will never drown." So saying, she granted the Nagah the gift of breath within her waters.

No other spirits would honor the Nagah with gifts.

Without great Gifts, the Nagah could not serve their function well. Devi prepared to throw away the snake as a concept altogether when she heard the thunderous voice of Typhon, the great Dragon King of storms crackling from the sky. "Do not abandon this new child, for he is one of ours. We will give this humble one *our* blessings. It will need no others'."

With such assurances from the Dragon Kings, Devi retained the notion of Snake and kept the Nagah as her punishers. When the time came for them to learn Gifts and begin fulfilling their duties to the Emerald Mother, the first Nagah, blessed by the Three Mothers, entered the Dragon Realm and presented themselves before their terrible scaled patrons for instruction.

The High Dragons, the Wani themselves — part storm, part dragon — resided in enormous caverns or immense stone palaces in their realm of Xi Wang Chi. Great spirits of all ophidian, crocodilian and saurian descriptions attend the Dragon Queens and Kings, including Tiamat and Typhon, and our terrible foremothers, the scaled and punishing Furies. As the highest-ranking lords and ladies of the spirit world, the Dragon Kings are granted absolute respect. And in the presence of their esteemed children, they attentively give it as well.

Though you would know better than I, Sesha, I am led to understand that the Wani are creatures of both random, violent chaos and terrifying intellectual focus. By alternating one with the other, or by filtering one *through* the other, they can be most… awe-inspiring.

It was in Xi Wang Chi that the Dragon Kings first taught the Nagah to be venomous. The Serpent People were, and still are, taught that our venom is a badge of honor, the mark of our status as wise judges and lethal assassins. The most important thing a young Nagah learns after her first change is to never rely on venom. Doing so with any frequency is the sign of a sloppy assassin and leads to obvious patterns in the chain of dead Khurah that trails behind us, an egregious violation of protocol that the cleverer among our prey could piece together, with results that could best be termed… regrettable. The Wani gave us venom in recognition of our station as Devi's assassins, not as the primary tool of the execution of our duties.

The Dragon Kings taught the first Nagah well. That had its own drawbacks. There was so much to know that had to be always held in mind that the Memory of our forebears, the Mokolé, had to be given up. Nagah still have extraordinarily keen memories, but we have to. As the tenders, hunters, judges and executioners of the Khurah, we are obligated to know things about the other Breeds that they would kill us for in the twitch of an eye, including the names of the lost Breeds and some of the Bastet's great secrets. Most of us no longer have access to the deep pools of Memory that the Mokolé have, but where the transgressions of the Khurah are concerned, our memories are quite long indeed.

When the Nagah returned from Xi Wang Chi, nearly four thousand years ago. they settled for a while in the Indus Valley in the north of what is now called Bharat, or India. After cultivating Kinfolk, they spread across the face of the world in order to maintain watch over the Khurah. Our ancestors, when given the opportunity, congregated near water, rivers mostly, but, because they had to be, they were also found in the deserts, jungles, forests, swamps and plains. Wherever the Khurah operated, the Nagah had to be there to watch, to judge and to strike when needed to maintain order among the Changing Breeds.

The Impergium

When the Garou decided to keep the human population down by thinning the herd, they thought it was an idea that all Khurah would support. When only the Ratkin and Apis noticed their efforts, the Garou grew sullen and snide. It was not out of a sense of duty or responsibility to manage Devi's opus that they opted to keep the humans in their place — it clearly had nothing to do with their role as "the Warriors of Devi." I feel they did it out of malice, out of arrogance and because they enjoyed the sense of power it gave them over creatures that were weaker than they. Even then, when the world was still young, the Garou were the problem children among the shapeshifters. Had our insight been greater then, we would have observed a subtle Impergium of our own against the Garou. As it was, for every single rogue member of the other Changing Breeds that our ancestors were obligated to weed out — from *all the other Breeds combined*, Apis to Rokea — our ancestors had to execute nearly three Garou. And consensus among most nests today is that we should have been sterner judges. I cannot be telling you anything new, Sesha, when I say that Nagah nests speak constantly of it today in hushed tones: too many of our ancestors were lax and indulgent of the Garou's untempered arrogance.

We have concocted extenuating circumstances for their lack of insight as means of pardoning them. Soldiers are expected to die for their cause, and those who are willing to die in the defense of others have always been granted an extra measure of indulgence by those they're expected to die defending. The same phenomenon still plays out among soldiers in the modern world; it's called furlough or shore leave. The harshness of combat is reflected in the laxity shown, as well; the harsher the fight, the more lenient the authorities tend to be on the warriors. Our ancestors allowed the Garou a great degree of leeway before meting out punishment, and the other Fera and we have suffered for their mercy ever since.

In hindsight we feel the pattern should have been obvious and therefore preventable. Garou lords, fresh from some great battle, would grow hostile, cruel, drunk on their own power. The minions of the Corrupter were relatively rare in those days, leaving the Garou with too much time on their bloody hands. When the Wolves grew bored, Devi's other creatures made easy targets. In time, small infractions became larger infractions and the transgressions of the leaders diffused throughout their packs and from there through their tribes. The Nagah of some regions were clearly more aggressive in monitoring their charges than were their peers. The Nagah of Africa and the Pure Lands were much stricter in their adherence to their dharmic obligations than their counterparts in Europe. There was no Sesha yet and, consequently, no way of setting standards by which all Nagah could judge the Khurah's infractions. It was supposed to be intuitive, but, as often as not, it wasn't.

Watching the Khurah was not all our ancestors did. The wereserpents' obligations rarely brought them into conflict with humans, giving the Serpent People greater leeway to interact with them constructively. The Nagah's interest in dance and art began early. Every culture in which we had Kinfolk developed drumming, and from drumming came music and from music came dance. Describing themselves as the Dancers of Devi was initially a joke among the Serpent People, but when inquiring Khurah came around asking inappropriate questions, it became the common answer. At no point has the Nagah's true function among the Khurah been made explicit, but some of the craftier among them — the Camazotz and the Mokolé for certain, possibly the Corax — probably put two and two together. These days it's only the hengeyokai who even know we're

An Opposing Viewpoint

Sesha, it's very easy to condemn the Garou for the Impergium, and to say that we were kept very busy slaying them for betraying their duty. I believe my nestmate finds it a little harder to admit that the Impergium was not a betrayal of the Garou's role of warriors any more than a Mokolé's fight against Devi's enemies is a betrayal of his role as a rememberer. Did the werewolves abandon the war on Devi's foes? Did they make war on the wrong targets? No. They culled a herd, just as clever humans today cull the herds of deer to prevent the deer from starving.

The sin *I* see is not that the Garou began the Impergium, but that they did not let the Ratkin assist them. Had the Garou and Ratkin cooperated instead of slaying one another, then perhaps we would still have cities and medicine and art, but not quite so many people choking the world. I am no champion of the Garou race, but to call the Impergium the beginning of all ills seems to me the judgement of a modern person with modern sensibilities.

So did our ancestors truly punish quite as many as my nestmate claims? I'm certain *I* don't know. I wasn't there.

— Indra's Dart

alive, and as long as they're content not to broadcast that fact or confront us about our role in Devi's tapestry, we're content to let them live with their little secret.

During the Impergium, the Nagah interacted peacefully with humans more often than any other Breed except for the Apis, a situation that benefited all involved. Though thinning the human herd was properly the task of the Ratkin, the Garou made it their own. And… my nestmate does make a strong point. Except for particularly gruesome excesses, which probably indicated the Corrupter's influence anyway, it was not the Nagah's place to interfere with the Impergium. It was and still is the role of predators to moderate populations of prey animals, and humans hadn't yet ceased being prey. We did, from time to time, punish those Wolves who committed atrocities against the human tribes, particularly if those tribes contained Nagah Kinfolk. Beyond that, we paid little or no attention to the Impergium.

Most curiously, though our serpent Kinfolk have frightened them for millennia, proper Nagah have little history of terrorizing humans. It makes me wonder why the Delirium comes on those who view our Azhi Dahaka form — it is seemingly some great ancestral memory, but from where does it spring?

The Age of Kings

Ultimately, it was our peaceful and open coexistence with human communities in India that resulted in what we can only call the Nagah Golden Age. As much as some of the Khurah, notably the Garou, scorned us for doing it, most modern Nagah have come to feel that it was precisely what our ancestors *ought* to have been doing. Many Nagah still resided in the wild, outside cities, but a large percentage of our ancestors welcomed the interaction with humans, many of whom had a great deal to share with us, particularly their assorted arts and other cultural elements. It was also an effective way to monitor the Apis, Ratkin and Garou.

Throughout India, the Nagah were open about what they were. Our ancestors shifted form before their chosen associates without shame or fear, and so we entered human legend as wise teachers, spiritual guides and intermediaries to the spirits. I have heard that as the Hindus adopted their caste system, Nagah were automatically assumed into the highest two castes: the Brahmin priests and the Kshatriya warriors. Our real concerted move into the circles of power had to wait for the guidance of Silappadikaram, whom I shall discuss presently.

Other shapeshifters, most particularly the Garou, were openly dismissive of our gracious participation in the developing human culture. We were accused of abandoning Gaia and our serpent Kinfolk, neither of which was true. Our ancestors never forgot or abandoned their duties to the Emerald Mother, and our cobra Kinfolk in India were revered just as we were. There was no conflict of interest as there may have been for Ratkin or Garou living in a similar manner. It was always the Garou who went out of their way to tell us what contempt they held us in for taking advantage of the comforts of civilization. They called us, among other things, Weaverlovers, which was ludicrous. With a single, reviled, exception, the Serpent People have always taken pains to revere the true Triat of the Creator, Preserver and Destroyer while ignoring the dark reflections of the Corrupter and the Trapper.

Once more our function among the shapeshifters became an issue as the Garou and certain members of the other Changing Breeds tried to accuse us of dereliction of our duties… and promptly realized they had no idea what our duties to Devi were. Were we really the dancers of Devi? The artists of Devi? Devi's temple prostitutes? There were Khurah who believed all of those things, but ultimately they had to concede that they did not know. They couldn't ask the spirits, because the spirits had little to do with us unless commanded to do so by the Wani. Those Khurah who had the effrontery to ask the Wani about our business were either rebuffed and rained upon or blasted to cinders, depending on the mood of the Dragon Kings and the tone of the inquiry. Our cousins the Mokolé knew that we did not perform the same task as they, and they may have been wise enough to figure out what it was we were doing. They at least had the good form not to wonder aloud.

Kala

The first Nagah, those who had gone to Xi Wang Chi to study with the Dragon Kings, had unofficially adopted as their leader Kala, the favored of the Wani. It was he who led them in consolidating their place among the people of the Indus Valley.

Kala was, and still is, considered one of the wisest and most highly skilled Nagah ever to have been given to us by the Three Mothers. Under the tutelage of the Wani, Kala had distinguished himself as a cunning tactician, a potent mystic and an excellent assassin. When the Nagah returned from the realm of the Dragon Kings, they all looked upon Kala as a leader, which, according to legend, he found frustrating. If other Nagah came to him for advice, he would give it, but he did everything in his power to avoid becoming that which he is called to this day: the King of the Nagah.

Kala is a cultural hero of the Serpent People. His legends, while fantastic, have a ring of truth to them that Nagah find deeply inspirational. Over the course of his enormously extended life, Kala judged many Khurah, sparing those whose potential outstripped the magnitude of their transgression and killing the rest as compassionately as possible. He was also an ardent foe of the rakshasa, the illusion-using demons that infested India and many Kala tales are accounts of the clever ways in which he vanquished his enemies by seeing through their subterfuge.

While there are no tales of Kala's death, it is recorded that he left civilization and became a *sannyasin*, a renunciate, shortly after the invasion of India by Alexander the Great. There are some Nagah who like to think that he was called back to Xi Wang Chi where the Dragon Kings made him one of their lieutenants, but most feel it likely that he either died in the War of Rage or just returned to Devi's cycle naturally.

Whatever else he may have done, Sesha, Kala established a precedent among the Nagah of acknowledging one of their own as a de facto ruler. King really is too strong a word, but it's the simplest and conveys the notion of someone that oversees and guides. The Nagah King never *ruled*, *per se*; it was always much more subtle than that — more like *suggested*. The Nagah King was more a gray eminence who, rather than dictate his will, nudged events toward certain outcomes. Those same strategies of statecraft later came to number among the Nagah's most powerful tools in the execution of their obligations to Devi.

Kala was far too busy judging Devi's enemies — and becoming a legend thereby — to play the role of the Nagah King for more than the first few decades and thus a great deal of early Nagah history became the responsibility of his "successor."

Silappadikaram

The Nagah King's de facto abdication opened the way for a new force to guide the Serpent People, and the new Nagah King epitomized his people's character in ways that even the great Kala never did. Silappadikaram was a sensualist, a dancer and a manipulator par excellence; more importantly, he had a clear vision of where he wanted to take his people.

The Serpent People are a sensual race, and have been from our very inception — it is one of the blessings of the River Mother who taught us to enjoy the feel of the river sliding over our scales as we glided through the water. That had always been a pleasing and enjoyable fact of life for our kind, but it had never been particularly important otherwise. Silappadikaram, being a master strategist, was keen on turning all of the Nagah's native inclinations into strengths that could be used to our benefit. At their new king's suggestion, our ancestors began using dance, poetry and other arts as ways of shaping their own destiny among the humans in whose midst they so frequently lived. By mastering, and subsequently teaching, their culture's arts and body of knowledge, the Nagah were able to, in many ways, take charge of that culture. Thus, in India we taught dance and created the discipline of Yoga.

From there it was a very short leap to charming and marrying into the existing power structure of whatever place we were in.

According to Silappadikaram — and I believe this is fact, not just prejudice, Sesha — the Three Mothers had made the Nagah stronger, wiser and more knowledgeable than humans for many reasons, not the least of which was to help guide the human race to greater enlightenment and sophistication and correspondingly less barbarism. It is, consequently, the duty of the Serpent People to gravitate toward the highest positions of leadership in any human society in which they live.

Given that such leadership positions also typically came with the additional benefits of comfort and a relatively sumptuous standard of living, it wasn't hard to convince the Nagah to charm their way into the bedrooms, staterooms and halls of power. The Nagah were already members of India's highest castes — the Brahmin, who mastered and transmitted the Vedas and associated ritual practices and the Kshatriya, the masters of weapons and statecraft — and from there they rapidly incorporated themselves into the country's royal power structure.

It was a resounding success. Under the guidance of the Nagah, the Indus Valley civilization became a thriving nation at the center of important trade routes. Silk, gold, perfume and rare spices passed through India, many of them winding up in the hands of Nagah royalty, who knew how to appreciate such finery. In the course of three generations, not only was the Azhi Dahaka form an essential sign of royalty throughout India, but also being Nagah Kinfolk became a sign of good breeding. For centuries — until the War of Rage, in fact — wherever the Nagah went the symbol of the serpent (or dragon, in areas where the serpent seemed too… humble) became the symbol of wisdom, sophistication and leadership.

There were times during the Age of Kings when the Nagah, because of their roles as kings, came into conflict with the Ratkin. The Rat Folk would feel the need to thin the human population, the human population would look to its rulers for help and the rulers, almost always Nagah at that time, would be put in an awkward position. The Ratkin were not ignoring their obligation to Devi, but, on the contrary, fulfilling it. While nothing resembling open hostilities ever broke out between our ancestors and the Rat People — not in India, in any case — I feel it's safe to say that Ratkin who brought plagues or famine too frequently to populations ruled by Nagah were frequently judged… harshly. While I do not believe our ancestors' twin obligations to Devi and to their people ever resulted in clearly unethical behavior, the appearance of impropriety is at least as problematic as impropriety itself. That fact has generated resentments that have effectively kept us from ever growing close to the Rat People.

While the Nagah were inclined to do everything in their power to repel the Ratkin, the temptation with the Apis was to do the opposite. The Apis, commonly called the matchmakers of Devi, watched over the human population and made sure that romance resulted in proper couplings and, subsequently, appropriate family bonds. Clearly, those communities tended by the Apis were healthier than those that were not and, as kings of humans and judges of Khurah, powerful motivation existed to ignore infractions on the part of an Apis as long as it was performing its duties well in the Nagah's kingdom. What our ancestors' exact relationship with the Apis was is unknown. Given that the Auroch People were entirely wiped out by the Garou during the War of Rage, the point is moot.

The Age of Kings, while clearly advantageous for our forebears in many ways, required much of their self-discipline. Historical accounts of the time, written by our ancestors in Sanskrit, tell us that they refused to shirk either duty, to Devi or to those they ruled. While the lives of most of the Khurah were relatively simple at the time, many Nagah attended to matters of state by day and slipped away in the river to attend to shapeshifter matters by night. It was as draining as it was rewarding. Sesha, how could it have been otherwise?

The Exodus

At the peak of the Age of Kings, there were more kings than there were kingdoms. Silappadikaram announced that there was to be an exodus from Bharat. Our fellow Khurah were scattered across the globe, and if we were to fulfill our obligations to the Three Mothers, then we had to be where they were as well. Just as the Nagah had become kings in India, so were there other lands that called out for our wise guidance.

Some believe that Silappadikaram called for this exodus primarily for strategic reasons — having so many Nagah clustered in one place could have been catastrophic under certain circumstances. But there were many reasons why it needed to happen, the foremost among them being proper performance of our duties as judges and assassins.

Many small Nagah kingdoms became fewer, but larger Nagah kingdoms and the Serpent People, slowly began leaving their home, traveling both by land and by ocean. Many settled in the Middle East, where they established the Yamilka and battled with the Persian sand wizards and their djinn servants. Others found Egypt and availed themselves of its advanced culture and beautiful river; I understand that many of our people became fast friends with the others there. Others made it to Crete, where civilization was thriving already, although they found Garou there in large numbers.

The most adventurous of our kind took to the oceans, ultimately finding themselves as far away as Australia and the Pure Lands.

Surprisingly large numbers of our kind found their way to England and Ireland. They could not be as open as they had been in Bharat, but they thrived there, incorporating themselves — where the Garou would let them — into royal houses. While England had nowhere near the level of civilization that India had attained at the time, our ancestors took up the challenge. Before the War of Rage, there were several kings and queens of Ireland, Scotland, England and Wales that were Kinfolk. The black hair and green eyes of the Welsh and Black Irish are still there as visible remnants of Nagah blood.

The exodus was, all things considered, quite successful. The proud Serpent People dispersed throughout the world with relative success and found viable Kinfolk almost everywhere they went. Our ancestors considered it a time of great promise. What Silappadikaram could not have foreseen, however, was the catastrophic timing of the emigration. The population of Indian Nagah was reduced to a fraction of its prior size and the wereserpents who had scattered outward never had time to establish significant numbers in their newfound homes before suffering from the trials to come. They had gone from being almost common in India to being thinly spread across the globe, and therein lay our undoing, because not more than a handful of centuries later came…

The War of Rage

Sesha, I admit that my learning is imperfect here. According to many of our own legends, the War of Rage came well after the Impergium, when human civilization was in full flower. According to the tales of many Khurah, the War of Rage was a thing that happened not long after the Impergium's end, before there was an Egypt and a Sparta. I cannot reconcile the stories — I can only presume that the war was not like human wars that begin and end with proclamations, but more like the war of the Garou that has raged since the world's dawn and never yet ended.

Here is the story I know:

When the raging Wolves came swarming into Bharat, the Nagah Golden Age arrived at its abrupt conclusion. In India, the Khan, the Makara Mokolé, a handful of Apis and Camazotz and even human armies under the direction of the Nagah Kshatriya largely repelled the indignant Garou. The Apis, Camazotz and Ratkin, though they were determined fighters, were not on par with the Garou's martial prowess; they suffered enormous losses early on and never recovered. The Khan, Mokolé and Nagah, however, were at least somewhat more enduring. We made the werewolves suffer for every life they took in our land. Though our numbers were decimated, we had driven back the Wolves. In India, it felt as though we'd won the War of Rage, or at least weathered it relatively well. That was the only thing we had to hold on to. Everywhere else, the Serpent People had been savaged, ravaged and slain by the marauding Garou.

Or they had gone into hiding. Water hides us well. Garou fancy themselves matches for any of us, and on land, in a one-on-one, face to face fight, if we're cornered and our venom is spent, they might well be. But even a pack of experienced Garou is taking its collective life in its own hands if it enters our Ananta, one hundred feet below the water's surface, while even one of us, no less a nest, quietly awaits them in Azhi Dahaka form with full venom sacs. At this stage, however, I suppose such consolations are moot. Our ancestors died in the War of Rage, and they died *en masse*.

Once the war began in earnest, there was little that could be done to salvage the situation. Ironically, we were obligated to punish the Garou's arrogance, but once they arrayed themselves against all the other shapeshifters, we could not act from stealth, the place of our strength, any more. Punishing or executing one corrupt individual — even if that individual is a powerful Garou — is not difficult for a Nagah. It is, after all, what we're made for. We have, for lifetimes, studied the arts required to take down a target directly or indirectly. A significant portion of what the Nagah were created to do involves stealthily eliminating corrupt Khurah while creating neither waves nor martyrs. We know full well how to stalk prey, implode reputations, arrange accidents and topple tyrants and rogues. However, Nagah methods, effective as they are, require thought, strategy and tactics; above all, they require time. Meeting pack upon pack of battle-ready Garou, unified by shared self-righteous rage and madness, on a battlefield does not play to our strengths, which explains why so many of our kind died despite the training and Gifts of the mighty Dragon Kings.

Consequences of the War of Rage

Other shapeshifters were hit by the War of Rage far worse than we, ultimately, but we were among the Garou's prime targets. They seemed to reserve a special hatred for those of us who would not share our secrets. At the war's inception, we appeared to be the easiest targets among all the Breeds, and our composure and our appreciation of a somewhat finer quality of life had long been a smoldering source of resentment among the Garou. To their eyes, we were fops and dandies, effete snobs, aesthetes, human lovers, the Changing Breed that was content to sit back and lead the life of royalty. While much of what they said was perfectly true, it didn't interfere with the execution of our duties to the Triat or to Devi and, frankly, it was none of their concern anyway.

When packs of enraged Garou began entering wereserpent castles and palaces and slaying us and our Kinfolk, the Garou soon discovered that we were not the comfortable targets they thought us to be. They underestimated us egregiously — at the outset at least. Nagah legend includes a few accounts of a single skilled wereserpent slaying entire packs of cocky young werewolves; how many others can boast that? We are the children of dragons, and the Wani gifted us generously. Our venom is not to be ignored, nor is our skill with weapons. In India particularly, our ancestors made heavy use of the bow and arrow, mitigating the Garou's greater destructiveness at close range. Another advantage that we used occasionally during the War of Rage but make much greater use of now is comprehensive nest fighting strategies. The Garou commonly assume that outnumbered means overwhelmed, and they use their greater numbers in the bluntest manner possible. Nagah practice interdependence. Every nest stays attuned to, and performs in accordance with, its members' strengths and weaknesses. By so doing, a nest of three can defeat a pack of four. Unfortunately, that was one of the few lessons that ever made it through the wolves' thick skulls.

A nest of three cannot fight a pack of eight. Toward the end, we were fighting war packs of twelve, sixteen, even twenty Garou. Before the War of Rage, traveling in nests at all was relatively uncommon for our People. Nagah simply did not tend to travel together in such numbers; it's generally unnecessary. In those days, the Garou had the luxury of numbers. We never have.

The Wolves were outraged that we would *dare* fight back against them and declared, quite directly, that they were going to wipe us from the face of Gaia. They called in every favor from every spirit, hauled out every lethal fetish, talen and rite that they could muster to savage us. Against most of the other

Khurah, the War of Rage was, at its root, about arrogance, but against the Nagah — and to a degree against the Grondr as well — it was more to do with expressing a vendetta. The Garou led a very focused campaign against us, entering lands they would generally steer clear of just to make war on the Serpent People. And, for the most part, it worked. They *are* the warriors of Gaia, after all. And She made them well.

In regions where Nagah and Garou had once co-existed, the Nagah were all but rendered extinct. Our people in Europe were wiped out almost entirely. The Fianna were particularly bloodthirsty, not resting until they had wiped out every last Nagah and *all* of our serpent Kinfolk in Ireland, destroying all but vestiges of the once-rich culture there.

Europe and Central Asia, in particular, were the worst; where the Wolves went, the Nagah were left decimated, if not exterminated entirely. Only in those places that the Garou found utterly intolerable — oceans, jungles, deserts — were we left unmolested. Our people survived only because our territory extends across so many vastly different regions. Had our territory been as narrow as that of the Grondr, we, too, would be extinct by now.

Imagine our shame, then, when we discovered that the blame for this tragedy lay firmly with one of our own.

Though we wish it were not, that dark account, too, is a part of Nagah history. It is drilled mercilessly into the heads of young Nagah, and I will tell you that tale, too, Sesha.

Listen —

The River Flows Red

Generations after the reign of the Nagah King Silappadikaram had come to an end, which itself took place many generations after the exodus of the Nagah from India, the presiding Serpent King of India, Takshaka, had sent his lieutenant, a Nagah of the Kshatriya caste by the name of Vinata, to Persia to hold a consultation with the Yamilka. Takshaka was ascertaining whether the Yamilka's charges had the numbers required to act as necessary against the Garou whose behavior toward the other Khurah had been growing increasingly outrageous throughout most of eastern Europe. The matter had been discussed, and Vinata was on her way back to Benares to tell Takshaka that, yes, in fact, the Yamilka did need more Nagah. Many Garou, some of them quite powerful, had violently and destructively overstepped their bounds in relation to the other Khurah, and they were being targeted for assassination before the problem became critical.

Vinata was a particularly powerful and trusted advisor to Takshaka. When she stopped — on her way back to Benares with critical information — at the southern edge of the Caspian Sea and told her retinue to wait there for her until she returned from a long swim, they assumed she was acting within her authority to do so. She assumed the Kali Dahaka form and entered the water.

The Corruption of Vinata

I have heard a story of Vinata's temptation, my Sesha. I do not think it is literally true — I believe it is more allegory and parable. But you may judge the story, and it is this:

The Corrupter had been working its way into Vinata's mind for decades. It had chosen her as its champion among the Nagah because she was hungry for power in a way that legitimate means could never satisfy. It made her cruel and inclined to judge Khurah with a lethal harshness. Every time she carried out a rash or questionable assassination, it was able to creep a little deeper in. It told her that if she would perform a single important service for it, that it would empower her and her alone to be the primary destroyer of all the wayward Khurah. Each time she made a kill — and Vinata had made many more than most Nagah her age — the voice of the Corrupter would add another promise to the long roster of the amazing things it would do for her if she would perform a single small task for it. It promised her instant access to the mind of any other individual, the better to know if they were plotting anything she could destroy them for. It told her that after her wise, noble purge of the traitorous ones, there would be no need at all to watch over many of the Changing Breed, because they would be so fearful of her great power — and, consequently, so well-behaved — that peace would follow in her terrible wake. The other Nagah would then bow before her, thanking her for the sacrifice that allowed them to devote themselves completely to the pursuits of royalty without the distractions of their karmic obligations to the Three Mothers.

The Corrupter teased her mercilessly with visions of power. It made her hungry for such might, made her crave power more than anything else. Initially, Vinata said she might consider doing some small act of service for it. Later, after it had not made her any further offers, she gave it a definite yes. In time, Vinata was begging the Corrupter to let her do its bidding, promising that there was nothing she would not do. By that point, she would have vivisected and eaten her own children in its name. And that degree of loyalty was exactly what the Corrupter wanted. When it asked for nothing more than the death of one young Garou, Vinata was almost disappointed. She'd begun to hope that it would ask something truly horrific of her.

Only later did she realize the degree to which it had done just that.

— Dragon Boat

Her retinue had quite a while to wait. Her intended destination was a village on the *north* shore of the Caspian Sea.

She was on her way to meet a great enemy of the Corrupter. And kill him.

Oddly, we have more information about the other half of this equation, the Garou, than we do about Vinata. Because of the role he played in this tragedy, his is one of the few names we know besides that of the traitor and the barbarian general. His name was Petros the Unyielding. He was a member of the Silver Fangs Garou tribe, one of their full moons — what we typically think of as the Kshatriya caste.

Petros was, by all accounts, the epitome of what werewolves like to think they are: he was chivalrous, charismatic and an excellent warrior. Though he never knew it, he had been judged by a Nagah perhaps a year before, and his actions had been found above reproach. He was a prince, the son of some great Russian werewolf king whose name has been lost in the flow of history. He was acting as an emissary for his father. The message he carried, in a leather bag, was an admonishment from his father to the barbarian commander of the Silver Fangs farther west — those exact werewolves that the Yamilka were requesting help to punish.

That letter read:

"Konstantos —

You are out of line. We have real foes, dangerous foes, who deserve your Rage far more than the other [Changing Breeds]. Unless you are unfairly attacked, cease hostilities."

His initial — A. — and his royal glyph marked the bottom of the skin the message was written on.

We know the text of this letter because the letter itself was among Vinata's possessions. It was, in fact, the deciding factor in the determination of Vinata's guilt. And it has been translated into Sanskrit and chiseled onto tablets that are, in fact, kept here in your Ananta, Sesha.

When Vinata got to the top of the Caspian, she discovered that she had missed Petros. The Corrupter was, presumably, irate.

Remaining in Kali Dahaka, Vinata raced after Petros at a tremendous speed for nearly three days before she caught up to him.

Once finished, Vinata took Petros' horse, rode at full speed back to the Caspian, changed to swimming form and returned to her retinue, still waiting for her. Just over a week had passed since she left them.

Garou Kinfolk found Petros' body less than a mile from his destination. It was whole, but it had been… desecrated.

Not realizing that the bloody consequences of her deed would spark an investigation, Vinata claimed that she had been called by Devi to judge a particularly wayward Garou. It wasn't a natural thing for a Nagah to say, and the members of her retinue were not impressed. They rode back to Benares in silence.

Meanwhile, the Silver Fangs under the command of Konstantos the Savage blamed the death of Petros on a young Bubasti man, whom they slaughtered. Konstantos, while little more than a barbarian at heart, had heard of the Gurahl's ability to resurrect the dead, and — in an urgent attempt not to have to explain the death of Petros to the king (whom he felt did not particularly care for him as it was) — headed north and tracked down three different Gurahl over the course of the following week.

Konstantos was not a man gifted with the social graces. He demanded that the Bear People either resurrect Petros or teach the necessary Gift to their Theurge so the boy, who was well liked among the Garou, could be brought back.

The Gurahl apologized but respectfully refused to resurrect Petros *or* share the knowledge of the resurrecting Gift, which Konstantos interpreted as an intolerable act of spite. The Gurahl tried to explain themselves, but Konstantos' pack rapidly became agitated, then violent. The fight that followed was, according to the histories, spectacularly brutal. Two of the three Gurahl were killed at the cost of the lives of five Garou, including Konstantos.

The surviving Gurahl escaped and begged for sanctuary from an old Grondr. He took her in and she related what had happened.

A call went out. Gurahl and Grondr from across the region gathered to discuss their options in the face of growing Garou hostility. The Grondr were indignant at the Garou's arrogance and unprovoked violence. At their urging, the two Khurah launched a terrible counterstrike against the Garou, and the wheel of fate rapidly spun out of control.

The Garou's response was, to say the least, impressive and largely final. We call it the War of Rage.

The cause of the ordeal, Vinata, was by that time back in Benares, wearing luxuriant silks and spending hours combing her long black hair. The Nagah all sensed that something was deeply wrong with her. She was sullen and unresponsive to social interaction. The Corrupter, finished with its fine game, had decided that while it was happy to grant Vinata great power, It didn't want to give her the vast abilities it had said it would. Those, It promised her, she would have after she performed one more small task.

It would be weeks before the bloody consequences of her actions made it from the Ukraine to Benares.

Vinata Discovered

Takshaka could not allow himself to have a lieutenant whose judgment and behavior were so clearly unstable. In an effort to determine the nature of Vinata's problem, he sent her to Sri Lanka on a mission of no consequence. While she was gone, he searched her chambers. He found Petros' letter from the king to Konstantos, but it made no sense to him.

Taking the letter, he sought an audience with the Wani.

Takshaka entered Xi Wang Chi and expressed his concerns for Vinata. One of the Serpent Ladies summoned a series of cloud and wind spirits that had seen Vinata's actions, and the spirits recounted for Takshaka and the Wani exactly what had transpired.

As they listened, the Dragon Queen grew ashamed for all of serpentkind. Takshaka was humiliated that he had chosen his lieutenant so poorly.

Even as the Serpent Lady and Takshaka stood there, the sky in the realm of Xi Wang Chi grew increasingly storm-ridden and the cavern of the Furies began to shake with the fury of their sibilant rage.

The Punishment of Vinata

When Takshaka returned to Benares from Xi Wang Chi, he knew of the approaching War of Rage as well as its likely outcome. The Wani had shown him the advance of the enraged Garou. They would be in Benares by dusk and the moon was full.

Takshaka's last act as Nagah King was to welcome Vinata back from Sri Lanka.

When Vinata entered Benares in Azhi Dahaka form, it became clear that the Corrupter's touch had left her changed. Her features were sharper, her scales darker and her voice seemed pinched and cold. Lethality dripped from her every languid gesture.

Nagah, humans and Kinfolk, warned by Takshaka, stayed out of sight.

The Nagah King had no intention of confronting Vinata physically. She was, by then, too powerful for even him to overcome. Her abandonment of balance was her damnation — a fact obvious to those who watched her enter the city — but it made her the favored daughter of the Corrupter — and whom the Corrupter loves, It empowers.

How do you convince someone that she has gone down the wrong path, Sesha, when all the physical signs of power and success spring up at her very step?

Takshaka met Vinata at the gates of the city and accompanied her to the grand hall where he granted audiences. The two talked idly about small things as though he had no knowledge of Vinata's treachery. When they entered the audience hall, the doors closed behind them. Vinata heard a low hiss and the fevered buzz of tail rattles. When she looked up at the dais where Takshaka normally sat, she beheld the most terrifying member of Typhon's and Tiamat's Brood: The Kaliya, the many-headed spirit of vengeance. It is the Kaliya who judges errant judges, punishes cruel punishers and executes corrupt executioners.

Realizing Takshaka's duplicity, she smiled and turned to gut him with her talons. The Nagah King stood there, steadfast, preparing to defend himself to whatever degree her twisted power allowed… but her blow never connected.

In less time than passes between heartbeats, the Kaliya snatched her up in its barbed coils and spirited her away to its cavern in Xi Wang Chi to begin punishment. Since the Corrupter's favor had made Vinata so resilient, it would take her decades to die under the Kaliya's excruciating ministrations. Ironically, though she spent every sliver of every hour of every remaining day of her life wishing that she could die, the traitor lived longer than the majority of her kind.

By preventing Vinata's killing blow, the Kaliya extended Takshaka's life by another handful of hours. By dusk, the Garou had arrived in the city and the slaughter of Nagah began.

Aftermath

The War of Rage turned us from wise judges to skulking victims living by stealth alone. In the face of oncoming swarms of enraged Garou, there was nothing that could preserve the way of life we had grown so fond of — not our royal status, not our tactical training and certainly not our prowess at assassination. Our ancestors initially hoped that India was being singled out for attack and that the exodus of Nagah to the limits of the world had turned out to be a wise strategy after all. Only later did we discover that the exodus had served only to spread our kind too thinly and all but doomed the Serpent People entirely.

For a time, there was little or no communication among the Nagah. We were so well hidden that we couldn't even find one another. Ultimately, most Nagah turned to their serpent Kinfolk and left civilization almost entirely. For years, the formerly rich, sensual and artistic culture of the Nagah simply ceased to be as our people fled into the embrace of rivers, deserts and holes in the ground. The War of Rage essentially sent the Nagah into a rapid slide into our own dark age. For a very long time, the Serpent People were severed from one another, fulfilling our obligations to Devi haphazardly, if at all.

To the world, we were dead. That was, at least, a small blessing.

The Founding of the Sesha

The end of that dark age came about with the founding of the Sesha.

Long after the War of Rage, Mandrodari Ma — one of the few truly old Nagah to have survived that event — swam from her island of Sri Lanka to the mainland to see what had become of the Nagah. She found snakes afraid to take human form. She found an ancient sage living in the gutters of Ranchavati. She found ascetics in the jungle who had undergone the Rite of Sannyasa, not because they were wise old snakes ready to learn the secrets of asceticism, but because they were too terrified of the Wolves to live otherwise.

She was embarrassed by her own people.

Being a powerful priest, she was able to enter Xi Wang Chi, the Storm Realm, and address the Wani. During those brief moments when the wind and thunder both grew calm at the same time, the sound of Vinata's shrieks of agony could be heard emanating from the cavern of the Kaliya.

She stood before the Dragon Fathers in a tattered robe. She explained that Devi's punishers had experienced a regrettable turn of fortune and she humbly asked for his help in rectifying that situation.

The Dragon Fathers were tired, Sesha. They looked at Mandrodari Ma's heart, looking for corruption so that they could judge her, kill her and be done with it. What they saw there was nobility and compassion.

The Dragon Fathers agreed to help the Serpent People, but only by granting them the ability to organize and only if they agreed to monitor one another much more closely, to prevent such disgrace as Vinata had brought upon the Serpent People. The one that stood forward to direct this help was Seiryu, the great Blue Dragon of the East.

Seiryu lashed his gigantic tail at the churning ocean of Xi Wang Chi, severing a portion of its waters from the realm. Those waters would become the Nandana, the Ananta of the Sesha. Then he ordered legions of Kolowissi, Inadu and thundersnake spirits to go find the three wisest Nagah from each breed and bring them back to Xi Wang Chi. Then he hesitated and told them that he had one of the wisest Balaram Nagah in front of him already, so he only needed two others.

Those revered nine became the first Sesha.

Seiryu reminded them, unsubtly, of the laws they had forgotten. He asserted that the Serpent People should be wise and fair judges as well as subtle and lethal assassins. He built the Nandana in his coils so that the Sesha would have a place to assemble and from which they could direct the Nagah, allowing the wereserpents to act in concert.

Finally, Seiryu told the Sesha that Nagah would henceforth have to cluster together in nests. The bonds that linked them would have to be strong to keep the Serpent People together, but they would be obligated to protect one another, nurture one another and scrutinize one another for the Corrupter's influence, which had led to embarrassments in the Nagah's history. To make his point, he had the Kaliya bring out the wretched and flayed form of Vinata. She cringed and cried out hoarsely with every step.

The Blue Dragon of the East pointed to Vinata as an example of what could happen to even a noble Nagah if any of the Triat is able to seduce that individual to its side. The words he spoke then, Sesha, have been firmly stamped into the minds of every Nagah since: *Loyalty to any facet of the Triat makes a mockery of true justice.* So saying, he crushed Vinata's body beneath his gigantic claw, thus ending her misery forever.

The establishment of the Sesha put an end to the dark age among the Nagah of the West and even the Pure Lands, but the Nagah of the hengeyokai were slow in accepting the necessity of such a system. It would take a tragedy to convince them of the wisdom of this new way. That tragedy was called…

The War of Shame

The Nagah of the Eastern Courts were not affected in the slightest by the War of Rage, which the majority of them had never even heard of. While their Western brethren were being slaughtered and effectively banished from civilization, the Nagah of the Beast Courts flourished.

For a while.

There were cankers in even that cultivated rose. A different tragedy befell the Serpent People in the East, and while it was far less destructive, in some ways it was worse.

The shapeshifters of the Middle Kingdom, called the hengeyokai, fell prey to the manipulations of the greedy Wan Xian. They wanted control of our sacred places, and if they couldn't defeat us to take them — and they couldn't — then they would have us defeat ourselves. It worked. The Serpent People made the thinnest nod to their duties as they claimed they were simply judging those they killed.

They killed Nezumi for not keeping tight enough control on the humans and for dealing too strictly with the humans.

They killed Okuma for not healing all that were sick or wounded.

They killed Tengu for conveying messages too slowly.

It was, in short, hypocrisy beyond measure.

Still, even during the darkest moments of the War of Shame, Nagah would not slay those who were completely without blame, and at no point did Nagah turn on other Nagah, nor did they turn on their respected older brothers, the Zhong Lung.

Those exceptions notwithstanding, the War of Shame elicited from the Nagah of the East the most atrocious, treacherous, unjust, self-serving behavior serpentkind has ever shown.

The worst excesses of inauspicious judging during the War of Shame we reserved for the Nezumi, with whom we were locked in a vicious shadow war. Nagah slew scores of the Rat People — and vice versa — until neither of our Breeds could stomach it any more. The origins of that conflict remain unknown, Sesha, but we can only assume that somewhere the Wan Xian were chuckling at their own cleverness.

We, of all of the Breeds, should have recognized the manipulative tactics, the smear campaigns, the careful fanning of flames of resentment and pride — but we didn't. We are adept at using such tactics, but apparently blind to them when we are their target.

Interlude

Sajita paused in her narrative, raising a finger to her chin. "Sesha," she finally said, "I realize that I am being inattentive to the shifting fortunes of humanity as I tell our history. But as you must certainly know, when the Age of Kings ended, so did our closeness to the human race. No more did we guide the development of cities and bloodlines; no more did we indulge ourselves in the luxury of manipulating our human Kin. Our business is now the fortunes of the Khurah, not that of the humans. Since the end of the Age of Kings, we have lain at the bottom of the river, concealed ourselves among the reeds. If war and famine befell our human Kin, we mourned — but we did not intercede, not in any way that would betray our presence. If there have been Nagah who made themselves players in human history, who have started or ended wars, then they were truly masters of anonymity, for I do not know their names."

A faint hiss filtered down from the seats of the Sesha. "Continue."

The Second War of Rage

Blindness can come easily when it's our own faults we're trying to see. That's true for the Nagah, and it's certainly true for the Wolf People. Many Khurah and spirits alike believe

the Garou sealed their own fate with the Second War of Rage. Children are allowed to make mistakes, and an indulgent Mother could attribute even the horrors of the First War of Rage to the folly of a young and somewhat overly boisterous race. The lands across the Atlantic presented the Garou with a second chance, the opportunity to get it right. With the Second War of Rage, however, the Garou showed themselves to be pathologically incapable of working with Gaia's other children. The death scream of the last Camazotz was nothing but a prescient echo of the death scream of the last Garou — and they brought it upon themselves.

When the Garou began acting in what they called the "Pure Lands," resuming their tireless crusades against the Camazotz and the Gurahl, the Corax were kind enough to spread the word openly. And we heard them, though they did not call our names.

We traveled to this "New World," because we heard that we were needed there. To our surprise, we discovered that we had been there all along — to some degree. Several of our kind had traveled along secret Umbral roads to the West, knowing that wherever the Khurah went, they would be needed. Though they had lost contact with the Sesha, they still maintained their bonds with the spirit world through their contacts with certain water serpent spirits who still spoke with the Wani. It was a delicate dance we shared with them when we first learned of one another, each one of us not daring to share too much of our true natures but deathly curious about the other. When we had finally established that we were still all Nagah together, the youngest Crown was founded: the Zuzeka.

And with the formation of the Zuzeka and the coordination of nests in the Americas, the American Khurah were able to finally benefit from our full and organized attentions once more.

The Industrial Revolution

I know that it is not given to us to judge humans as we do the Khurah. But I imagine that when industry began to rear its head in such scope as it did during the Industrial Revolution, our forebears must have been sorely tempted. They poisoned the rivers, Sesha — they violated the waters of the mother that gave them life as well as us. Their factories tore up the ground, their cities swelled like wombs heavy with demons, their smoke filled the air. It was as if all the hells of the underworld were threatening to break free, pushing up the earth into wells of manmade toxin.

As the situation grew worse and worse, nests reported their misgivings to the Crowns, and the Crowns relayed their own worries to the Sesha. The Sesha in turn, in its wisdom, forbade the Nagah from taking direct action against the humans who devised these horrible buildings and machines. The reason given was that to take up arms against humanity as a whole would be to usurp the position of the Ratkin — just as the Garou tried so long ago. But even Nandana shakes with the tremors of industry, and the Sesha were wise to foresee that the difficulties would only grow worse. It was at this time that the Sesha unveiled the latest of the Sacred Laws — "Strike Against the Corrupter if the Opportunity Is True."

Though we obeyed the law and struck when and where it was given to us to do so, still the human population has boiled out of control. Mass industrialization has now usurped enormous regions of land that the Serpent People once occupied. I regret that we are unable to prevent this growth, that we could only slow it at best and still remain true to ourselves. It has been a dark period, one that I pray we may yet be allowed to end. While we still respect its parent, the Destroyer, the Corrupter must not be allowed a free hand any more.

Death of the Bunyip

The other children of Rainbow Serpent, the Bunyip, were allies of the Australian Nagah. We felt that they might be a connection between us and the other Garou, but those hopes were dashed after the initial blows were exchanged between the Bunyip and the invaders. They were dashed further when it became clear that the likeliest outcome was the death of the Bunyip.

But Sesha, if ever there has been a powerful argument for the necessity of learning as much about a target as possible before passing judgement, then Australia would be that argument.

On the surface, it seemed that the conflict between the Bunyip and the newcomers was all too typical — that the European werewolves were ridden by impulses more of the Corrupter than of the Destroyer, and that simple prejudice brought the Bunyip low. And that assumption proved at least partly true. But we owe a debt to the wisdom of the Shining Rainfall nest, for it was they who learned the truth — that the Europeans had been goaded into their war by their own fallen tribe, the Black Spiral Dancers. One of the Dancers, an exceptionally cunning beast named Mara the Scream framed the Bunyip for the murder of a ranking Red Talon's sister. It was his fury that set tensions to all-out war, and that led to the fall of the Bunyip.

Sesha, I do not wish to imply that the European Garou were not to be held accountable for their actions. We judged many during the War of Tears and found them lacking — although I have heard it said that the Europeans blamed the deaths of our targets on the Bunyip, and thus their fury intensified. I would like to think that we were prudent in our actions then, and that we did not ourselves contribute to the Bunyip's extinction — or that they would have died anyway. Whatever the end result, our actions were too little, too late. And once the Bunyip passed into extinction, we left off our judgement — not because the Bunyip are forgotten, but because their ghosts appear to be avenging themselves without our help.

But I will say this much — Mara the Scream did not escape in the end. When I think of the Bunyip and mourn, I like to console myself with the thought of the Dancer's bones crunching in the jaws of the Kaliya.

The Modern Age

The world wars are the major punctuation marks of the twentieth century for most of the world. The horror they caused, particularly the Second World War, stole away the final vestiges of innocence from many world powers. The first left our people largely unaffected; the second one was devastating.

The First World War

Our numbers in Europe have never been more than a small fraction of what they were before the War of Rage. The prevalence of Garou makes the kind of long-term secrecy we'd need to observe burdensome. Consequently, the First World War, concentrated as it was on Europe, left us relatively unscathed. There were stings, of course: the death of a single Kinfolk, a poet of some talent, was mourned by many Nagah around the world who otherwise knew nothing about Europe or those that served their under the Nemontana. Thanks to colonization, and the subsequent emigration from India, England was also the funnel into harm's way for Indian Nagah and Balaram Kinfolk, although most of them, members of the higher castes mostly, had the good sense to remain in India.

But our people could not remain far from the battle lines for long.

The Second World War

World War II came to *our* lands, and for once the brutality of modern warfare was made evident on the flesh of our kin. The jungles we have frequented throughout the ages were overrun with soldiers: Americans, Japanese, Australians, Russians and Chinese. The atrocities of war ground down innocent humans, testing us all with the temptation to slay as many soldiers as we could find. We had our Ananta, so remaining hidden was not a true issue — but humans weren't the only ones involved in the war.

Yes, the youth of many nations were conscripted— but it is my belief, Sesha, that among the Changing Breeds, only those who truly wanted to fight came to the battlefields. How difficult can it be for a person who also walks as a beast, who enters the spirit world at will, to evade the clumsy press gangs of the human military? And if recruited, how easy would it be for one whose breast burns with Rage to successfully pass through training without incident? How would one conceal his true nature on the battlefield? No, it's foolish to presume that the Khurah — much less we — would be drawn *en masse* into the conflict against their will. Only those whose territory and Kin were threatened would be present in numbers.

And yet — the Khurah came. Not in great numbers, but they came. Some stowed away on military vessels, eager to leap into the Pacific Theater and hunt down whatever of the Corrupter's children they could find there. Others found their way here through the spirit world, sure that their enemies would do the same. We, and the Beast Courts, watched the newcomers carefully. Some were judged — and found wanting. Others proved themselves allies by their actions, even if we never approached them to call them such. For many of the Vritra, this was the first time we had seen the Western Khurah in anything other than song. Some were noble; others were more monster than man or beast. And we now knew first-hand that the time to reveal ourselves was no closer than before.

The Corrupter's Victory

Forgive me, Sesha. I cannot describe the horror that came over our kind when the first atomic bomb was deployed against living targets. I was not yet born. I can only make a poor attempt at summation.

An entire city — blasted with fire and radiation. Men, women and children, beasts and birds — slain both quickly and slowly. The hopes of an entire people died that day, and a cloud of fear descended over the entire world. To many — and forgive me if I speak falsely, Sesha, for I know some among you might even have been there — it was almost a sign that the Final War was over, and that the Corrupter had won.

The spirit lands bordering the Middle Kingdom have not been the same since. The Corrupter's greatest lieutenants, the mighty spirits called the Yama Kings, feasted on the horror and misery reaped by that outrage and grew bloated with power. The Dragon King of Umi, the spirit ocean of the South Pacific, bellowed in agony as the once-rich spiritual landscape of Nippon was twisted beyond recognition. The Wani shrieked with pain and rage, and many of us passed judgement much more harshly in the years afterward, trying to soothe our great patrons with offerings of blood and vengeance.

If only it had been the last time….

Viet Nam

The final tenet of the Sacred Laws was sorely tested once more when the United States came to Viet Nam. Yes, a few Khurah came to the battlefield there, but at no time did the Westerners outnumber the hengeyokai. Once again, I give thanks for the territorial nature of the Garou; with their own sacred sites under continual attack, only the most foolish abandoned pack and caern to fight a war in an unknown land against unknown enemies.

But they weren't needed. The Corrupter had weapons aplenty without their presence. Napalm. Land mines. Agent Orange. Young men killing and raping, children being slaughtered and raped — so many of us were driven to action. Many soldiers on both sides vanished in the jungles, never accounted for — and rightly so.

I have been told that the Sesha of the time took particular interest in scrutinizing nests for undue ties to the Corrupter. While no nest was condemned, many Vietnamese Nagah were required to undergo several extra Shedding the Past Samskara to purge the Twisted One's poison from their system. We learned more about the Corrupter's tactics after that one war than we had learned in the preceding two centuries.

The Punishment of Black Tooth

It can be hard to recognize the effects of history on the present, Sesha. During our quiescence after the War of Rage, the Nagah became overly accustomed to being unable to affect the world beyond our immediate environment. We were certainly more than capable of defending ourselves; power and force both serve important roles in the assassin's repertoire of disciplines, but ultimately they are hollow if they do not further our long-term goals. Stealth had become our overriding concern, and, so shackled, we began ignoring incidents by other Khurah worthy of punishment.

It was you, Sesha, who formally rededicated the Nagah to the judgment, punishment and execution of those who would betray Devi. The target roster, ordered according to the magnitude of the target's transgression, was given to all Nagah nests as we received our annual audience, and I imagine all of us expected the first ten names all to belong to Garou.

They did not; the first name belonged to a Bastet.

Imagine our surprise.

Black Tooth was a powerful Simba who had learned magic and Gifts well beyond what most of his kind would ever learn. That, alas, was part of his imbalance; power interested him more than justice and it showed. For decades he had allowed his own uncontrolled lust for power to guide his actions and he was not concerned with serving Devi in any of Her incarnations. He allied himself, albeit indirectly, with the Corrupter and took it upon himself to conduct his own War of Rage upon the Ajaba. The decision was not an easy one. With the Final Days upon us, the decision had to be made whether it was more likely that his strength would be lent to ours in the last battles or whether his lust for power would lead him to fight for the Corrupter. He was supposed to be a king among kings, ruling through nobility and wisdom; instead, he embodied *every* failing of the Khurah: arrogance, bloodthirst and cruelty being among the more obvious of these. For these reasons, Black Tooth was marked for assassination.

Every Nagah nest — including our own, Sesha — considered "passing through" southern Africa to carry out the will of Devi. All but the eldest and most powerful nests ultimately decided to set their sights lower on the list of Devi's enemies. We are taught from a young age that knowledge of one's own limitations ranks among an assassin's most valuable assets, and Black Tooth was one of the most powerful of the Cat People.

Ultimately, two nests of revered Nagah — Shiva's Eye from India and Flowing Edge from Brazil — coordinated their efforts against the rogue Simba. They met for months in a small village in Brazil, a few kilometers up the Amazon from Manaus, to minimize the possibility of Black Tooth's spirit allies overhearing anything. The old cat was exceedingly perceptive, so until proximity to the kill site became necessary, they opted to remain far from the Simba's territory. They spent their days determining where the assassination could best be carried out and how to lure Black Tooth to the kill site. They contrived plots to deal with the Endless Storm, the gang of Simba thugs he called his pride. They debated how best to counteract the influence of Black Tooth's spirit allies, what to do about his control of the weather and how to neutralize the mighty powers given to him. I understand they had no fewer than five contingency plans prepared by the time they left Brazil — the Simba king was just that terrifying.

Once the strategic planning was done, the two nests held practice drills with each individual Nagah playing the part of Black Tooth at least once and voicing, at each step of the way, what he or she would do in Black Tooth's position. Once they knew their roles in Black Tooth's assassination, the nests went to Congo to begin their work.

But — and Sesha, this was such a surprising thing — when they arrived, Black Tooth was already dead. The slayer of the Hyena King, the master of the Endless Storm — he had fallen to the vengeful teeth of the Khurah he had wronged. I have asked many nests, including Shiva's Eye, if they know the details of Black Tooth's fall, but none can answer me. All that is known is that the Ahadi, a new alliance of African Khurah, seems to have been opposed to Black Tooth in the final days of his reign. He is now dead, and the Ahadi is still alive.

Did they usurp our role, Sesha? Of course not. Our job is to punish those who would otherwise escape justice; if justice is able to find a wrongdoer without our help, all the better. And yet, I still wonder — the Yamilka has been persistently close-mouthed about the Ahadi and its merits or failings. I believe — and I may be wholly in the wrong, Sesha — that perhaps the Ahadi had the assistance of a few of our own, though they never knew it. But I have no proof whatsoever; merely a hope that some of ours might have contributed to this great deed.

That, Sesha, is the direction the Nagah pursue, as always. Those who have turned their backs on Devi, those who have betrayed Her, who shirk their duties to Her, will now be dealt with in the ways that the Nagah know best.

However, while our duties among the Khurah are our primary focus, they are not the totality of our existence. Judging the Khurah is our primary role in the world, but we must also act in Devi's best interest in other ways, acting as judges, punishers and executioners of those who side against any of our three mothers. And of course the recent developments so near to the heart of our territory have caught our interest.

The Rise and Fall of the Rakshasa King

The general details of the event were impossible to miss. However, we possess specific knowledge of those unnatural days due to the power of the Wani. When the elements themselves were loosed, the Dragon Kings had no choice but to take notice.

In July of 1999, five months after Black Tooth's death, Bangladesh became the site of a series of unnatural occurrences of most extreme magnitude. An ancient rakshasa king, an unspeakably powerful demon of illusion, shredded the fetters of somnolence that bound him and awakened. Some called him Ravana himself — as if Rama had failed in his endeavor! The name I have heard is Ravnasa — and I do not recognize it.

Whatever his name, this monster was of a power so great that he would have challenged Vasana himself. His rampage was short, however; very soon after his awakening, in accordance with the principles of Destiny, three enlightened demon warriors arrived from China to engage him in combat.

It was, in no uncertain terms, cataclysmic, the sort of thing one expects rather more of in these climactic days of the Kali Yuga. It was also inappropriately interfered with and almost made much, much worse by an outside agency.

The initial violence and madness of the incident were awesome, in the most powerful meaning of that term. Our Mokolé cousins have seen confrontations of that magnitude, Sesha, but few others have been so… blessed. The champions from the East summoned enormous dragon storms into the region for use as screens and weapons against the rakshasa. The resultant typhoon sank ships, flooded shorelines, ripped up villages and toppled whole tracts of jungle. It was considered a once-in-a-millennium storm.

And that was the least of the peculiarities associated with that conflict.

The Walls between worlds were dissolved and the bright and dark Umbras were called into our world. Spirits, demons, ghosts, dreams and odder things flooded into this Realm. A number of other Khurah, particularly Garou, arrived in the region to protect Devi's interests, in whatever way they thought they might be able to do that. It is believed that most of them died without achieving their goals.

And as the Dragon Kings relate, "Above the thickly-packed typhoon clouds, four suns blossomed and shone at night."

It was then that the cataclysm went oddly awry. Someone or something, a third party of unknown origin, unleashed a series of enormous explosions that devastated vast swathes of the Penumbra in the region. It was almost comparable to Hiroshima and Nagasaki all over again. The three Chinese demons were slain by the barrage of spirit energy; the rakshasa king survived a while longer. But once the dragon storms dissipated, allowing the four suns to shine down on him, none of his illusions could save him. Even the mightiest rakshasa falls beneath the direct glare of Surya, and when that glare is fourfold, there is no hope, even for the most ancient rakshasa king.

Once the battle concluded, nothing remained but the aftermath and consequences. The dead — from the battle, from the storm, from the melding of the worlds and from the explosions — numbered in the thousands of thousands. Had the interfering party's tactics failed — after it had killed the combat's rightful champions — the devastation would have been much, much worse — a possibility to which we take violent exception.

This third party's actions are profound violations of the natural order. Dragon wizards of our acquaintance, seers, tell us that two of the Chinese warriors would have fallen in battle to the rakshasa, but the last, the Dancing Dragon, would have defeated him. This expected destiny never manifested as it should have because of unexpected interference. Not only did the interlopers kill the rightful champions of the conflict with their bombs, but they killed many Khurah — and Nagah — and thousands of humans as well. Only through the blessings of Fortune were their explosions and four suns enough to destroy the rakshasa; otherwise the chosen champions would have been dead and the rakshasa would have been free, at least for a time, to ravage as he chose.

It is the Kaliya's task to punish the gravest violations of the natural order — of which there were several during this handful of days. It is the Wani's place to govern the storms of the world, and their duties have been severely interfered with in this event. And thus the Dragon Kings — through you, Sesha — have granted us *carte blanche* in locating, identifying and punishing the agency responsible for interfering with the proper outcome of this conflict. Regrettably, the investigations are proceeding quite slowly. We have heard that the explosions were the work of the Corrupter's agents, turning on themselves in a blind parody of the Destroyer's role. We have heard that the Trapper sent this devastation, blindly lashing out at the great disturbance caused by the rakshasa king. There is really no evidence to guide us one way or another.

But as we have been since the beginning of time, we are driven to succeed. We *must* keep the laws, for if not us, then who?

And that, Sesha, ends my account of our history.

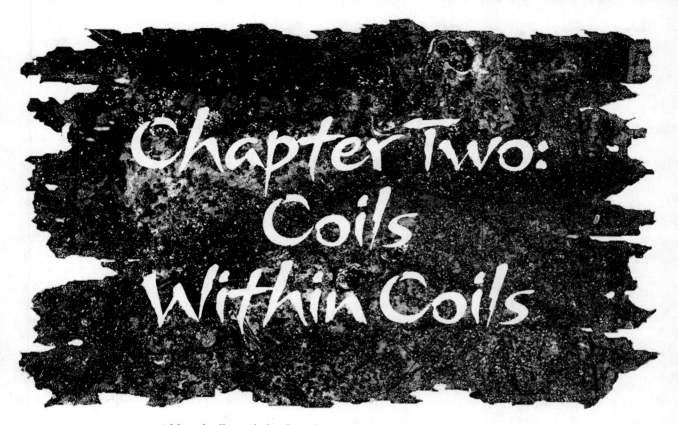

Chapter Two: Coils Within Coils

Although all people hanker after a magistrate's office,
Few realize all that is involved in solving criminal cases:
Tempering severity by lenience, as laid down by our law makers,
And avoiding the extremes advocated by crafty philosophers.

One upright magistrate means the happiness of a thousand families,
The one word "justice" means the peace of the entire population.
— Dee Goong An (Celebrated Cases of Judge Dee), translated
by Robert Van Gulik

Her narrative finished, Sajita stepped back to stand alongside her nestmates. The Sesha offered no further words to her; instead they shifted slightly in their high seats, offering only small gestures and glances to one another. Finally, another of the cobras, her snaky brow set with a tiny gem, lifted her head higher from her hanging basket and stared directly at Dragon Boat. Her spirit-voice resounded in the nest's minds.

"Announce yourself."

He bowed deeply. "I am Dragon Boat, born ahi, born Kamakshi. I have had the honor of serving the Sacred Laws for ten years, all of which I have spent with my nest, Night's Passage. The Sesha has judged my deeds in the past, and I shall not tire you, my Sesha, by repeating them in the vain hope of currying favor."

The cobra's posture did not change, and not even another Nagah could read the emotions of a snake's face.

"You have taken the responsibility of keeping the law for your nest."

"I have."

"You are acquainted with our customs and laws; you know where we gather and why we hold to the task of judgement."

"I am; I do."

Again, the silken rustling. "Tell us."

Shedding the Skin

In the womb, we are Nagah. In the egg, we are Nagah. We are made Nagah at the moment that we are made at all, and none may undo that crafting.

But it is not given to us to know all that we are from the moment of our hatching. We must be taught what we are, why we are here, how to complete our lives. For the ahi such as myself, this instruction begins early, while we pass our childhood in the Serpent Waters. But my brothers and sisters of other births must grow in ignorance before they mature and learn themselves.

This is the Final Turning of the Age, my Sesha; the world will soon be remade, and only the efforts of the Khurah will determine whether it is remade into a world that can heal itself or if it will become as cinders. There is no more dangerous age to live in. And so each one of the Changing Breeds, Nagah and Khurah alike, must do what they can to keep their enemies from finding them. We, like other beast-people, raise our balaram and vasuki children in ignorance of what they are, in the hopes that silence will keep them safer.

When we are children — or hatchlings — we are troubled. A balaram child finds it difficult to relate to the human children around her, and watches herself grow cool and aloof without ever really knowing why. She does not understand the growing tension within her breast, and cannot truly know why her neighbors treat her with something akin to dread. A vasuki hatchling has impulses that confuse it as well, although it is unable to define them until the time it matures and becomes Nagah. Fortunately, a vasuki grows to maturity swiftly, for it would be a true struggle to endure for years with the conflicting impulses within his bones. We ahi are no different; we are confused if our parents visit us in forms that are unlike our own, we do not understand why we cannot leave the tiny realms that serve as our nursery, and our lessons are troubling to accept — until we Change at last.

As children we are distanced from our own kind, human, serpent and Nagah, because we still wear the First Skin. My Sesha, the First Skin is a thing of spirit, unseen by us and invisible even from the spirit world. It is with us when we are conceived. It cuts off our perceptions to some extent, as an aging skin clouds serpentine eyes. It keeps our Rage from rising to the surface prematurely, but it also seals us away to some extent from those around us. But the greatest gift the First Skin offers is that it protects us from detection. A Nagah who has not yet shed his First Skin is indistinguishable, even through divination, from a mortal human or cobra. And so we are able to hide.

I have learned that the Changes that come upon Khurah are hot things of blood and pain. For us, the first time we change is a struggle, perhaps most akin to a vasuki's struggle to push his way free from the eggshell. A choking closeness — that is what I remember. I remember feeling the First Skin for the first time, and struggling against it for freedom. So it is with all of us. We peel away the First Skin, and are reborn. The First Skin dissolves into spirit mist as we shed it and rise into our new form. Sometimes our own power overcomes us, and we reflexively kill whoever is unfortunate enough to be at hand — but not always.

It's a frightening time, yes. My own change terrified me; the worst of it was when I mistakenly took on the Vasuki and realized I could no longer hear anything around me. But with the fear and pain comes such a blessing, a newness — I don't think I have the words for it. I can say, "When I shed my First Skin" to another

Nagah and they will know immediately what I mean, but to try and summarize it in human words....

As you know, my Sesha, when a snake — one of us, or an animal — sheds his skin, it takes time for him to adjust to the way in which his senses have changed. As a skin grows old, the plates over the eyes become clouded and difficult to see through. When the skin is finally shed, the eyes are sensitive and not as well-protected — but they are able to see so much more!

This is what it is like to become truly Nagah — one becomes vulnerable during those first feverish moments, but he is also granted the gifts of health and sharp senses in such potency that he may well compare his prior life to being ill and half-blind. The balaram discover that they are finally capable of tasting the world in the manner it was meant to be tasted — not with dull human noses and tongues, but with the tongue of a snake. The vasuki are given an even greater gift — they discover that they can finally listen to the world, hearing its songs and screams and sighs in ways that a serpent could never imagine. And the ahi, who were already blessed with a portion of the senses of each, are finally able to leave the Serpent Waters, to walk in the cities or slither in the fields as others do — they are given the rest of the world.

Breeds

The greatest refrain sung throughout the universe is a harmony of three voices. Many human societies, when they think of balance, picture a balance between two things — yin and yang, light and dark, and so on. Their scales have two weighing pans, they have two hands — they choose two as a number for balance, because it represents symmetry.

We, however, are taught that balance is a matter of threes. Three Mothers — Earth, Moon and River. Three worlds — human, beast and spirit. Three great forces at war; three layers to the spirit world. And there are three ways to be born Nagah.

For our race to be balanced — and thus healthy — the breeds must be in balance. This is a hard thing to govern; there is no guarantee that any coupling will produce a Nagah, even between two Nagah parents. But we must try.

Balaram

Those of us born to human parents, the balaram, are children of the fortunes of the world. Where life is good for our Kin, a balaram might enjoy a childhood that is almost happy. Where life is bad for our Kin, the struggle to shed one's First Skin can be crushing.

Once we bred exclusively with nobility; all our balaram were the children of princesses and rajahs. But those days are no more. It became obvious many centuries ago that noble blood among humans was not enough; would that the kings of the Garou had learned that lesson! We now choose our human mates with an eye for the traits they may offer our offspring; so it is that there are Nagah born of almost every human race on the planet. Still, our strongest Kin bloodlines lie in India and the Middle Kingdom. It is a difficult choice between furthering a bloodline — which offers a greater chance of a child breeding true — and choosing a parent who may add many strong traits to the line, but has less chance of producing a Nagah heir.

A balaram's childhood is not a simple thing, my Sesha; so it is with all of us given Devi's blessings. Other children, other parents and teachers unconsciously sense the serpent within, and they fear it. The First Skin prevents any from sensing anything more — but we cannot walk among humans for long without disturbing them. The fear of snakes is too deeply buried within.

And we are not good parents, I fear. We have no time to devote to the proper raising and care of a child; the nest and our duties call. For secrecy's sake, we do not tell our children what they are; they are raised unknowing, perhaps by foster parents or perhaps by a Nagah's abandoned mate. It is not an easy childhood — but no part of our lives is easy, and the balaram are in this way prepared for what they are to be.

Ahi

How much can I say of the ahi? I am ahi — I could recount the tale of my entire life to you, my Sesha, and it would be the tale of each of my breed, more or less.

We are the center of the race. It is our task to reach out the left hand to our balaram brothers and the right hand to our vasuki sisters, and to draw them together and join their hands in ours.

Like others of my breed, my Sesha, I was born of two Nagah of the same nest. Perhaps there have been ahi whose parents were of different nests, or even sannyasin, but I find that hard to understand; even those of our race who are not of our nest are, to some extent, outsiders that will never understand us. My mother knew the moment she was pregnant by my father; this is a great gift given us by Devi, that we may prepare for our ahi children. Within minutes, she knew that I was ahi. If the mating had not been "true," then she would have performed the Rite of Bearing within a day, to choose whether to bring a human child or a clutch of cobra hatchlings into this world. But I was ahi, and so she knew that she would have to bring me into the world as a single egg, laid by a mother wearing the Azhi Dahaka.

In fables such as the Ramayana, it is said that the children of the gods are born within a day. It is not so easy for the mother of an ahi, but the pregnancy is easier than bearing a human child. My mother carried me for six months, during which time she was still able to take on the Balaram, Silkaram, Azhi Dahaka and Kali Dahaka. At the end of this time, she laid a single egg in her Ananta, and nursed it until I hatched three months later.

I was raised in a "jeweled pool," a spirit cavern of Serpent Waters. Each year, on my birthday, my mother came and carried me across the Gauntlet into the physical world for a day, that my flesh would prosper and not fade into spirit. I shed my First Skin when I was eight years of age; I joined my nest after a year of apprenticeship and final lessons. And now I am here.

My childhood was peaceful, though it was not "happy." Yet I do not regret the experience. My only regret at being born ahi is that my mingled blood and life in the Serpent Waters have ill-prepared me for the outside world's toxins; I blister and burn at the touch of toxic chemicals and pollutants, as do all my kind. And that, Sesha, can be said to be more the world's fault than my parents'.

Vasuki

Those of us born of serpents' eggs have, in some ways, the most difficult time adapting to life among the Nagah. All the skills that allow one to function effectively in the human world are doubly hard to learn for one who is still becoming accustomed to having limbs or hearing speech. It can take some time for a vasuki to learn to tie a knot or wield a knife, much less drive a car or operate a computer. The vasuki are in many ways the most spiritually potent of us all, but the time it takes to educate a serpent-born in full is an extensive investment. Although it is rare for us to reach old age peacefully, the Crowns encourage those who become too slow to perform their duties effectively to take on the position of teacher, devoting their time to teaching vasuki the ways of the human world. Regrettably, this is not an ideal solution — how can we ask a Nagah born before the Second World War to adequately explain everything a vasuki should know about computers? — but it is something.

Just as our balaram have gone from a few select families to a mix of bloodlines from around the world, the vasuki of the modern age are a remarkable picture of diversity. First and foremost, we are the children of Cobra — we all bear hoods as the mark of our greatest serpent forebear. But over the centuries, we have learned that we are capable of breeding successfully with almost any species of venomous snake. The Nagah serving under each Crown have developed their own personal preferences; the Zuzeka's charges are particularly fond of rattlesnakes, for instance, while those under the Nemontana prefer adders. To be certain, the majority of vasuki — and of all other breeds — still wear the cobra's form, but there is no longer a stigma of shame for being born of other blood.

I know vasuki largely from afar; my nestmates are both balaram, after all. It has been my experience that they are still more snake than human; they are not very sociable outside their own nests. This imbalance, however, is a necessary one; it counters the necessary more-human-than-serpent imbalance of the balaram, and the more-spirit-than-either imbalance of ahi such as myself. To be whole as a race, we need one another.

Auspices

The circumstances surrounding our birth are very important, my Sesha. Not only does our breed influence the talents and learning we bring to our lives as Nagah, but it also influences our predisposition to the things of spirit. A balaram will know more of how to influence and prey upon man's ways while an ahi finds he has a closer connection to storms and elemental power. So too does the time of our birth influence the path we walk.

When my First Skin was peeled from me, I felt many things, as I have said. But woven among the tangled cloth of my thoughts was a refrain of wakefulness, a feeling of restoration and renewal. It was later that I learned that because I had been born in the spring, and because I had shed my First Skin in the spring, that I was now attuned to the spring and its spiritual resonance.

That is the way of most of the shifting races; we are given to certain feelings, certain impulses depending on the auspices of our birth. The Wolves are ruled by the moon's phase; the Mokolé, by the face of the sun. The Bastet draw upon the hour of their birth, and we are influenced by the seasons. And not the seasons of the tropics, as one might assume. No, we are bound by the four seasons recognized in East and West alike, by a cycle that includes both fiery heat and icy cold. These seasons have a lingering hold on most of the Umbra, and on us as well. Of course, we do not let our auspices affect our duties — some Khurah may consider auspice a mandate for a specific role, but we are Nagah, and have but one role among us.

I understand that most Nagah shed their First Skin in the season of their birth — it is seen as unlucky should it happen otherwise. I have heard tales of Nagah born in the winter that changed for the first time in the summer, and how the conflict in their spirits maddened them. I sincerely hope they are but rumors.

Kamakshi

My Sesha, I am Kamakshi. I find it difficult to judge how deeply the season of my birth has affected my fortunes and my talents, but I will try.

The Kamakshi are the Nagah born in spring. This is the time when hibernation ends for those serpents in colder climes, when young are born. The Kamakshi reflect the warming of the world; we take pleasure in healing the ill, or in the presence of children. We dislike spending too much of our time sleeping, preferring to remain active. The element of our auspice is earth, and our virtue is generosity.

Do not think, however, that I mean to imply that Kamakshi are too fond of life to bring death. We do not confuse business with pleasure. Perhaps, just perhaps, we regret the necessity of a kill more than others — but regret is not mercy, particularly where a well-earned fate is concerned.

Kartikeya

After spring comes summer, the time of war, the season of the Kartikeya. We are not a passionate and demonstrative people, I fear — at least, not when compared to our human siblings and cousins — but those born in the rising heat of the summer are perhaps closest to the human feelings of passion and temper. The Rage of a Kartikeya burns hotter than that of any other Nagah, and when the killing fever is upon them, they are more terrible than any of us. Fire is the Kartikeya's element, and their virtue is vigor.

Some have said that the Kartikeya can make poor assassins, as their fervor injures their subtlety. That is not so. A Kartikeya's zeal leads them to sing songs not of mourning, but of inspiration. Though they are still far from being as demonstrative as humans or Khurah, the Kartikeya say what the rest of us might only think. They are warm as the sun on rocks, as swift as a forest fire. I am glad to have them among us.

Kamsa

With autumn, the blood cools. This is the season of the Kamsa, those of us born to an aspect driven further by logic and introspection. The autumn mind is a cool mind, one that coils about the thoughts of others and applies pressure to guide the others' actions this way and that. None knows the mind of a target, or of the Corrupter itself, like a Kamsa. The Kamsa's element is air, and their virtue is insight.

My nestmate Indra's Dart is Kamsa, born late in the autumn and almost into the winter. Though this is not the time to praise or criticize him, I can say I have learned much of the Kamsa from his presence. None could accuse a Kamsa of suffering overmuch from the "failing" of compassion; such thoughts don't occur easily to the autumn-born. Perhaps this impairs the Kamsa; my nestmate certainly has more difficulty dealing with humans than even an ahi such as myself does. But it was he who discerned the patterns in the old Nuwisha's thinking, and he who set the trail of false snares that tricked the coyote into our true trap. It would have been very difficult to catch a Khurah as slippery as this one without a Kamsa in our nest; I feel sorry for those nests that are not as fortunate.

Kali

Finally the cycle comes to winter, the season of the Kali. Where the Kamsa are cool, the Kali are cold, but it is a cold with purpose. In their own way, the Kali are as active and determined as the Kartikeya — they are driven by a desire for excellence, and are perhaps more devoted to our duties than any other auspice may be. They require such drive, for winter is not a good season for serpents, and it takes great perseverance to excel in the winter months. A Kali wears a sharpness like that of broken ice in her heart, and her fury is that of a soundless blizzard. Their element is water, and their virtue is clarity.

My nestmate Sajita Jadavi is Kali, born in midwinter. I see the marks of her auspice clearly upon her. She does not set a task down unfinished, and though she is offended by failure, she insists on carefully studying whatever mistakes she may make, however insignificant, that she may learn not to repeat them.

There are few vasuki that hatch in the winter, and so they are underrepresented among the Kali. This is not an issue of balance, if I may be so bold as to assume as much. It is simply the way things are; it would be ridiculous to ask snakes to hatch in the season least suited to support them.

Organization

Such are the traits we are born with, my Sesha. They influence our very being, our personality and even our ties with things of the spirit. I realize that they say little of us as a whole, but I cannot adequately explain how we come together without first describing what we are as individuals.

And we are individuals — not completely solitary, true, but far more scattered than the tribal societies of the Garou and similar Khurah. Our hierarchy is simple and limited; there are no more than twenty-seven Nagah in all the world whose role is simply to govern. Each nest must be self-sufficient, capable of operating without constant governance, but ultimately tied to the elders and the Wani to ensure that the laws are upheld over all.

The Wani

Above us all are the Wani, the Dragon Kings, the Great Storms. They are not Nagah — but we are their creatures. We are not *truly* their children, of course; our Mothers are Earth, Moon and River, not monsoon and ocean. But the Dragon Kings serve as our spirit patrons; they guide and command us as a werewolf's tribal totem might. Their home is Xi Wang Chi, a realm of clouds and wind, rain and thunder, a place where no shapeshifter is strong enough to endure more than a brief visit.

If not for the Wani, we would stand revealed to all the other Changing Breeds — for we would have to strike pacts with the other spirits, and their alliances with the Khurah would endanger our secrecy. I have at times lamented the lack of relations between our people and the remainder of the spirit world — save the elementals friendly to our auspices, of course. Only a fool does not desire more friends than he has. But I draw solace from the knowledge that the Wani *are* our allies, that they favor us above all others save only the Mokolé, and even then they will not endanger us to the Dragon Breed.

The Wani have served as lawgivers to the Nagah, but they do not govern us. They acknowledge our deeds and set spirits to aid us or to teach us new Gifts, but they do not intercede to judge our lawbreakers or make decrees unless the circumstances are dire. The business of our race is left to you, my Sesha, to the Crowns and to the nests themselves.

I have never counted the Wani. Our accounts say that there are as few as three, or as many as a hundred and eight. Who can say for certain? They show themselves to us in the forms they find comfortable, and an audience may be granted by one Dragon King or by as many as nine. Their names are innumerable, and only the scholars among us can keep track of them all. They are ultimately unknowable — but it is not our task, or our place, to name them.

The Sesha

You are the Sesha. You are the voice of the Wani, the many-headed serpent that governs our behavior. By tradition you are three in number; three balaram, three ahi and three vasuki. By law you are the heads of the race.

Your duties may well extend beyond my knowledge, but most are publicly known. You guard, administer and oversee Nandana, the greatest Ananta of all; by your law, it is kept as a place of respite for those of our kind who have earned the right to a few moons of rest. You keep the laws of the race, and decree punishment for those of us who betray their duties as Nagah. You oversee our progress like aunts and uncles, decid-

ing when we have earned an increase in station and increased privileges. You oversee the gateway to Xi Wang Chi, and ensure that none speak with the Wani who have not earned the honor.

Each spirit servant of the Wani is your servant as well, and they act as your messengers. The gates to Nandana do not open unless you decree it, and when you do so, Nandana's doorways may open into any Ananta in the world. You remain here, keeping this realm safe; should one of your number require the freedom to attend to outside affairs, he must first find a successor. I may only presume that you touch your feet to earthly soil from time to time, in order to maintain your fleshly bodies — but it *is* a presumption, and I beg pardon for mentioning it.

The Crowns

Below you, my Sesha, and below all other Sesha that have been and will be are the Crowns. They too are lawgivers, but on a regional scale; the Crowns were established so that the concerns of all nests in a given area could be more properly monitored and addressed. Each one is a council of Nagah, although they number but three; the world turns too quickly for us to spare more.

As you, my Sesha, keep your realm in the spirit world, the Crowns keep headquarters in the physical world. They too have the power to open gateways between their courts and the Ananta of their charges, although they do so much less frequently. If a nest must pursue a target from one Crown's jurisdiction to that of another, it is etiquette to inform each Crown of the chase. Not just etiquette, but common sense — for a Crown may know things about the target's flight that a nest might not.

The Vritra are your seconds here, in India and throughout Asia. The Yamilka oversee the Middle East. The Sayidi watch over Africa, and the Nemontana coordinate the activities of Nagah in Europe. The Zuzeka reside in the Americas. The Jurlungur oversee Australia and the Southern Pacific. It is difficult work, serving on a Crown — so much area to govern, and still with the limitations of any mortal Nagah. I feel a guilty relief that I am unsuited to do so, for I am not certain that I would be worthy of the challenge.

Nests

Below the Crown and the Sesha lies the nest — the foundation of our very society. The fall of Vinata taught us that, though we may not be pack animals like the Garou, we cannot afford to travel alone. It is as hard for one to know one's own internal balance as it is to know, to *truly* know the color of one's eyes. How often do we look into our own eyes? How often do we *look* there, to see what others see every day? Though it is a sacred charge to maintain our own balance, we *can* fail.

Thus we form nests, at once less and more than the "packs" of certain Khurah. We are not bound together by pack instinct or totem spirits. We come together by necessity, and our isolation from others brings a nest closer together still.

My Sesha, the bonds among nestmates are almost akin to those of a husband and wife. We are each other's closest friends, companions, helpmates and, more often than not, lovers. No marriage to Kinfolk can last as long or inspire such loyalty — at least, in my experience. I have heard of Nagah who have renounced their nests to remain with the humans they love — but I fear for them. I see my nestmates as extensions of myself, and I know they view me in the same light. To betray them is as alien a concept as betraying my hand by severing it at the wrist.

Of course, these bonds are not evident to those who do not know us well. We are, after all, subject to our own cool blood, and overt displays of powerful emotion are simply not intuitive to Nagah. But a nest's bonds run deeper than most humans would understand — few humans can call another human being friend, lover and sibling all at once, much less two. But what human could serve the role we do for years upon years, with none but his fellow assassins to hold him close?

A nest may be two or three; three is the luckiest number for a nest, but sometimes we must make do with two. It is a difficult to lose a nestmate, and the sole survivor of a devastated nest must sometimes rest in the Serpent Waters for years before he is able to accept the bonds of a nest once more.

Nests enjoy great autonomy in the field. By carrying our own havens with us in the form of the Ananta, we are not tied to any given locale. We are free to pursue targets wherever they may flee. Most nests settle in a specific locale, be it city or province, for a time, observing the local Khurah and following the Crown's directions. A nest may undertake many assignments before being called by the Crown or Sesha to relate their latest deeds, or crossing paths with another nest. As I said before, we are few in number, and cannot spend too much time fretting over formalities.

We cannot rely on coincidence or regular social gatherings to exchange information. When a nest has something vital to report to another nest, or to the Crown or Sesha, it tends to rely on encrypted messages carried by spirit messengers; mundane means are unreliable and not as secure as we require. In this way do we exchange information, but only when necessary to do so; optimally, a nest should be able to perform its missions in utmost silence.

Sannyasin

Despite our very real need for the companionship — and watchful eyes — of a nest, there are still Nagah who live alone. They do not *operate* alone, my Sesha; to hunt and punish without companions is forbidden by our laws. No, the Nagah who has chosen a life of solitude — the sannyasin — no longer serves as a judge and assassin. He becomes a hermit, an ascetic, never to kill again.

To become sannyasin is to die, to perform one's own funeral rite. Most who undergo Sannyasa have lived beyond the prime of their years, and feeling the touch of time upon them, choose to leave our world. Those who are crippled in battle may also choose to become sannyasin, fearing that their impaired faculties will endanger their nestmates — or worse, the Sacred Secret. I have even heard it said that some sannyasin were the sole survivors of their nests, and could not bring themselves to go on with another nest.

I, like many of my peers, look upon sannyasin with a mixture of pity and respect. I cannot imagine life without my nest, without my duty — but at the same time, I must admire their wisdom and strength of character in seeing when their time has come and being brave enough to accept it.

Kin Relations

Yes, my Sesha, I feel as though my heart is too much that of a Nagah to ever be close to humans, serpents, Khurah or beasts. But the Nagah cannot survive alone. Though we perform our duties in secrecy and seclusion, we require the bonds with our Kinfolk to continue as a race. There is little enough bonding to do with our serpent Kin, for obvious reasons — but to maintain the ties with our human mates and relatives is more difficult.

In all things, our relationships must be proper; it is unseemly and dangerous to develop relations with a human, mate or no, that endanger one's ability to work effectively with one's nest. It is a rare Nagah who has true friends outside his nest and Kin mate, and he who maintains such relations is a gambler. Such risks are highly discouraged by the law, and rightly so. This, I imagine, is one of the reasons why we seem so mysterious to the hengeyokai who know of us — but it also preserves the Sacred Secret, which is vital.

There are… internal reasons why we are poor companions to humans, as well. We understand emotions as serpents do not, but we also lack the great capacity for passion — excepting Rage — that humans possess. Each one of us, balaram, vasuki or ahi, is little closer to humans than we are to cobras. When we take a Kin mate, we are not unaffectionate, though the ties of blood or children are but a tenuous bridge across a wide chasm. Some of us are able to cross that bridge, and love our mates as we love our own nests, perhaps even more so. These must be the happiest of all our kind. I envy them.

When there is no love, however, we must still strive to treat our Kin with honor. Without them, there will be no more generations of balaram raised well. Many of us allow our mates to take other lovers, or even to marry publicly with us as their secret partners. In these cases, however, it becomes vitally important that each child born has the strongest blood possible. A Naginah may allow her Kin husband to impregnate his human (and preferably Kin) wife or lover without fear. But a Kin woman must strive to conceive her Nagah mate's child and not that of her human lover. It is much to ask of her, but we have no recourse.

There is also the question of faith.

Mortal Religion

It is no exaggeration to say that humanity has lost its collective way. Once they had the spirit world itself brushing against their fingertips; once they caressed the living world within the world and called it friend. No longer. Now a pit yawns within the mortal breast, a cavern that compels the human to devour all he can in the vain hope that he might satisfy his hunger. He eats more food than he needs to survive; he takes more lovers than he requires to attain solace. He sires more children than is necessary for the continuance of his race, and he gathers more goods than he needs to live comfortably. The human perceives that he has *need*, but he deceives himself into believing that his need coincides with his *want*, that the things he desires are the things that will make him whole.

Humans are clever, however. They are perhaps not as divine as they should like, but they are not completely blind. Many perceive that they hunger for a connection to the living world, or to the unseen. They go in search of that connection. Some wise few find it.

The humans understand the word "Gaia" — or at least, some of them do. Most understand the concept of the Earth Mother, even if so many discard the idea as a "primitive belief" unsuitable for their modern conceits. But in India, where our human Kin are most numerous, the strongest local faith has found a face of the Earth Mother. They call Her "Devi," and so too do we name the face of Gaia that is knowable as Devi. They understand the triune forces of Creator, Preserver and Destroyer, and they do not reject them as superstition.

It is arrogance to claim that we guided human religion in the years since the Severing. It was not our task; it was the task of the Apis to nurture humanity's connection with the spiritual world, and only they were properly suited to do so. Not being a historian, I cannot say whether the humans learned the name "Devi" from us, or whether we learned it from them — I would presume the former, but as I say, such a claim borders on arrogance.

Whatever the origin of these similarities, in some ways, they make the transition for our Indian balaram much easier. The beliefs they grew up with need not be discarded wholly — merely adapted to recognize the facets they did not previously see. The most difficult transition, however, is recognizing the flawed faces of the Destroyer and Preserver — the Wyrm of Corruption and Weaver of Suffocation, if you will. A young balaram's faith may be sorely tested in his first year; but I would be surprised if the same were not true of any human-born Khurah from any land.

Nagah Spirituality

What, then, of our faith as a whole? We share all the Changing Breeds' faith in Gaia; we believe we were crafted to serve Her will. We recognize the Triat of Creator, Preserver and Destroyer, and the unfortunate aspects each one has taken on in these dire days. We respect the mighty Incarnae and Celestines, though we are part of no pact with any save the Wani.

I am not a philosopher, my Sesha; my strength lies in the law, not in the shifting of celestial beings. I am ashamed at this failing, but I am certain that the things I know are shared by almost all our kind.

Three is a sacred number to all shapeshifters, but to us most of all; we owe our existence to Gaia, who birthed us, to Luna, who kissed us with spiritual power, and to Apsa, who gave us a home. Though their broods do not act as our servants, the Three Mothers are the most sacred beings in our faith; I would gladly die for them, as would my nestmates.

We are not alone in venerating Gaia and Luna; Gaia is sacred to almost all our Khurah cousins, and most of them are Luna's children as well. But Apsa — Apsa is *our* mother. No other Changing Breed, not even the Rokea, venerate Apsa in their prayers; none share our ties to the running water that is her domain. Gurahl fish from her rivers, Rokea may venture along their length, Mokolé may even hunt and sleep in Apsa's bosom — but only we make our homes at the bottom of her riverbeds. There are old stories of humans who could take the forms of freshwater fish, exterminated in the War of Rage — but they are cloudy rumors, which cannot even guess at what purpose such folk would serve the Mothers. No, I believe that we are Apsa's most precious children; she

serves the whole world with her blessings, but we are the only ones granted her dearest gifts.

Why us, the Serpent People? Why not fish or otters or other river-dwellers? I cannot say. Perhaps it is because we are the only ones with sharp enough teeth to serve her purpose; perhaps it is because our vasuki forms emulate her rivers. A snake may not be able to breathe water, but since the beginning of time human legend has painted serpents as creatures of water, attributed us with the power to call down rain, regulate the tides and alter the flow of rivers. Even before the Age of Kings, this was so.

Human legend is, once in a great while, extremely accurate.

From the river and fresh water we gain solace as does no other shapeshifter. It is our hidden strength, as well as our hiding place. I can imagine no more sacred place to be than lying on a riverbank under the full moon, water above me and earth beneath me. Those who violate Apsa by violating her rivers — in the name of their own enrichment — my Sesha, I think every Nagah believes in my heart that such people *must* die, even if it is not our task to ensure their deaths.

The Solace of Art

I think I cannot speak of our spirituality without mentioning our tradition of pursuing the arts. As I say, I am no philosopher — but I understand the lure of creation.

In many ways, we are compelled to create works of art and beauty. It serves the balance we hold dear to do so. After all, we are destroyers; and by filling that role, we also preserve the world and its inhabitants. The only thing lacking from our duty is the process of creation — and so, in our free time, we create. It suits our balance to do so.

Balance....

Your pardon, my Sesha. Balance is only part of the reason. We play music, we sing, we paint, we write poems, we practice calligraphy and sculpture and weaving because we cannot remain silent forever. Our serpent blood

does not desire to call out to others — but our human blood does. The Mothers did not remove our emotions from us entirely, and the Sacred Secret can be stifling in its silence. So we practice the arts because we must somehow express the desires in our hearts. We sing because we cannot speak.

The Sacred Laws

"You say you keep the laws for your nest." The speaker wore human form, and she was very young — perhaps in her twenties. Certainly she seemed far too young to have a place on the Sesha. She had not spoken until now. "How do you recount them?"

Dragon Boat almost smiled. Of all the things the Sesha might have asked him, this was the only question he'd been certain would come.

My Sesha, it is my duty as Nagah to understand the laws that bind all shapeshifters. My teachers taught me the laws of each one in turn, and I was a dutiful student. I can tell you the Garou Litany; I can recount the Duties given the Dragon Breed. I can say with certainty that the Coyotes are perhaps given too few laws, and I can criticize the Spiders for following laws that were perhaps given to them by the wrong sources.

And I know our own laws. We have many of them; we would be poor judges without laws to govern our sense of justice and fairness. The Wani give us laws for speaking to them and availing ourselves of their Gifts, the Sesha gives us laws for conducting ourselves, each of the Crowns lays edicts upon the nests under its guidance in order to increase their efficacy. But the Sacred Laws are those that bind us all, that we may not ignore. The original versions of these laws were given to us in the beginning of all things, and as the world has changed, we have made quite certain that our code has kept pace. Yet I believe in the truth of these laws, that each change made to their form is a change that was destined to happen at the right time. Like the dharma of all things, they are true to our hearts.

Preserve the Sacred Secret at All Costs

In the West, it is folly to let the Wolves, the Cats, the Rats or even the Ravens learn that we still live. Death would come upon us in a torrent — for the Khurah would reason that we still live because we have made a pact with the Destroyer, or that we have remained silent because we mean them ill.

The penalty to violate this law is death, and I do not challenge the wisdom of such judgement. Far, far too many people, human and shapeshifter both, are fools — fools who do not know how to hold their tongues, who cannot be trusted. But not all people are like this. It is my belief, my Sesha, that we do wrong to silence those who *are* wise, and temperate, and able to bear our secret with us.

Alas, I lack the wisdom of the Mothers, and I cannot claim that I am able to sift the trustworthy few from the silt of the rest with exact accuracy.

Honor the Three Mothers

We are born of earth, moon and river. We are made of the best traits of human, beast and spirit. We are given tremendous gifts to use in the observance of our duties. We would be ungrateful indeed if we did not honor the mothers who gave us these things. This law is not simply a mandate to say prayers on a regular schedule — it is a decree demanding that we defend the integrity and honor of the Three Mothers.

The most blatant abuse of this law I have seen is that of the nest who demands justice for Apsa and proceeds to destroy every human building along a riverbank that they can find. This is excessive behavior; I feel it would be more productive spending our efforts on those who pose a threat to the remaining Gurahl, so that the healers might yet have a chance to cleanse the rivers in full once more.

Punish Those Who Betray Their Duties

It seems odd to explain this tenet to my Sesha, but misinterpreting this duty has led to downfall before. It is our role to punish those who deliberately betray their duties to the Earth Mother and who are unlikely to receive justice from their fellows. We must punish those who have broken the laws, not their companions or relatives; we must punish in accordance to the crime; we must not let mercy or wrath interfere with proper justice being done. We must be certain of the guilt of our target and we must strike before he gains the chance to betray his duties further. They are simple guidelines, my Sesha, but not all Nagah obey even these.

Never Hunt Alone

Vinata fell because she did not trust other Nagah. We cannot afford to repeat her mistake. We must trust one another precisely because we cannot trust anyone else.

I wish I could say this law is inviolate, but I have heard many stories of Nagah whose nestmates died in the course of a mission and who decided to persevere and complete the judgement to honor their loss. This is, in my mind, forgivable — but he who takes other missions upon himself without rejoining a nest courts a fall.

Remain Humble

The assassin who overestimates his own abilities is a walking dead man. We must at all times retain a realistic assessment of our own skills, and given that the survival of our race is at stake, it is better to err on the side of prudence.

It is also noteworthy that many of the greatest disasters to befall the Changing Breeds — and of course

I speak of the War of Rage — stem from pride. No other justification for this law is necessary.

Abhor Imbalance

The laws that bind the other Changers bind us as well. The Nagah must remain in balance, in body as well as in spirit. It is not for us to breed irresponsibly, siring or bearing children from lust rather than necessity. There must always be a balance between the balaram, ahi and vasuki. Should the numbers of our breeds grow too far unbalanced, they must be set right.

This is obviously a preventative law, my Sesha, for it may apply to behavior in any number of situations. It is regrettably easier to recognize a Nagah who ignores this law than to acknowledge one who follows it virtuously.

Strike Against the Corrupter if the Opportunity Is True

This is the most recent tenet added to the Sacred Laws, my Sesha, and it is good advice. We are not the chosen warriors of the Earth Mother; that job has fallen to others. It is not our task to purge the Corrupter's minions from the land, sea and sky. However, the Khurah are far too few in number to stand any true chance of victory in the Last War if we do not assist them. This law charges us to strike against the Corrupter's minions and schemes, but only if we do not endanger our own mission in the process. To abandon the task of judgement in order to remove a spiritual cancer from the world is a grave temptation — but it is also an arrogant choice. Still, I must commend those who follow this tenet obediently, if not always prudently; it is a better thing than ignoring the corruption of the world entirely.

Punishment

The silence carried on for a minute or so before being broken by another of the Azhi Dahaka. Her speech, like that of her colleague, had no sound to it, but conveyed the feeling of distant thunder.

"You have spoken well, Dragon Boat, and you have proven that you understand who you are and why you do as you must." The ahi bowed deeply in reply.

"One question remains unanswered." The statement floated in the air like a silken scarf. Dragon Boat bowed again.

"Yes, my Sesha."

"If we are to understand your dilemma, then you must explain how it is you interpret our First Duty — and why your course is not clear."

Dragon Boat's breath hung high, in the tops of his lungs — and slowly slid out as his face tightened.

"Yes, my Sesha."

The Emerald Mandates

The Nagah who move among the Beast Courts of the Emerald Mother must balance the laws of their own kind with the Mandates that govern the shapeshifters of the east. This double burden is not an easy one to bear, given the inflexibility of Nagah law, but the wereserpents are used to the heavy weight of duty.

Shirk Not the Tasks Which Have Been Given You

The Nagah of the Beast Courts take the First Mandate extremely seriously. Their task is to enforce the First Mandate, and by enforcing the mandate, they obey it. To obey it, they must enforce it. That is the Law. As a result, almost every Nagah among the hengeyokai knows the Rite of Quiet Burial.

Guard the Wheel, That It May Turn in Fullness

Eastern Nagah obey this mandate with particular reverence, relating it to their task of punishing the errant. Several Asian nests have made it their exclusive purpose to assassinate those of any race who threaten to halt the Wheel in the Sixth Age.

Presume Not to Instruct Your Cousin in His Task

Needless to say, the Nagah find it difficult, even impossible to reconcile perfect obedience to this mandate and to the First Mandate. Their task *is* to instruct their cousins, albeit in lethal fashion. Therefore, most Nagah of the Beast Courts interpret this mandate to mean "do not rebuke small things — wait to punish the larger offenses."

Honor Your Territory in All Things

The rivers of the East are particularly sacred to the Nagah, who have found themselves hard-pressed to contain their righteous anger in recent times. Only the words of compassionate balaram have pre-vented the ahi and vasuki of India from going to extreme lengths to stop the humans from befouling the Ganges any further.

Let Mercy Guide You in Our August Mother's Court

The Nagah know full well that any acts of violence that so much as seem unwarranted might well turn the rest of the Beast Courts against them a second time. This mandate further reinforces their rules of secrecy and prudence; no Nagah wishes to be seen as a corrupt judge.

Honor Your Ancestors and Your Elders

The Nagah are dutiful children, and pay respect to their deceased forebears as proper relatives should. However, a Nagah will not overlook the actions of an elder should they be worthy of punishment. Nagah don't like to strike against those that outrank them, but they will pass the news on to *their* elders....

Honor the Pacts with the Spirit World

Eastern Nagah do indeed honor their pact with the Wani, but since they have no pacts with any other spirits, they do not observe most of the common rites and rituals. Most prefer to remain unnoticed by spirits that are not their allies.

War Not Upon Human nor Beast

The Nagah rarely kill in passion, and rarely in numbers. This mandate suits them well.

Let No One or Nothing Violate the Sacred Places

Though they prefer not to take open action against invaders, the Nagah are as dedicated as any other hengeyokai to defending the sacred sites of the Emerald Mother. Those who lay siege to a court's caern must watch their backs as well as their flanks and front line.

The Wolves fight. The Cats stalk. The Ravens watch. The Sharks endure. So it is with each one of the beast-people who were given great spirits by Gaia. The magnificent gifts given each of us are not pure largesse — they are tools given to craftsmen, weapons issued to soldiers. With these comes duty.

Our duty, as it has been since the first Nagah bowed before the Dragon Kings, is to punish.

It is, of course, more complicated than that. If we were to punish every living being, be they human, werebeast or monster, for violating the laws its people holds sacred, the rivers of this world would run with our venom and their blood and people would *still* sin. It is simply the nature of the free-willed — as long as there is a choice, some will choose dishonor or even evil.

It is *our* task to punish those who have violated the rules of their own kind, and whose affronts to the Mothers would, without our intercession, go unpunished, unnoticed, or even rewarded. And to properly serve our duty, we must observe, judge and deliver punishment.

The first, and perhaps most vital, stage of any task is to observe the target. That is, this is the first stage if we already know his name and crimes — if not, then *locating* the target is the first step. But they are both mostly the same thing. We are bound by duty to watch our target closely, to properly establish his routine, his abilities, his resources, and even his crimes if they are left unclear. This takes time, of course. It is a poor Nagah who is willing to rush to judgement without performing proper surveillance first. The only force that could convince me to abandon observation before the proper time would be a direct order from the local Crown or from you, my Sesha.

When the target has been properly identified and watched in his affairs, then judgement may proceed. It is proper — even necessary — that nests retain a great deal of autonomy in delivering judgement. The fate of a target of the Nagah lies entirely within the hands of the nest that watches over him; we cannot drown our superiors in constant requests for guidance.

Forgive us, Sesha. We believe we have no choice.

When all the information has been properly shared, then judgement is usually swift. A nest is, as I have said, often of one heart and mind; we are rarely in disagreement. The verdict is almost always "guilty"; if enough evidence has been tallied to proceed to the judgement, then it is usually enough to damn the target. All that remains is to decide upon the sentence — which is almost always death, my Sesha — and how to carry it out.

Execution is a most careful affair. A nest must plan the means of isolating the target, the counters for his strengths, and the method of execution itself. Although we have been granted potent venom for the pursuit of our duties, it is not always the ideal choice; certainly not if the body is to be found. If we poison a target, or crush him in our coils, or rend him with our claws, then we must destroy the body as well, in order to preserve the Sacred Secret. The veils of the Wani extend only so far.

It is in many cases preferable, however, to arrange a more mundane-seeming "accident." These are *much* more difficult to arrange, of course; the Khurah are not soft targets. But if we can see to it that the body is found amid the evidence of his crime, seemingly slain in a way most coincidental and fitting, then the other Khurah have learned a lesson from their brother's fate. Foolish Nagah, or perhaps the inexperienced, are the most likely to poison first and then try to cover their tracks with the Wani's veils. But the accomplished and renowned among us know better.

● ● ●

Dragon Boat sighed and spread his hands helplessly. "Which brings us to the Nuwisha we have brought before you. We caught him spying upon us — but we have had no time to observe him. His death would preserve the Sacred Secret — but is it just?

"My nestmates and I are in disagreement. Perhaps Manyskins is indeed a liability, one who will pass word of our existence on to the other skinchangers. If he does so, then he is arguably not only a threat, but in need of punishment — for instead of teaching as is his duty, he will be fomenting a third War of Rage. Perhaps, though, he does not intend to reveal our secrets — in which case killing him would be, in my estimation, practical but of questionable virtue.

"But I wonder — in learning our ways, in stealing our secrets, is this Nuwisha trying to teach us something? Is there a lesson in his paws that we have yet to unravel?"

Dragon Boat bowed his head and spread his hands. "I cannot know. This is my dilemma, O my Sesha, and the dilemma that faces our nest. Do we slay the Coyote and call it justice — or necessity? Do we let him live? We ask you to understand why it is that we cannot agree — why our laws fail us. Command us, and we shall obey."

Around the World

Dragon Boat waited for a few breaths. The cobra with the wide hood, the one that had first addressed them, mind-spoke again.

"Not yet, Night's Passage. There is more yet we wish you to tell us — the portions of your education that do not come from songs or law books. You are a far-ranging nest; what have you learned from your travels?"

Jadita stepped forward and bowed again. "Sesha, permit me."

Nagah in the Wild

Sesha, the world is large, and we can be found across more of it than not. We are blessed with a degree of flexibility unequaled by any one of the Khurah. We are found on all continents but one, and we've made forays even there, and recently. There are Nagah in the densest jungles, in the deserts and across nearly every stretch of fertile plains. We are in the rivers, the lakes and the oceans, places commonly — though falsely — believed accessible only to the Rokea and some few Mokolé.

There are few places that are not habitable by the serpents that are our Kin: tundra, the high mountains and other places where frost covers the ground year round, and a handful of islands. But our human Kinfolk can be found even there, and there is no place on this planet that a Nagah cannot go, if necessary, to fulfill her grave responsibilities. My nest alone has visited locales as inhospitable as Arabia's Rub al-Khali, the Canadian tundra and, most recently, the white gem called Antarctica.

It is a great help that we are gifted by Gaia with the Ananta, the underwater home that gives us shelter and access to the Velvet Shadow's secrets, that small world we carry within ourselves and speak forth into the waters with the Ananta mantra. Since this small realm goes everywhere with us, we are not tied to any one place, Sesha; we may weave our way through the world, shifting and roaming as needed, arriving and taking our leave as easily and as quietly as the stars.

It should be no surprise that we are found everywhere, Sesha. Snakes and humans are both marvels of adaptability, and that alone is suitable explanation for our kind's seeming ubiquity. As my great teacher Jaya Devi once told me, the greatest secret of the Nagah is that of being everywhere while not appearing to be anywhere. It is our finest mystery.

Human cunning enhances the serpents' wisdom. We watch. We adapt. We improve. We pass unseen and thrive. Where our prey goes, there go we. We burrow, we climb, we swim. With such variation among our number, how could our success ever be in doubt?

Our human and serpent heritage serves us well. Our Kin extend across the world. We are not shackled, as some Khurah are, by small, isolated pockets of Kinfolk here and there. Our vasuki Kin are everywhere, including the turquoise waters of the tropical seas. Our balaram Kin, while moderately less common, have spread throughout Eurasia, Africa, Australia and South and North America.

And that, Sesha, is as it must be. As Gaia's appointed judges and executioners of rogue Khurah, we must be where they live, where they operate and where they go to hide. Given the role the Nagah play, it is essential that we be capable of entering any nest, den, warren or caern as balance and justice demand. And we *are* capable. My nest alone has poisoned a psychotic Garou in Wyoming, blown apart a Wyrm-ridden Mokolé hiding in the Atrocity Realm and, in Japan,

removed the head from a babbling Tengu whose chatter nearly betrayed several of his kind to the Wyrm.

I do not think, Sesha, that this old Nuwisha is inclined to spread the word of our existence. The Coyote Folk — and we know them well, thanks to the Nagah who reside in America's Southwest — are tricksters, but they are not stupid and they are not malicious to Gaia's children. It is not curiosity that is a crime, but betrayal. I believe that if he is released, he will remain quiet about the Nagah. But I say that knowing that if he is not, then there is no place for him, or anyone he speaks with, to hide from us. Not even…

The Cities

Though they are not the most hospitable environments, cities are home to many, many Nagah and many of our Kinfolk of both breeds. Historically, India has been the key cultural center of the Serpent Folk. That being the case, how could we not wind up living in the most overpopulated cities on earth? Calcutta, Mumbai and New Delhi swarm with activity. And, again, where there are Khurah, there are the Nagah, watching them and waiting. Serpents, after all, commonly eat vermin, and modern cities are host to vermin of all sorts.

We've been in these cities since the Impergium. We know them well. We know which Khurah fre-

quent which cities and where in these cities they go. In the Indian cities we know best — cities that are not full of pristine nature, cities that do not have extensive parks, cities that are not pretty or serene — you will not find many Garou. The noble mystics among them find that such plebeian living clashes with their romantic natures. Likewise, there's not enough glamorous business to attract many Glass Walkers, certainly not a pack's worth — and they hate that. They are, by nature, pack animals, and being alone leaves them feeling vulnerable. The one or two who have come in to check out the city appear to have had business setbacks or personal issues call them back to a "real" city like Hong Kong, London or New York. We have noticed that about the Wolves: they're quite fierce in packs, but if you put one or two into a strange new situation by themselves, they get most uncomfortable. The pack tactics that are their greatest strength can also prove a liability. The so-called Fangs of Gaia are arrogant and vicious when the advantage of numbers is theirs, but, when you get one alone in a strange environment, he rapidly becomes the "coward of Gaia."

So, in these crowded cities, reeking with the assorted stenches of humanity, you will find the Ratkin, the Khan, the Ananasi, the Corax — and you will find us. In such crowded places, largely abandoned by the Wyld, the Garou are blessedly rare.

Obviously, we are most familiar with these over-populated places, but we are found in cities of all sizes. Many of us are bred and reared in the hearts of the most densely populated cities on Earth. Those of us who grew up balaram under those conditions are often uncommonly streetwise, and any place less crowded, then, feels almost bucolic in comparison.

India

This vast country was once the setting of the Nagah's greatest achievements. Our history in India — including those regions now belonging to Sri Lanka, Pakistan and Bangladesh — boasts, I think, the apex of interaction between humans and the Changing Breeds. Mutual respect and appreciation prevented most of the difficulties that could have arisen. We lived openly, recognized and respected as servitors of Devi. Our wisdom and strength were honored and we claimed the two highest castes: the priests and warriors — the Brahmins and the Kshatriya — as our Kinfolk. To this day we remain a part of their cultural history. Since our sudden disappearance following the War of Rage, we have come to be thought of as quaint mythological figures.

There are scholars among our kind who assert that too much emphasis is placed on India's place in Nagah history. I cannot say. We have always been found around the world, of course, and we have played a role of one sort or another in most cultures, but in India we were common enough that our existence was taken for granted. There were many times in ancient India when we were called upon to act as intermediaries between the humans and the other Khurah. I believe was no city or significant village that did not have its Nagah guide. Our goal was not to rule the humans or conduct some strange variant of the Impergium; we simply wanted to bridge the gap between the world of Devi's servants and those we shepherded. Since our duties to Gaia do not bring us into conflict with humans the way those of the Garou and Ratkin do, our association with the humans was a relatively simple matter. That the deeds of one of our own brought such harmony to an end is a heavy burden of knowledge for us to bear.

After our exodus from India and after the War of Rage brought the Age of Kings to an end, Indian Nagah seemingly disappeared from India just as completely as they did from all other places. Still, there are many more Nagah and Kinfolk scattered throughout India than any other single place. Wild wolves, you may note, are notably absent from India, although a few Silver Fangs arrived with the waves of British colonization. Our own efforts to resist the machinations of the Corrupter, combined with those of the Bagheera, Khan, Makara Mokolé and Ratkin have largely made the Garou presence unnecessary and unwanted. While the campaign against the Corrupter necessitates allowing some Garou in, we attentively monitor the Wolves' numbers to prevent any unhealthy accumulation that might compromise our secrecy or effectiveness.

Grand Nagah history aside, this is a wondrous land. There are jungles, rivers, plains and hundreds of miles of coastline. The king cobra, while not as numerous as in days gone by, is not so endangered as the Kin of many Khurah, and our human relatives are, quite literally, everywhere. There exist lineages of our Kinfolk descended from the Brahmins and Kshatriyas who know of our existence and arrange marriages strategically to keep the cobra blood strong in our Kin.

I wish that I could speak as beatifically about the overpopulation here. A billion people, Sesha! Even China is hard-pressed to contain such a large number, and India is not so large. Where the people are crowded too close, the suffering comes. We are not a people intrinsically prone to corruption, but so many people, so densely packed — the spirit world grows thick with the spirits that prey upon human misery. Even if no greater percentage of India's population is in misery than elsewhere, that is still a percentage of a vast population in a small place — which cannot bode well.

Asia

Asia is a somewhat different story. We are rare in the north; this is largely true of our kind in Asia north of the thirtieth parallel. We have serpent Kinfolk up there, obviously, and some small number of human Kinfolk, but full-blooded Nagah are scarce. Much of the area — Afghanistan, Kazakhstan, Mongolia, Russia — is too mountainous, too cold and too inhospitable for our heat-loving kind. The Garou also become more numerous and more powerful the farther north one ventures into those lands. Northern China, Korea and Japan are all essentially empty of wereserpents. Much of that is due to the efforts of the Nezumi during the War of Shame. While nests do travel there to perform duties, we find such places hostile and leave them relatively quickly.

The South, particularly the Southeast, however, is a different story. We are stronger in the lush jungles and warm rivers of Southern China, Burma, Cambodia, Malaysia and Viet Nam. We are scattered throughout the islands, too; Indonesia, Sri Lanka, the Andamans, the Nicobars, the Philippines and the Maldives — all are Nagah territory. Between the rampant green growth and the plentiful water, we could hide in such places forever. We thrive along the verdant banks of the Mekong, the Si Kiang, the Salween and the Hong rivers. There is a small village in the Irriwady River Delta in Thailand whose population consists entirely of human Kinfolk and a number of Nagah nests. In such places, free of Garou aggression and protected by a close-knit network of extended family, we may yet increase in numbers to levels unheard of, as though the Emerald Mother soon expects to have need of many judges and executioners. This village, whose name we all know but which shall go unnamed even here, is where Nagah go when they are recovering from wounds, when they are looking for nestmates and when they need to regroup. It is possible that future Nagah will look upon Southeast Asia as we currently look upon India: the epicenter of Nagah existence and culture. We are justifiably vigilant in our guarding of this fact, as we must be. If *this* were the information that Manyskins had stumbled upon, his bones would already be cold.

The Beast Courts

The territory of our greatest visibility — and, therefore, vulnerability — is in the Beast Courts of the Emerald Mother. Nowhere do we maintain a higher profile. Our existence — even our role — among the Hengeyokai is an open secret to all of our East Asian cousins. We are free to participate as fully or as minimally as we choose in the Beast Courts' business. Not only do we not keep our existence secret from the hengeyokai, but the rare Nagah who has not participated in a nestbinding may even become a part of a large, temporary "nest" — called a sentai — with Khurah. Such risky behavior is rare — for the most part we remain firmly in the shadows, an accepted and unmentioned fact of life, quietly carrying out our duty to Devi. But you, Sesha, gave this arrangement your blessing, citing that where the Nagah may be effectively reintegrated into the lives and consciousness of the Khurah, it is our duty to attempt to do so.

In theory, we are capable of acting so brazenly among the hengeyokai only because of their deeply ingrained sense of honor; we believe, *in theory*, that we can trust them. We have a tacit understanding with the hengeyokai, from the chattiest Tengu to the wiliest Kitsune, that they will keep the presence of the Nagah secret from outsiders as part of their duty to the Emerald Mother. Thus far, it has been miraculously effective. They keep our existence secret from the Sunset People and all other *shen*, and in return we monitor the hengeyokai most closely for imbalance and correct or purge it as necessary.

What I find myself wondering, Sesha, is why we feel we cannot trust the wisdom of even a wise old Nuwisha like Manyskins when, in the Beast Courts, we entrust even young Kitsune with the knowledge of our existence. Honor is honor. I do not believe that the Sunset People, on the whole, are ready to accept our existence or our role among the Khurah. But I do believe that if we are willing to share the secret of our existence with the likes of the Tengu, the Hakken and the Nezumi, that we should certainly be able to rely on the discretion of one wise, proven Nuwisha.

Australia

Australia, once a treasure, is a very sad place for us now. We once shared the continent with a tribe of very wise Garou called the Bunyip. The War of Rage didn't affect Australia, and our folk there were not wiped out and for centuries did not need to hide. Bunyip and Nagah existed harmoniously, perhaps even amicably, in part because their totem was the Rainbow Serpent, said by some to be one of the Wani themselves.

When the Europeans arrived with their Garou, we knew enough to disappear immediately. The Sesha advised the disappearance there to avoid a Third War of Rage. Living unmolested for centuries had allowed our numbers to attain an equilibrium of sorts and, as much as our Folk didn't want to go underground, it was better than being warred upon by rabid dogs.

They did not know our particular responsibilities to the Emerald Mother, and it was only infrequently that we were forced to act against the Bunyip because they were quite attuned to the balances of their tribe, and they policed themselves efficiently. It was, we believe, that same combination of honor and self-discipline that made them blind to the other tribes' imbalance and ultimately led to their extinction. Their naïveté blinded them to the significantly less noble motives of the other Garou; they were unprepared for the aggression, greed and malice of their cousins. Only in the last years of their existence did the Bunyip realize that the other Garou were behaving as they were out of imbalance and lack of insight. By then, of course, it was too late.

In retrospect, there was no good resolution to the conflict once it began. We could easily have ignited yet another War of Rage had even our small part been discovered. The Bunyip would still be dead, and many more Garou and Nagah as well. That is no consolation. Rainbow Serpent has no more Garou children and there is nothing we can do to change that now. While our Australian brethren would still be happy to avenge the Bunyip, they do not. Curiously, the vengeful ghosts of the Bunyip appear to be doing that themselves, and for that we are pleased.

Australia has an enormous population of Nagah Kinfolk. Highly venomous sea snakes are quite common just off the Australian coast. Almost all of the snakes of Australia's mainland are extraordinarily venomous, and two of them, the taipan and the tiger snake, rank among the deadliest snakes on the planet. In the modern era, it is not uncommon for Nagah to travel to Australia just to mate with such potent serpents. We have a number of Kinfolk among the aborigines of Australia as well, mostly in the jungles to the north, far from the major cities.

Africa

In the far distant past, several millennia ago, Africa was once nearly as great a homeland as India. Egypt, in particular, with the rich Nile flowing through and flooding the land, was home to many Nagah and their Kinfolk. The War of Rage never quite reached into the depths Africa, where the Simba and the Mokolé were powerful and numerous enough to repel the Garou's incursions. It was not the werewolves who decimated our population in Africa, but vampires in the east and mortals in the west.

Egypt had long been a home for the Nagah. Human and serpent Kinfolk were both relatively common, and the relatively sophisticated civilization was a new high for the humans. It attracted curiosity seekers among the Khurah, fascinated by the Preserver's influence among our human cousins. Where the Khurah were, then, so were we.

When the Nagah heard rumors of a terrible serpent god, we felt certain that one of our own number had been claimed by the Destroyer. When we moved, *en masse*, to destroy the corrupted one, we discovered not a mad Nagah, but an extremely powerful vampire with the ability to assume the Kali Dahaka form and use other serpentine Gifts. Many nests of Nagah tried to destroy this pretender, but to no avail. We destroyed legions of vampires, many of them extraordinarily powerful, but to no end. In time, the Nagah of Eastern Africa either died combating the vampire or left. The hardest part of conceding the monster's victory was watching as the serpent fell from its position as a symbol of wisdom to a symbol of corruption. Devastating as it was, we still fared better than the Bubasti.

Most wereserpents, particularly those of African and Asian extraction, nurse an icy vendetta against this vampire — Sutekh — and those who serve him. Nagah still go far out of their way to destroy vampires who follow him.

Eastern Africa was all but cut off to us. Western Africa, then, became the homeland for African Nagah. It wasn't as comfortable for our human Kin, but we managed. We lived for some time in relative peace among our human Kinfolk, the Yoruba, and our serpent Kin, the mambas, kraits and others.

Then the slavers came looking for trade fodder. They sought out the strongest, healthiest individuals they could find. Those of the serpent blood were particularly prized for their strength, their health and overall fitness. While Nagah were able to kill their captors and escape, our Kinfolk were not. The culling was ruthless, and nearly every Nagah Kinfolk from the western coast of Africa was stolen from his family, village and people. We have heard tell that the Mokolé suffered the same form of predation. Some of our kind went along with the slavers just to see what had become of their Kinfolk. The Nagah of western Africa were left with only serpent Kin to mate with. To this day, the Nagah of Africa are still somewhat more connected to their cold-blooded Kin than their human relatives, and they share certain insights in common with the Garou of the Red Talons tribe for that reason.

South America

While not as numerous as in the rest of the Southern Hemisphere, we are still strong enough in South America. It took our ancestors a very long time to discover South America; they did not discover it immediately after the exodus from Bharat, but once they found it, they took to it immediately. The lush rain forests extend for miles, hiding our serpent and human Kin alike. As with Africa, the Second War of

Rage had little effect on our Kinfolk or us in the jungles where our mastery of guerilla tactics protected us from the Garou. We certainly didn't meet the same fate as the Camazotz, though we've avenged a few. Oddly enough, our Kinfolk in Brazil benefited from the slave trade. Just as a large number of those taken from West Africa were Kinfolk, so were those same Kinfolk delivered to Brazil and other areas of South America. The vigor of new Kinfolk was a great boon to the Nagah of South America, and one that still serves them well.

The Nagah of South America, however, do not travel or reveal much of themselves. With so many Ananasi and Bastet to keep track of, and so many tools of the Corrupter at work, they are thoroughly enmeshed in their obligations. Developments are unfolding there in the war between Gaia and the Wyrm that demand constant attention. The Bastet, Mokolé and even the Ananasi are all playing their parts in the turning of the great wheel, and as they do so, some buckle beneath its weight and fall to the Wyrm. For those unfortunates, we arrange endings.

Our position in South America is strong also because of the protection of Uktena. He, like the Rainbow Serpent of Australia, is willing to speak to us. Many of his brood — including the feathered serpents, the wingless dragon spirits, sea serpents, Kolowissi and Inadu — are simply servants of the Wani wearing different masks. There were times in the Second War of Rage where Uktena, and the Garou who follow him, would hide or protect us out of respect for the spirits we jointly revered. We appreciated the gesture. It's a pity the Camazotz were not deemed fit to receive the same consideration.

The Caribbean

The slave trade took many of our Kinfolk from Africa's west coast and delivered them to the Pure Lands. They took their knowledge of the Nagah with them and sometimes incorporated it into their spiritual beliefs. Yoruban religion was infused with Christian mythology to create hybrid beliefs including voudoun, Santería, shango, umbanda, macumba, batuque and candomblé. Throughout the Caribbean, and even in Louisiana, our Kinfolk have infused their communities with an awareness of snake spirits and reverence for the serpent god, whom they call Damballah.

North America

While we were never numerous in North America, there was a time, before the second War of Rage, when we were relatively evenly spread across the continent. There would be far fewer of us had we not dropped out of sight when we did. Many insightful Nagah, heeding the words of the Corax, anticipated the second War of Rage. They contacted the Sesha and shared their knowledge. Through the intermediary of the Sesha, they invited all Nagah to disappear with them for a while, even as the Garou began murdering the Gurahl, Pumonca and Qualmi, even as they annihilated the Camazotz — over nothing. Nagah nests faded from sight throughout the world, but they became particularly silent in North America where the Garou were especially strong. When our absence was noted, the Corax were the first to announce that the Nagah were dead. The first to say so were allies of the Nagah who'd been asked to do so as a means of atoning for their… questionable behavior during the War of Rage. They passed that bit of information on to the other wereravens who spread the word, and within a decade, it was a known fact that the Nagah — variously mourned as the artisans of Gaia, the dancers of Gaia, the diplomats of Gaia and the thinkers of Gaia — were extinct.

It was a distressing departure. The Nagah of Europe and Asia had been devastated by the first War of Rage; they were keeping a low profile already. For the Nagah of North America, the disappearance was difficult. Leaving their Kinfolk along the Mississippi, the Columbia, the Colorado and all the other great rivers was difficult, but necessary. Watching the change in the temperament of the Garou we thought we knew was also quite disturbing. Before our strategic disappearance, we had amicable dealings with the Uktena, though they never entirely shed their aloofness, despite their Totem's advocacy on our behalf. Our relationship with the Croatan was cordial and occasionally even warm, particularly throughout the Mississippi river basin. The Wendigo we rarely encountered, and when we did, we found their ways questionable. Their cannibal totem may be guiding them in directions that are unwise, and though they are more numerous than we by far, the day may come when we are required to act against many, many of their number.

Our secrecy has not yet resulted in a general Nagah repopulation. Though our Kinfolk, serpent and human, are not overly rare, the population of Nagah has been slow to recover due, in large part, to the social barriers we have erected between our Kin and us. Nest bonds are so tight that outsiders, even Kinfolk, are kept at a distance. In addition, many of the poisonous serpents of the land, such as the eastern diamondback rattlesnake, are now in grave danger.

Many, perhaps most — though I hope not — of the new Nagah being born in North America are ahi. I fear the consequences such imbalance might bring.

Europe

The War of Rage hit us harder in Europe than anywhere else, and we never have recovered. The odd thing about Europe is that it still has relatively large numbers of Kinfolk, both human and serpent, but very few Nagah. Ireland is obviously an exception here. In the last century, a few Nagah have gone to Europe from India and Pakistan. They've taken to breeding with the local Kinfolk with some success. While this helps in some small way to restore Europe's meager Nagah population, it does little to restore the cultures that once held the serpent sacred.

The Oceans

The Rokea are not the only shapeshifters living in the ocean. While it is their stronghold more than it is ours — particularly the depths — we are quite capable of living our entire lives beneath the ocean's waves. There are Nagah who go out of their way to mate with the sea snakes of the tropical oceans, which are both perfectly adapted to their watery existence and extremely venomous. Those Nagah who prefer the oceans to the land live predominantly in the southern Pacific and Indian Oceans. Malaysia, in particular, is home to a large portion of our sea folk. Their Kinfolk are mostly islanders. They tend to be inspired artists, though their nests are even more insular and reclusive than is typical for Nagah.

The Umbra

Though we are less adept at entering the world of spirits than, say, the Corax, Nuwisha or even Garou, fulfillment of our duty requires that we be able to enter the strange waters of the Umbra. The Nagah are the only ones able to reach certain spirit waters. The Rokea cannot easily reach the Umbra, nor are they typically found in fresh water; the other Changing Breeds are found almost exclusively above the surface. Guardianship of the other waters of the Umbra, then, falls to the Nagah.

Our passport to the world of spirits is the watery door, the jewel of passage: the Ananta. If we have taken the Ananta into ourselves, we are able to will ourselves into the spirit world just as the Garou do by entering through the reflecting doors; the underside of clear water is ideal.

If we have breathed the Ananta into the water, then it becomes the place we must pass through to enter the Umbra. If we have breathed out the Ananta and we are not near it, entering the Umbra requires extreme measures.

Nagah are not prone to exploration of the Umbra's mysteries. We are, by nature as well as construction, close to the Earth, and only rarely do our duties require us to enter the Umbra. My own nest has executed its responsibilities to Gaia only once while in the spirit world. That said, there are two strong reasons — and one less urgent one — when Nagah may venture into the spirit world for extended periods.

The purpose of the Nagah is to judge and kill shapeshifters who have turned against the Emerald Mother. Stalking the Umbra is sometimes the only way to track down certain targets. Nests of Nagah, disguised as mages, Mokolé or something altogether different, will enter the spirit lands for extended periods, if required, to hunt down one whose life we are responsible for ending. As you know, Sesha, this frequently requires a great deal of adaptation and skill, particularly if the prey we seek is Ratkin or Corax; both of those Breeds are capable of going places the Nagah usually do not, but we are more than equal to the task. Serpents have been preying on tunnel rodents since the dawn of time, and even Corax need to land sometime.

Hiding is the second reason we may enter the Umbra. Disappearing into the Deep Umbra saved the lives of countless Nagah during the War of Rage. Some learned an exotic Gift from the Wani that allowed them to curl into fetal position and exude a shell around themselves. The Serpent's Egg, as it's called, allowed them to float, unaging and well-protected, through the farthest reaches of the Umbra for decades — if not longer. It is my understanding, Sesha, that these strange voyagers still return from time to time bearing tales of Nagah history that they recount as though the exploits transpired only a week ago.

The third, and least pressing, reason for a lengthy stay in the velvet shadow is the re-creation of the self. Judgment and assassination of wayward forces of nature — in essence what all shapeshifters are — is a heavy burden, nor does the current age, the Kali Yuga, provide us with a shortage of urgent targets. To prevent the twisting of the soul, many Nagah retreat to certain safe regions of the spirit world to divert themselves.

Ananta

It is not surprising that many of us are found in the water. It means freedom to many of our kind. On the land we are slow, whether walking or crawling, the ground sets limits for us. Those of us used to crawling find walking awkward and a bit precarious, though it is faster. Those of us used to walking find crawling to take far too long and to give no perspective on where we're going.

In the water, however, we can take advantage of our full dexterity. It is also the water that gives us access to the spirit world. The Ananta, the little dream world we carry within ourselves and breathe into the water, is our doorway into the Umbra. We carry them where we need them within ourselves. When we settle in a new river or on a new stretch of coastline for a time to attend to business, we breathe out our home beneath the surface of the water. Within that sacred serpent space, we are the masters of the water, knowing what is within its bounds, able to travel from edge to edge at the speed of thought. Better yet, once a group of Nagah is nestbonded, they share each other's Ananta. When three Nagah establish an Ananta, it can take up a large stretch of a river or coastline.

In the Ananta, slipping into the Umbra is just a matter of wishing it so. We don't even need reflective surfaces. On the other hand, if the Ananta is established in the water and we are *away* from the water, we are not able to enter the spirit world except through extraordinary effort.

The Ananta is heavily warded. Those the Nagah want kept out are kept out. Those the Nagah want kept within are kept within.

Permanent Ananta

Other Ananta, like great Nandana, Sesha, do not get moved. It is made of the Anantas of several Nagah and since it is unmoving, structures may be built within it, and the Nagah masters of the Ananta are attuned to every building and every visitor to the realm. The masters of such permanent Ananta are quite powerful. Within their private realms, they may control who enters, who leaves and who has passage to and from the Umbra. Entering such a place unbidden is the act of one who is unafraid of death.

The Serpent Waters

The Near Umbral reflections of certain bodies of water have proved themselves to be safe havens for us. Those that we have claimed for our own and sanctified we call the Serpent Waters. These are typically the reflections of pure tropical rivers or small lakes, though a number of Serpent Waters exist in the reflections of many coral reefs, particularly in the Indian Ocean and the tropical Pacific. Those are the refuges of the sea snake Nagah.

Serpent Waters are watery Glens. Being in the Umbra, the water takes on hues that it cannot in the physical realm. Swimming through the Serpent Waters is like gliding through liquid sapphires and flowing emeralds. Younger Nagah, seemingly driven to translate everything into their own argot, call Serpent Waters the "jeweled pools."

The Serpent Waters are dedicated to the Nagah and our flesh or spirit kin, including the Zhong Lung. All serpent folk who serve and revere the Emerald Mother, including feathered serpents and sea serpents, are welcome. All others are given ample motivation to turn away. Those who cannot be dissuaded are killed. Uktena himself has swum in the Serpent Waters on rare occasions.

Xi Wang Chi

The most powerful serpent spirits, whom we call the Wani, or the Dragon Kings or Long Lu reside in a realm of storm and water. Their Realm crackles with elemental power. Enormous primordial rivers wend their way to a vast and frothing ocean beneath eternally stormy skies. Weathered peaks of elemental basalt rise into the mists of low, gray clouds. The tranquility of the Serpent Waters is not to be found anywhere in Xi Wang Chi. This is the place where the great water storms are forged: anything that could not withstand the constant raging of monsoons, typhoons and hurricanes has long been swept away. In addition, the bottomless oceans are prone to whirlpools and waterspouts. Lightning flashes through rising steam and whirling clouds as it did during the most tumultuous periods of the formation of the physical realm.

Most of the eldest Dragon Kings have been in slumber for centuries at this point, although I have heard, Sesha, from one of our Mokolé cousins that this time of sleep is soon to end. You would know that better than I.

Umi, the Dragon Kingdom of the Sea

Like an unhealthy reflection of Xi Wang Chi, Umi is home to a Dragon King in the Near Umbra. Permeating the Pacific Ocean throughout most of the Southern Hemisphere, Umi includes the tropical oceans where we have located our safest havens.

Most of those who serve the Dragon King of Umi (or his lieutenant, Gajyra) are Mokolé or Rokea, but, as favored children of the Wani, Nagah are there as well, although mostly in a ceremonial capacity. South Seas spirit politics being what they are, it is the most prudent approach.

The Nagah who do reside their report that there is a strange pall over the place, as though it is moving slowly, trapped in a dream. This sense has grown increasingly strong over the last sixty years since the Second World War. Something seems to be wrong, but no one knows how to say so or how to attend to the problem. Most Nagah deal with Umi by avoiding it to whatever degree possible.

And that is what I know of the world, Sesha.

Stereotypes

Quiet fell over the audience chamber then. When the next spirit-voice sounded in the nest's heads, none could say which member of the Sesha was speaking; none had leaned forward or shifted upward to indicate their interest.

"You have said little while your nestmates have made their declarations, Indra's Dart."

The stony-eyed Balaram stepped forward, sinking to one knee, then rising again. "My nestmates are prettier speakers and better educated than I, Sesha."

"Nonetheless, we are interested in your words as well. In what topic do you consider yourself well-versed?" There was a slight pause, marked only by the sound of shifting coils. "What of our cousins — those who share the world with us?"

Indra's Dart bowed his head. "Then judge my knowledge, Sesha."

The Khurah

We have seen these places and done these things. We care for Gaia as we can, even as the Wyrm thrashes in his jagged crystalline maze. We do not judge the humans who have remade this world in their image. They are not our responsibility. But our brother Khurah are our responsibility. We force them to do their duty and let them guide the humans as they see fit.

Yet my objectivity withers as I contemplate what effect Manyskins' treachery might wreak on our place among the other Khurah. Sometimes, I can scarcely remember their duties well enough to hold them accountable to them.

The Ajaba

Adjua Ka, the hyena's mightiest king was a fool. Rather than leading his people to do their duty, he fought his sister-cousins for dominance of the savannas. He deserved to die. His people, however, did not.

Brief surcease has been afforded them with Black Tooth's death, but will the remaining survivors capitalize on it? If they do not forgo their dreams of revenge and get back to work, we will show them what it means to tend those who suffer and lead the infirm back unto Gaia's embrace.

The Ananasi

They are only Clotho and Lachesis. Atropos' role is ours.

The Bastet

All I know of the Proud Brothers is that they are the keepers of secrets. That is good enough for me. If they discover our secret, they will not share it but with each other. If they divulge our secret, they will die. Gaia is kind to allow us to pursue this self-serving end in a world that is not ours.

The Corax

We need not fear our secret falling into any Khurah's hands more than those of the Whispering Winds. Like us, they watch and remember, but they do not respect what they learn. They give up every secret they uncover, so that what one knows the rest of the flock will soon as well. And what the flock knows, the other Khurah will find out soon enough.

They hold a particular grudge against Manyskins as well. He has pulled the greatest coup of all time against the Ravens, and they have only just realized it. For centuries, the wereravens have crowded around the Tower of London, although we know not why. What we do know is that Manyskins crept furtively into the tower very recently, and he told them something that stirred them into a frenzy of activity for months. We do not know what he said, but we know that the Whispering Winds have uncovered his trickery at last. Many of them have made it a singular pursuit to hunt Manyskins down for this "outrage" and "scatter his bones on every wind." We are familiar with Corax hyperbole, and we know that they mean only to expose his every secret to any available ear. I say "only," but for this reason especially, Manyskins must be eliminated. What he knows, the Corax will find out soon enough.

The Gurahl

Some claim that we owe the Mountain and the Thunder a great debt. It was to them that the ancient Silver Fangs turned when She Whose Name is Remembered but Never Spoken had slain their kinsman. The ancient Garou demanded that the werebears return their fallen comrade to life. The Gurahl refused, and this refusal — some say — testified to the Gurahl's faith in our right to judge. They relied on us to do as Gaia commanded, and they would not make our efforts meaningless with the gifts our Mother had granted them.

Others have more perspective. The Gurahl should never have refused this request. She Who Is not Named of was of the Wyrm. Her judgment was false and undeserved. Had the Gurahl realized this, and raised the fallen Fang, there would have been no War of Rage. We could have excised She Who Is not Named of from our ranks and put the rest of our kind above reproach. The Gurahl's shortsightedness brought us to this low state despite their every effort. Now that they are rising once again from their slumber, we must watch them carefully, lest they once again bring us to harm.

The Kitsune

Toddlers. Gaia created them so long after the rest of us that we seldom know how to judge them at all.

The Mokolé

Eclipse's Children respect us and keep our secret, for they would be no less subject to the werewolves' wrath than we if that secret got out. They have never forgotten us or what our sacred duty is, for it is their sacred duty to remember for all time. Their old and their young hold in their hearts the accumulated wisdom of all the preceding ages of the world. But unlike the Corax, it is not in the Mokolé's nature to give their knowledge away recklessly. Even should Manyskins come among them with a loose tongue, they would not be moved. They would remember always who it was that told them, but they would not continue his work for him.

But when I think on Eclipse's Children, I cannot help but despair. Why would Gaia not give us all the potential to see the tapestry of time as they see it? Why parcel Her memory out solely to them? The only answer I can fathom is that She knows that only they will survive the wars and devastation that are to come when the Wyrm breaks free of the Weaver's web at last.

The Nuwisha

We will not be mocked, honorable Sesha. Our survival is not the punchline of a joke, nor will our death be any laughing matter. Many Nuwisha could respect this, but only in the abstract. Most would laugh at the thought that what they know could doom an entire species or rekindle the War of Rage and doom the world entire. But Manyskins is in just such a position. He is too old to maintain any sense of perspective on this matter. He will tell others that we still live, and to Malfeas with the consequences.

He must be silenced. I honor the Lonely Skies for the duty they perform, but the Old Man is too dangerous. I will not allow the tears of his laughter to salt the earth where I lie dead. I will not allow his laughter to be the last thing Gaia hears before the Wyrm strangles Her to death.

The Ratkin

The Fires that Cleanse are repugnant, vile, scurrilous and entirely within the bounds of their duty to be so. Gaia created them to destroy humans when the humans grow too populous, and they relish their work. We cannot punish them for their zeal, but that same zeal is simultaneously attractive and repulsive to the Wyrm. When a Ratkin enjoys his work, we respect him. When a Ratkin revels in his work, we become his shadow. When a Ratkin lusts after his goals and the means of achieving them drive him more than the ends, we enable another zealot to take his place.

They do not know of us because they do not care that we exist. We are casualties of the war that has so embittered them. We are a rallying cry for them against the Garou they hate. We respect them as they respect our memory, but we do not shy away from judging them. They are the Fires that Cleanse, but they may be the next to take the path that the Garou's White Howlers traveled.

The Rokea

The Ever-Waking are our second-closest cousins. Where we make our homes in Gaia's lifeblood, they revel in Gaia's very heart. Their duty does not bring them ashore, nor does our duty take us out into their territory. They live and thrive alone there, and they police their own.

Only when one of the Ever-Waking abandons his rightful home and evades the pursuit of those who come to take him back do we have any right to judge them. But even then, we trust the Rokea most and fear them least with the secret of our existence.

The Garou

The Fenrir and the Silver Fangs build empires proudly on stacks of shapeshifter bones. The Furies and the Bone Gnawers envy their powerful cousins and withdraw their support out of self-righteous bitterness. The Shadow Lords are envious as well, but they sniff constantly for the scraps their betters drop. The Glass Walkers gladly tangle themselves in the Weaver's webs, just as the Red Talons lose themselves among the dreams of the Wyld. The pretentious Children of Gaia vie for peace among the Garou, but their efforts serve only to point out the conflicts. The Fianna are lazy and unmotivated. The Silent Striders are ever distracted by dreams of revenge for a home lost. The Uktena and the Wendigo build walls around their caerns and brood when their brothers try to do their job for them. And the Stargazers… we will deal with them soon enough if they remain hidden in selfish, frightened seclusion.

But a storm is not one raindrop. A hurricane is not a single gust of wind. The werewolves are the Storms of the Apocalypse for a reason. They have not earned their fearsome reputation or the hatred of so many of their cousins by accident. They were created by Gaia to kill and make war. She commanded them to wet their teeth and claws all the days of their lives, and in this they have excelled. Every life they take honors Gaia in their hearts. It is only when they claim as much in vain that we sentence them to death.

We understand that the Storms of the Apocalypse are not evil — they are simple. They are focused. Even the War of Rage is a forgivable sin the wolves committed. We are more to blame than they are. No, the werewolves' greatest fault is that they lack the requisite control and perspective to guide their Rage to exalt Gaia as She most truly deserves. And for that reason, they must not be allowed to find out about us. Manyskins must be drowned and silenced before he incites the killing frenzy in the werewolves again.

Manyskins presumes to call us lax. He claims that our decision to hide from the other Khurah has encour-

aged them to eschew their duties. He will tell them that we still live, to remind them that their actions have very real consequences. If that happens, the wolves will hunt us down for Wyrm-friends and traitors. They will take their eyes away from their actual duty in the crucial moment that the Thrashing Corrupter needs to break free. When it does, it will find no front line of defense waiting to receive it. It will decimate the distracted Garou, and all hope will be lost for the rest of us. We need them to be ready, Sesha. Manyskins must die.

The Others

The others who exist outside the reckoning of man are known to us, but they are not ours to judge. The Hungry Dead of east and west compete with the Fires that Cleanse to cull the human herds. Like Eclipse's Children, the Waking Dreams struggle to remember the world as it was, although they will die if they ever forget. The Lightning People congregate and make their own wars, rivaling the worst of the Garou in their arrogance. Of the Restless Shadows, we do not discourse.

But there is another kind of man and woman that clouds my heart with despair. I have seen them in my dreams, making war on the dead and heeding the whispers of Gaia's noblest ministers. I have seen them judge Khurah and Hungry Dead and Lightning People alike. So many of them are doomed, yet their comrades never waver.

I fear these dreams, because this army does not know of the Nagah. It does not know of Gaia. It does not know of the Wyrm. It knows only "right" and "wrong". I fear what these people in my dreams portend, Sesha. They hint that Gaia is ill pleased with us and has replaced us as best She can in the time left before the Apocalypse. When I see the first of these people with my own waking eyes, I will know that we have failed. I will know that the End Times are coming no longer. I will know that the Apocalypse has come.

Epilogue

His testimony finished, Indra's Dart stood quietly at attention. The young girl nodded at him, and he bowed and stepped back to the side of his nestmates.

"You have said enough, Nest of Night's Passage." It was as if a single voice was speaking, then a chorus, then a single voice again. "We do not find fault with your decision." A slight pause.

"We are ready to pass judgement."

With bowed heads, the three Nagah waited for the Sesha to speak.

61

Chapter Three: The First Skin

I am the wound and the knife!
I am the blow and the cheek!
I am the limbs and the wheel—
The victim and executioner!
— Charles Baudelaire, *Les Fleurs de Mal*

There's much more to being a proper Nagah than simply dumping as many points as possible into Stealth, Subterfuge and Brawl. A true Nagah, one who follows the values of his race flawlessly is literate, artistic, cunning, diplomatic, resolute, swift, pleasing to the eye, and, of course, deadly. Brute killers and graceless murderers have no place among the Serpent People.

Of course, the Nagah's ideals are rarely met in completion; after all, the wereserpents are ultimately mortal, and perfection isn't something given to mortals. Even the Sesha are bound to be found wanting in one or two areas. A Nagah character should strive to excel in as many areas as possible, but should probably ultimately fall short in several. A proper mix of virtues and failings is the key to an interesting character — particularly one of the noble yet terrible Nagah.

Nagah Traits

Although the Nagah share a number of traits in common with other Khurah like the Garou, they also boast a number of abilities and liabilities all their own. Some of the traits peculiar to the wereserpents come

from simple biology; others are the result of their unusual spiritual heritage.

Amphibious

The Nagah are strongly tied to water — their patrons, the Wani, are great water-spirits as well as dragon-spirits, and the Nagah feel a special affinity for fresh water in their very being. Nagah are able to hold their breath twice as long as other people can (**Werewolf**, pg. 189), and are fully capable of breathing water as easily as air in their Kali Dahaka form.

Kin Species

Although most Nagah consider themselves the spiritual heirs of the cobra, the wereserpents are capable of mating with any venomous snake. A Nagah's forms tend to reflect her serpent heritage; hence, the product of a Nagah/rattlesnake mating will resemble a rattlesnake in Azhi Dahaka, Kali Dahaka and Vasuki, and will even have scales patterned like a rattlesnake's in Silkaram.

For simplicity's sake, the Storyteller may wish to assume that all Nagah have similar statistics regardless of their "stock" (that is, the species of serpent evident in their blood). Storytellers seeking more detail may wish to assign particular advantages according to the Nagah's actual stock. For example, Nagah born of crotalids (such as rattlesnakes and pit vipers) might be capable of sensing infrared radiation in their Kali Dahaka and Vasuki forms, while Nagah of cobra stock might enjoy an extra die on their Intimidation and Leadership dice pools. Nagah of sea snake stock might be able to hold their breath three times as long as other people, while Nagah born of the incredibly venomous snake species native to Australia might gain an extra dot of Rage at character creation. The exact bonuses are left to the Storyteller's discretion, although we don't recommend actual bonuses to Attributes or increased venom potency, which can prove unbalancing.

Language

Like other Changing Breeds, the Nagah are heirs to an instinctive language peculiar to their kind alone. However, the Nagah's speech (called simply "the Tongue") is much less reliant on vocalization and more reliant on pheromone releases, body language, coil-shifting and the like. Thus, Nagah are able to communicate with one another even in the deaf Vasuki form. However, Nagah cannot communicate with ordinary serpents beyond the very basics of threat display and similar concepts; snakes simply don't have the capacity for conversation.

Nests

The Nagah nest is in many ways similar to a Garou pack. Nests do not have pack totems, owing to the Nagah's distanced relationship with the majority of Gaian spirits. However, a nest is still considered to have a spiritual bond, which allows them to purchase pack tactics maneuvers (**Werewolf**, pg. 212) and nominate an "opener of the way" into the Umbra (**Werewolf**, pg. 228). Nagah pack tactics are usually Fur Gnarl or Wishbone; Nagah do not have the numbers or fighting style to support regular use of Harrying or Savage maneuvers.

Nests do not necessarily have a fixed leadership; the nest members themselves decide who among them should have the final word in crisis situations, and the "leader" position may change hands several times over a mission, depending on the nature of the tasks immediately at hand. Nestmates are usually far too close to make leadership challenges; a Nagah quickly learns to trust his nestmates implicitly and to behave in a manner befitting his nestmates' trust in him.

Rage and Gnosis

Nagah possess both Rage and Gnosis, and use them in much the same way that werewolves do — taking extra actions, attuning fetishes, and so on. Like a Garou, a Nagah's Rage is influenced by his auspice, while his Gnosis is affected by his breed. Nagah regain their Rage between stories or by becoming angered or frustrated as usual; they may also regain one Rage point per hour of meditation spent partly submerged in water. However, although Nagah possess a strong portion of Rage in order to carry out their duties, they have difficulty raising their Rage above a certain level; the experience or freebie cost to purchase permanent Rage is double what it is for Garou.

Like a Garou, a Nagah radiates a certain menace if his temporary Rage is higher than his Willpower rating. For every Rage point above his Willpower rating, the Nagah loses a die to all dice pools involving social interaction. However, where a werewolf whose Rage outstrips his Willpower radiates an aura of predatory menace, a Nagah whose Rage exceeds his Willpower projects a feeling of quiet, venomous presence. People instinctively avoid making contact with the Nagah, uncertain just why they dread his presence so much but unwilling to remain near him all the same. Nagah also are subject to frenzy (but not to the Thrall of the Wyrm), although the difficulty to enter frenzy is always a 7 (or a 6 if the Nagah is near polluted water).

Rank and Renown

Nagah have a system of rank that moves from one to five, with Rank Six achievable by only the greatest heroes of the race. At any given time, it is exceptionally unlikely that there are any Rank Six Nagah in the world that are not part of the Sesha.

A Nagah's rank is determined solely by the judgement of the Sesha (which is to say, the Storyteller). When the time comes for a nest to be considered for advancement in rank, the nest reports to Nandana, where each member in turn comes before the Sesha. The time is selected not by the nest, but by the Sesha; when the time is right, a door to Nandana opens in the nest's Ananta. The Sesha asks each member of the nest to recount the details of their deeds, to report other news salient to the race, and finally to evaluate her nestmates and their performance. Once each interview has ended, the nest is given one week to relax in the Nandana, conversing with other Nagah who might be there for evaluation or on business while the Sesha makes judgement. When the week is up, the Sesha takes each nest member separately into the Hall of the Wani, where the Wani inform the supplicant if she has earned a new rank, and teach her any Gifts she may have earned by her deeds.

[In game terms, the Storyteller is the one to decide when the time is right for characters to advance in rank. This shouldn't be a hasty business; most Nagah make several trips to the Nandana to report their deeds and learn new Gifts before finally advancing to the next rank. Nagah should advance no quicker than Garou, and probably even more slowly. Patience is a virtue, particularly in the Nagah's business.]

The Nagah ranks are, in order: Opening Eye (Rank Zero); Singing Brook (Rank One); Razored Arrow (Rank Two); Silken Noose (Rank Three); Thunder Chakram (Rank Four); Silver Coil (Rank Five); Mouth of the Sesha (Rank Six).

Regeneration and Silver

Nagah regenerate much as werewolves do, healing back bashing damage with ease and lethal damage with little more difficulty. Aggravated damage slows down a Nagah's regeneration, but given time a wereserpent can heal even that. Nagah characters use the healing rules given in **Werewolf** (pg. 188).

Silver is the bane of Nagah, just as it is the bane of Garou. The lunar metal causes aggravated damage to Nagah, and is unsoakable if the Nagah is in any form save his breed form.

Senses

The Nagah possess the best sensory abilities of human and snake — however, these abilities are often contradictory. A Nagah's eyesight is passably accurate in all forms, and most Nagah have good color vision even in Vasuki form. As the Nagah moves along the scale from Balaram to Vasuki, his senses of smell and taste become more and more acute. The difficulty to detect odors drops by 1 for each form removed from Balaram; hence, a Silkaram makes scent-based perception rolls at -1 difficulty, whereas a Kali Dahaka does so at -3 difficulty. Nagah in Azhi Dahaka, Kali Dahaka and Vasuki may track by scent. In Kali Dahaka, the Nagah's eyesight, sense of smell and sensitivity to vibrations are sufficiently acute that he automatically benefits from the effects of the lupus Gift: Scent of Sight.

Unfortunately, the Nagah also suffer from the hearing problems common to their serpent Kin. Although a Nagah in Azhi Dahaka can hear about as well as an ordinary human, in Kali Dahaka all auditory Perception rolls are at +3 difficulty due to the form's poor hearing. In Vasuki form a Nagah is deaf to any airborne sounds, and becomes reliant on his ability to sense vibrations and sound carried through solid objects.

Stepping Sideways

The Nagah lack the easy access to the Umbra that the Garou enjoy. To enter the Umbra, they rely on the connection they share with their Ananta, their pocket den-realms. While the Ananta stands, the Nagah who call it home can only step sideways when they are in its immediate presence, entering or leaving the physical world "adjacent to" the portion of the Penumbra where the Ananta has been established. If a Nagah is carrying the Ananta within himself at the moment, then he may step sideways in the usual fashion; his nestmates cannot, although he can act as "opener of the way" and lead them across the Gauntlet (**Werewolf**, pg. 228). Nagah can also step sideways freely into and out of Serpent Waters.

Venom

In any form apart from Balaram (and even in Balaram with the proper Gift), Nagah are capable of injecting supernaturally potent hemotoxins into their victims. The Nagah can inject venom only if the target has taken at least one health level of damage from the wereserpent's bite after soak. The venom moves through the body with supernatural speed, causing immediate damage. Poisoned victims suffer an additional seven health levels of aggravated damage, which is also soaked separately. The venom cannot affect spirits, even materialized spirits, but it does damage vampires (albeit the damage is halved), who are vulnerable to attacks to their bloodstream. Other Nagah are immune to Nagah venom.

Each Nagah has the equivalent of three full "doses" of venom in their venom sacs. Once depleted, the Nagah must wait 24 hours before their venom has replenished.

In some cases, the Nagah may spit their venom in their opponents' faces in order to blind them. In Vasuki or Kali Dahaka, only Nagah of spitting cobra stock can attempt this, but the versatile fangs of the Azhi Dahaka make spitting venom a possibility for all wereserpents. Spitting a jet of venom at an opponent uses up the equivalent of two full "doses" of venom, due to the amount necessary to properly cover the target area; it also requires a Dexterity + Athletics roll, difficulty 7 (or 9 when targeting a foe's eyes). If the Nagah successfully strikes the target with her venom, the target takes the usual seven health levels of damage, although there is a delay of one turn as the toxin seeps through the skin into the bloodstream. Quick-thinking targets may be able to wash the venom off before it takes effect. If the venom gets into the target's eyes, the pain and damage leave the opponent blinded for (10 - Stamina) turns, to a minimum of three turns.

Willpower

Regardless of their upbringing, all Nagah must have a certain fortitude of character to successfully shed their First Skin and graduate their apprenticeship. All Nagah begin play with 4 Willpower.

Character Creation Chart

- **Step One: Character Concept**
  Choose concept, breed and auspice
- **Step Two: Attributes**
  Assign Attributes (7 primary, 5 secondary, 3 tertiary)
- **Step Three: Abilities**
  Prioritize the three categories: Talents, Skills Knowledges (13/9/5)
  Choose Talents, Skills, Knowledges
- **Step Four: Choose Advantages**
  Choose Backgrounds (5), Gifts (1 Nagah Gift, 1 breed Gift, 1 auspice Gift)
- **Step Five: Finishing Touches**
  Record Rage (by auspice), Gnosis (by breed) and Willpower (4); spend freebie points (15)

Breed

- **Balaram:** You were born of humans, unaware of the serpent's blood within you. Now you have said farewell forever to the human world, preparing to begin your almost solitary life's journey.

  Initial Gnosis: 1

  Beginning Gifts: Cold Blood, Persuasion, Prehensile Body, Self-Mastery

- **Ahi:** You were raised in the Serpent Waters from the day of your hatching, with only a brief visit to the physical world every year. Both your parents were Nagah, giving your blood a purity that is both blessing and curse.

  Initial Gnosis: 3

  Beginning Gifts: Bones as Coils, Weaver Sense, Wyld Sense, Wyrm Sense

- **Vasuki:** You were hatched a serpent, and your life has been a struggle to survive until the shedding of your First Skin. Now you can hear the world as well as taste it.

  Initial Gnosis: 5

  Restricted Abilities: Drive, Etiquette, Firearms, Computer, Law, Linguistics, Medicine, Politics, Science

  Beginning Gifts: Death Rattle, River's Gift, Sense Vibration, Treesnake's Blessing

Auspice

- **Kamakshi (Spring)** — Touched by the forces of renewal, healing and earth.

  Initial Rage: 3

  Beginning Gifts: Ganga's Caress, Kind Death, Resist Pain

- **Kartikeya (Summer)** — The auspice of vigor, inspiration and fire.

  Initial Rage: 4

  Beginning Gifts: Brief Sensation, Eyes of the War God, Scent of the True Form

- **Kamsa (Autumn)** — The seasonal auspice of insight, psychological warfare and air.

  Initial Rage: 3

  Beginning Gifts: Executioner's Edge, Predator's Patience, Slayer's Eye

- **Kali (Winter)** — Touched by the influence of clarity, focus and water.

  Initial Rage: 4

  Beginning Gifts: Guided Strike, Iron Coils, Wyrm Sense

Backgrounds

- **Ananta:** The underwater den-realm that is your safest haven.
- **Ancestors:** The ability to channel the spirits of your ancestors to aid you.
- **Contacts:** People you know who may prove useful to your duties.
- **Fetish:** An heirloom of spiritual potency.
- **Kinfolk:** The humans and, rarely, serpents who share your blood.
- **Pure Breed:** The spiritual and physical prestige of your royal lineage.
- **Resources:** Money, possessions and other material goods that can aid you.
- **Rites:** The number and level of Samskara, or rituals, that you can perform.

Gifts

Nagah Beginning Gifts: Eyes of the Dragon Kings, Lizard's Favor, Scent of Running Water, Slayer's Eye, Snake's Skin, Sting of Sleep

Rank

All Nagah begin at Rank One.

Freebie Points

Trait	Cost
Attributes	5 per dot
Abilities	2 per dot
Backgrounds	1 per dot
Gifts	7 per Gift (Level One only)
Rage	2 per dot
Gnosis	2 per dot
Willpower	1 per dot

Breed

A Nagah's spiritual nature and aptitudes are heavily tied to their parentage. Those born of humans, serpents or Nagah/Nagah matings display a wide range of abilities and failings.

Balaram are essentially homids, with most of the same rules as homid Garou; they have limited Gnosis, a human breed form, and so on. They begin with 1 Gnosis.

Ahi are essentially Nagah metis, although the differences are profound. Ahi are not infertile, and do not suffer from deformities; however, only 10% of Nagah/Nagah pairings produce ahi. They are hatched in the Azhi Dahaka, which is their breed form. Ahi are raised mostly in the spirit world, and this practice, along with the intense "more Nagah than Nagah" nature of their blood, makes them particularly vulnerable to pollution, particularly water pollution and Wyrm-toxins. An ahi takes from one to three levels of lethal damage per turn to exposure to heavy pollution; the level should be appropriate to the pollution's severity. The damage rises to aggravated if the toxins are water-borne. Standing near a billowing smokestack would count as one level of lethal damage, whereas a dunking in the river downstream of an industrial plant would count as three levels of aggravated damage. This damage is soakable as normal. Ordi-nary levels of city smog and similar "background pollution" aren't damaging, although an ahi will be consistently coughing and miserable on a smoggy day or in a smoky room). To make matters worse, an ahi may use only half her Stamina pool to soak damage from Wyrm-toxins. Ahi begin play with 3 Gnosis.

Vasuki are the snake-born Nagah. There is only a 10% chance of producing a vasuki Nagah per *brood* of hatchlings, not per snake in the brood; thus, a brood that produces 20 offspring has a 10% chance of producing a Nagah, not a 100% chance of producing two Nagah. Vasuki begin play with 5 Gnosis, but also begin play with the same restrictions as lupus characters; they cannot purchase Drive, Etiquette, Firearms, Computer, Law, Linguistics, Medicine, Politics or Science at character creation unless they use freebie points.

Auspice

A Nagah's auspice is determined by the season of the wereserpent's birth, rather than by the moon phase. The seasons' influence tends to predispose the Nagah to certain spiritual connections, such as the sort of Gifts for which they have the most affinity. (An auspice may also have a slight effect on a Nagah's personality, but it in no way

PRESCOTT

defines said personality.) Unlike Garou, Nagah don't view an auspice's influence as a determinant of social role — it's a matter of affinity, nothing more. All Nagah have the same task within the race — to assassinate.

A Nagah's auspice not only influences the Gifts he might learn, but it also tends to give the wereserpent a subtle connection to one of the four mystical elements. Although elementals are no more bound by the Pact to assist Nagah than are any other Gaian spirit, spirits of a specific element tend to look a little more favorably on Nagah of a related auspice. Nagah still don't learn Gifts from elementals, and can't reliably summon them — but the Storyteller may allow a Nagah a certain amount of leeway if he finds himself trying to strike a quick agreement with an elemental of his auspice's element.

The Kamakshi are the auspice of spring. They tend to be slightly more empathic than other Nagah, and more commonly study the arts of healing. They begin play with 3 Rage, and have an affinity for earth elementals.

The Kartikeya are the Nagah born in summer. Their personalities run slightly more toward the intense or emotional, and they often focus on more overt forms of self-expression such as song. They begin play with 4 Rage, and are tied to the element of fire.

The Kamsa are the autumn-born Nagah. They tend to be more logical and introspective than their brethren, and are particularly adept at psychological warfare and preying upon an opponent's weaknesses. They begin play with 3 Rage, and have an affinity for air elementals.

Finally, the Kali are the auspice of winter. They are the most "professional" of the Nagah, and learn Gifts that increase their efficiency and skill in the killing arts. They begin play with 4 Rage, and are associated with the element of water.

Forms

The Nagah have five forms, not unlike those of the Garou. Each Nagah's serpent form resembles a specific poisonous snake. Most Nagah are obviously of cobra stock, although some are distinctly descended from mambas, sea snakes, adders, vipers and even rattlesnakes. When in any of its non-human forms, the wereserpent retains the coloration and markings of its snake form to some degree; thus, a Nagah who takes the form of a diamondback rattlesnake will have a rattle on the end of her tail in Azhi Dahaka, and subtle diamond patterning on her back in Silkaram.

• **Balaram:** The Balaram is the "human" form; a Nagah is indistinguishable from other humans when wearing the Balaram. Most Nagah are of Indian or Asian ancestry, although there are wereserpents of other ethnic groups scattered about the world.

• **Silkaram:** This form has the proportions of a human, but cannot truly pass for an ordinary man or woman. The Silkaram form is completely hairless, with bony ridges that strongly resemble scales covering its skin (even the lips, which makes human speech slightly stilted). The Nagah's fingers and toes become webbed, providing excellent swimming ability. The jawline extends substantially, while the nose recedes and widens, becoming near non-existent. The Silkaram's eyes lose their human coloration, becoming more like the eyes of the Nagah's serpent form. The canines lengthen into hollow fangs that can fold back when not in use, while the other teeth grow closer and almost fuse together.

• **Azhi Dahaka:** The Nagah's "war serpent" form is a terrifying beast resembling nothing more than a giant cobra complete with a barrel torso and a powerful set of "arms" (its arms being more like the flexible trunk of a snake than a human's limbs). Below the torso, the tail (thick enough to balance on) easily runs

Form Statistics

Silkaram	Azhi Dahaka	Kali Dahaka	Vasuki
Str: +2	Str: +3	Str: +2	Str: -1
Dex: +0	Dex: +2	Dex: +2	Dex: +2
Sta: +2	Sta: +3	Sta: +2	Sta: +1
App: -2	App: 0	App: 0	
Man: -2	Man: -3	Man: 0	Man: 0
Diff: 7	Diff: 6	Diff: 7	Diff: 6
Bite (Str)	Bite (Str +1)	Bite (Str+1)	Bite (Str +1)
Claw (Str)	Claw (Str +1)	Claw (Str)	
	Constriction*	Constriction*	
	Incites Delirium		

to a length of 16 to 20 feet; often more. The Nagah largely resembles his serpent form in Azhi Dahaka, although even Nagah descended from non-cobra bloodlines still sport impressive hoods in this form. Azhi Dahaka may unhinge their jaws at will, and are able to breathe water as easily as air. Regardless of the Nagah's actual serpent "stock," the fangs of the Azhi Dahaka are long and hinged like that of a viper. The wereserpent's hands sprout claws as terrible as those of any Garou, and their scales and scutes take on a supernatural resilience. Any scarification the Nagah has received stands out significantly in this form, often as patterns in the Azhi Dahaka's scales. The Nagah causes the full Delirium effect in this form; few humans can stand to look on such an embodiment of their primal fear of snakes.

• **Kali Dahaka:** The "great serpent" form more resembles an actual snake, albeit one that rivals even the largest anacondas in size. The Kali Dahaka is often thirty or more feet long, and as big around as a strong man's leg; it boasts the general appearance and dentition of the Nagah's serpent stock. The Nagah may, if he chooses, make a Stamina + Primal-Urge roll, difficulty 7, to sprout a slender set of arms like those of the Azhi Dahaka; these arms are not as impressively muscled or clawed, and are considered unsightly in most Nagah circles. The Nagah's ritual scars also remain, although they are muted and harder to pick out. The Kali Dahaka form is fully amphibious.

• **Vasuki:** The Vasuki form is indistinguishable from a normal serpent.

New Combat Maneuvers

• **Constrict:** In either of its "great serpent" forms, a Nagah is capable of constricting one opponent in his coils while biting, clawing or swinging at a second foe. To do so, the Nagah must first successfully catch his opponent with the constrict maneuver; the opponent must be of a manageable size and shape to feasibly constrict. A Crinos-form Garou or even Gurahl can be constricted, or even a Mokolé with Huge Size (if the Nagah catches the monster around the neck), but coiling around something like a Thunderwyrm is obviously not an option.

Once the opponent has been caught in the Nagah's coils, on the Nagah's successive actions he may fight another opponent (or deliver a finishing strike to the ensnared opponent). The Nagah cannot move from his current location while he constricts a foe, so he might not be able to easily reach a second target unless in close quarters. On each successive action, the Nagah must roll Strength + Brawl against a difficulty of his trapped victim's Strength + Brawl -2 (as a free action). If the Nagah is successful, he inflicts his Strength in bashing damage against the opponent; if he is unsuccessful, the victim manages to writhe free. While constricting a victim, the Nagah is an easier target to hit; the difficulty of any dodge rolls the Nagah makes are raised by two.

The victim may attempt to break free as an action; this usually entails a resisted Strength versus Strength roll. (The Storyteller may assign additional modifiers to the rolls based on the relative size of the two, and just how firmly the victim has been caught.) A victim caught in a Nagah's coils may or may not take other actions, again depending on relative size. If the Nagah attacks the target in his coils with a bite or claw attack, the difficulty of his attack is reduced by 1 (it's easier for him to shift the usually immobile victim to a good vantage). However, others trying to strike the constricted victim are at +1 difficulty, owing to the Nagah's coils getting in the way.

Example: Karna Shining-in-the-Sun is fighting a pair of Kuei-jin vampires. He is currently in the Azhi Dahaka. He wins initiative, spends two Rage, and declares that he will attempt to constrict the first Kuei-jin, claw her when she is in his coils, and then bite her partner. On his first action, he successfully catches the first vampire with his Dexterity + Brawl roll. Both Kuei-jin then act before his Rage actions. His victim tries to break free, but her Strength of 4 isn't sufficient to overcome Karna's Strength of 6; her action is done. Her companion strikes Karna and wounds him (Karna elects not to dodge, given his poor odds of success). On his second action, Karna first rolls Strength + Brawl to maintain his hold; he does so, and rolls his Strength, inflicting three health levels of bashing damage on his prey. (She, however, easily soaks this.) He then takes his second action, clawing his entrapped victim (at -1 difficulty to hit). On his third action, he again rolls to continue constricting. This time he fails the roll; the Kuei-jin struggles free, although he still bites at her partner as declared.

Usable By: Azhi Dahaka, Kali Dahaka
Roll: Dexterity + Brawl   **Difficulty:** 6
Damage: Strength   **Actions:** 1

• **Injection:** A Nagah's fangs are capable of inflicting great damage even when the Nagah doesn't inject any venom into the wound. However, Nagah can choose to bite gently into a victim as well. If not engaged in combat or other stressful situations, a Nagah can inject an unresisting target with venom without actually causing any aggravated damage from her fangs; the venom does the entirety of the work. This is particularly useful when using a non-lethal dose of venom such as with the Sting of Sleep Gift. The Nagah can also attempt such a merciful bite in combat, although it becomes more difficult than an ordinary bite attack. Still, wereserpents still capable of compassion find it worth the trouble in several situations.

Usable By: Any form capable of injecting venom
Roll: Dexterity + Brawl   **Difficulty:** 7
Damage: Venom only   **Actions:** 1

New Knowledge: Khurah Lore

"This is a crime?" Cottonmouth Jack settled down a little more comfortably as he peered over the rooftop's edge down at the alley below. The rending and gulping noises drifting up from below elicited nothing more than a bored stare from the Texan. "I mean, what's this supposed to be, cannibalism? He's a werewolf, not a human, so it's not like he's eatin' his own."

"Try to keep up," his partner sighed. "The Garou have a law against this — and not just a local ban, it's part of their Litany. 'Ye Shall Not Eat the Flesh of Humans.' I learned it back before my First Venom." She shook her head. "I swear, you're going to mortify me when you go in front of the Sesha, I just know it."

For Nagah to be able to rightly punish a Khurah's offenses against his purpose, they must first be able to understand that Khurah's purpose. Although the Nagah will never be as well-versed in a Changing Breed's society as a member of that Breed, they have still managed to compile a sufficient amount of information on the Khurah to help them in their jobs. This Knowledge reflects how well versed a Nagah is in identifying members of a particular Changing Breed, and how easy it is to determine whether they are betraying their duties or not.

There may be imperfections in the knowledge granted by this Trait; the Nagah are assassins first and spies second, and portions of their information may be out of date. If a particular Garou tribe has changed their methods of operation in the last century or so, the Nagah may well have missed many of the various ramifications of this change.

This Knowledge does *not* in any way convey the right to consult other supplements in play without the Storyteller's explicit permission. No matter how high his Khurah Lore, no Nagah is able to list off the tribal Gifts of a given Garou tribe or rattle off all three of a Bastet tribe's potential Yava. Storytellers should be careful to make sure that players use this Knowledge in the manner in which it's intended — to aid Nagah in punishing the crimes that truly merit punishment, not to provide a catalog of specialized information on a Changing Breed's organization and key weaknesses.

• You know the names and duties of all the surviving Khurah races.

•• You know that sometimes you have to use gold instead of silver.

••• You can tell an Uktena from a Wendigo, or a Makara from a Gumagan.

•••• You can quote the Litany, Ananasa's Laws and the Duties of Sun with equal facility.

●●●●● You know what the word "Yava" means, and you've heard the names of a secret society or two.

Possessed by: Nagah

Specialties: Garou, Bastet, Ratkin, Ananasi, Mokolé, Corax, Beast Courts, Europe, Africa

Backgrounds

Nagah may select from the following Backgrounds: Ananta, Ancestors, Contacts, Fetish, Kinfolk, Pure Breed, Resources and Rites. The self-imposed isolation of a Nagah nest interferes with the amount of maintenance necessary to cultivate a person as an ally rather than a contact. The cellular nature of Nagah society also tends to forbid true mentor-student relations, at least that extend past the apprenticeship period — a Nagah's former mentor will likely be inaccessible, on missions of his own, once the Nagah has undergone the Celebration of First Venom.

Finally, the Totem Background is unavailable; the Wani and their servants do not act as personal or "pack" totems, and no other spirits are entitled to do so. A Nagah nest counts as a bonded pack for purposes of pack tactics, nominating a leader into the Umbra and so on, but no totem bond is actually present.

Ananta

White Desert held tightly onto Juval's hand as the tension of the Ananta pulled over her. It was like walking through a waterfall that wasn't pressing downward. Juval had never let her into his personal Ananta before, and the sensation of being the led instead of the leader was remarkable. Then they were through, standing on a stretch of wide savanna under a warm sun and brightly visible full moon. A silk pavilion loomed over them both, the cool air from within scented like cinnamon. Juval pulled his hand from hers, then drew back the flap of the tent.

"Welcome to my home sweet home," he murmured.

This Background describes the general setup of the Nagah's Ananta, the pocket "realm" in the Umbra that she calls her own. Unlike the den-realms of other shapeshifters, though, the Ananta is a shared Background; all the members of a nest may contribute to a communal Ananta, or they may maintain their own. However, no Nagah may carry more than one Ananta within herself at a time, so one member of each nest must usually forego having a personal Ananta, instead being responsible for the transport of the nests' communal home.

The number of Background points spent on an Ananta determines the den-realm's size and ability to provide food; the most powerful Ananta can supply a nest with Umbral food and drink as nourishing as the physical equivalent, adding to the nest's self-reliance. However, although an Ananta may have a small pool or stream running through it, the spiritual water of such a feature does not count as fresh water for purposes of the Nagah's more sacred rites or regaining Rage. Only naturally occurring water will suffice. The Nagah of a nest may spend their points in this Background on personal Ananta, to contribute to a group Ananta, or both. However, the rating of any Ananta cannot exceed 5 without the Storyteller's explicit permission. (The Storyteller may choose to let the nest create a permanent Ananta by spending double the Background points on the Ananta, but the characters aren't *entitled* to such a rare and wondrous luxury.)

In the physical world, the Ananta has little to no actual presence — only a small space nominated as a "doorway," through which the Nagah may step sideways to enter the den-realm. This portal is invariably at the bottom of a river or other source of fresh water. Other Nagah are capable of sensing the presence of the entryway into an Ananta; it is otherwise invisible. The difficulty to step into an Ananta is equal to the local Gauntlet, -1 for every two points in the Background. The difficulty number cannot fall below 2.

Breaching the Serpent Wards

Passing through the wards of an Ananta if the Nagah owner doesn't want you to can be anywhere from moderately difficult to impossible. The hopeful escapee has the best chances if the Ananta belongs to only a single Nagah, otherwise her chances of entry or escape plummet sharply.

Passing the wards of an Ananta requires a contested Willpower roll against the controlling wereserpent(s). (This is true even if the Nagah is not currently home.) If the Ananta belongs to a nest of Nagah, then the strongest Willpower trait among the nest is used, with an additional +2 Willpower for each nest member beyond the first. (The difficulty for the invader's Willpower roll cannot go above 10, although the Nagah's communal Willpower die pool can.) While it may be possible for a strong-willed and lucky intruder to enter or escape the Ananta maintained by one or possibly even two Nagah, an Ananta belonging to a nest of three Nagah is almost inviolable. To enter Nandana itself, an invader would have to best the combined will of the Sesha — at difficulty 10 for his own roll, while the Sesha would have 26 dice to oppose him!

And if the intrepid ward-passer believes himself to be free and clear once she's through the wards, she's mistaken. A Nagah knows the moment and the location of the breach, and is likely to attend to the violator post haste.

In the Umbra, the Ananta is invisible from the outside; its perimeter is solid and yields slightly to strong pressure, like a thick rubber sheet stretched over water. Umbral travelers coming across the boundaries of an Ananta are unlikely to see it as anything more than a local boundary of unknown origin; spirits ignore the Ananta entirely, and are unlikely to believe that there is anything there. Given the underwater location of an Ananta, the den-realms are very safe from casual discovery.

An Ananta is in some ways part of a Nagah; once the wereserpent has created his (or his nest's) Ananta, he may "swallow" it to move it from place to place at any time. No roll is necessary; the Nagah simply moves through the outside wall of the Ananta into the Penumbra and draws the den-realm into himself. He may then regurgitate the Ananta at any point. While a Nagah carries his Ananta inside his body, he may step sideways freely as Garou do. However, if an Ananta is destroyed for any reason, each Nagah to which it belongs loses a permanent Gnosis point.

The contents of an Ananta are determined by the nest or Nagah to which it belongs. Most prefer décor reminiscent of Indian royalty, hearkening back to the glory days of the race, although local fashion is also quite popular. Fruit trees are the most common source of provided food, although a stream of Umbral fish is also popular with vasuki. The interior can resemble almost anything the Nagah chooses; although there are definite internal boundaries, the "outside walls" can look like wide-open plains, dense rainforest or anything else of the Nagah's choosing. The illusion is uncanny.

- A small and meagerly appointed Ananta; there might be room for a small cot, but little else. No refreshments are available.
- •• A modest Ananta, with roughly the size and furnishings of a guest bedroom. The Ananta may supply enough food and drink to entertain a visitor or two, although it is more illusion than nourishment.
- ••• An Ananta well-suited to a nest, roughly the size of a hotel suite or townhouse. There's enough "empty" food and drink for the whole nest, or enough truly nourishing food for one.
- •••• A pleasantly spacious nest, about the size of a comfortable house. The Ananta provides enough "true" food for three.
- ••••• A most luxurious Ananta, the size of a small mansion and appointed to look the part. The food and drink available is all as nourishing as the best mortal food, and can feed five people.

Gifts

The Nagah don't learn their Gifts as other shapechangers do. As Nagah are outside the Pact that enables shapeshifters to learn Gifts from friendly spirits in exchange for chiminage, virtually no spirit not directly in service to the Wani can teach a Nagah a Gift even if they wanted to. (Incarnae and Celestines are of course above such petty restrictions, but only the most foolish wereserpent would risk angering the Wani by scorning their pact to go begging to an outsider.) A Nagah learns her Gifts during her regular "review" sessions with the Sesha; even if the Nagah has not yet earned an advance in rank, she may be taken to Xi Wang Chi to learn more Gifts that might assist her. (In game terms, this entails spending experience to purchase Gifts as usual; the Nagah are simply more limited in terms of when they can do so.)

To learn any "outside" Gifts, the Nagah must successfully petition or coerce a spirit or other shapeshifter to teach her — in itself almost impossible. Spirits not directly under the Wani's orders see no reason to help Nagah, and given the inflexible nature of a spirit's mentality, this makes finding a spirit teacher difficult indeed. And, of course, learning a Gift from another shapeshifter violates the code of secrecy. Should the Nagah overcome these obstacles, she must still pay the Gift's level x 7 experience points to learn the Gift, and most Level Four or Five Gifts are completely off-limits. (Storytellers may allow a balaram Nagah to learn a Level Four homid Gift, for instance, but most Gifts of this level are exclusive to their "proper" owners.)

Nagah Gifts

• **Eyes of the Dragon Kings (Level One)** — With this Gift, the Nagah can see through almost any obstacle short of a solid wall. The Nagah can see through fog, smoke, and murky water without difficulty. This Gift also grants the ability to see in even total darkness. The Nagah's eyes glow with a faint golden sheen when this Gift is employed.

System: The player makes a Gnosis roll, difficulty 6, to activate the Gift; this Gift doesn't negate the need for other Perception rolls, although conditional modifiers for poor visibility may not apply. Gifts or powers such as Blur of the Milky Eye can still foil the Eyes of the Dragon Kings, though the Nagah's penalties to see the hidden character are reduced by 1 while this Gift is active. The Gift's effects last for a scene.

• **Lizard's Favor (Level One)** — Nagah value their secrecy highly. This Gift grants the wereserpent the ability to masquerade as a Mokolé by evincing certain lizard-like characteristics.

System: The player rolls Stamina + Primal-Urge and spends a Willpower point. For every success, the Nagah may develop some trait like legs, royal crest, frilled neck, fins or a back sail. This Gift does not grant physical characteristics that have any actual game effect; the most useful traits that can be developed are legs, which allow full bipedal or quadrupedal mobility. Characteristics such as wings, horns or armor are just shy of vestigial, useful for appearance alone. The changes last for one scene, or until the Nagah shifts into Balaram or Vasuki form.

• **Scent of Running Water (Level One)** — As the Ragabash Gift.

• **Slayer's Eye (Level One)** — As the Shadow Lord Gift: Fatal Flaw.

• **Snake's Skin (Level One)** — This Gift allows the Nagah to shed a layer of skin, allowing her to slip out of handcuffs and similarly tight bonds. The shed skin is instantly regenerated. This Gift may help a Nagah avoid being grappled, held or thrown by an opponent. If performed quickly, this Gift may also allow the Nagah to avoid taking damage from dangerous substances splashed on her skin (e.g., acid and poison).

System: The player spends one Gnosis and rolls Dexterity + Athletics; if successful, the Nagah slips free from the outer layer of her skin, allowing her to slip free of most bonds. Five or more successes may be required to slip free of extremely complicated bonds at the Storyteller's discretion.

• **Sting of Sleep (Level One)** — There are times when it suits the Nagah's purpose better to induce sleep than death in a victim. This Gift alters the Nagah's venom so that it does just that.

System: The player expends one Gnosis point; the Nagah may choose to change up to three of his venom doses. The altered venom causes sleep instead of death. Such venom is treated as lethal rather than aggravated for purposes of soaking and healing, although it doesn't endanger the victim's life. The sleep-inducing venom still induces wound penalties, although these are the result of overwhelming drowsiness rather than pain. If the target reaches Incapacitated, he falls into a deep, restful sleep for an hour (plus an extra hour for every wound level below Incapacitated given by the venom).

• **Burrow (Level Two)** — Snakes are at home both on and under the ground. Through the use of this Gift, the Nagah is able to tunnel through earth to follow prey, create an ambuscade or make a nest. While the specifics are largely different (snakes don't dig, per se, they just sort of insinuate themselves into the earth), and the Nagah must be in Kali Dahaka or Vasuki form to use this Gift, this Gift is otherwise like the metis Gift of the same name.

• **Gift of Breath (Level Two)** — While Nagah have no problem breathing underwater in any Kali Dahaka form, Gift of Breath allows a wereserpent to grant the ability to breathe underwater to others as well. This Gift saw the most use during the War of Rage, when the Nagah used it to transport certain of their beloved Kinfolk to their underwater dens.

System: The player rolls Stamina + Enigmas to extend the Nagah's ability to breathe underwater to another. One success allows a target enough air to survive as long as he remains relatively still. Two successes allow for normal movement including swimming or walking, and three successes provide the target with enough oxygen to support strenuous activity, like combat. The Gift's effects last for five minutes; if the Nagah is willing to expend a Gnosis point, the effects last for an hour instead.

• **Night Whispers (Level Two)** — With this Gift, the Nagah is able to communicate silently, through mindspeech, with any member of his nest (or anyone else he chooses). Unless the Nagah takes special pains, no one else can hear the conversation; the Gift's user must effectively "whisper" to one person at a time. Vasuki Nagah often take this Gift to facilitate communication with their non-vasuki nestmates.

System: The player must spend one Gnosis. For the cost of an additional Gnosis, the character may choose to speak to all within "earshot" at once. This Gift lasts for one scene. To speak to an unwilling target, the Nagah must roll Charisma + Empathy, difficulty of the target's Willpower.

• **Sense of the Prey (Level Two)** — As the Ragabash Gift.

• **Veil of the Wani (Level Two)** — This Gift allows the Nagah to erase the memory of her existence from the minds of others. While those who have seen (or fought) the wereserpent remember that an encounter of some sort took place, they misremember the exact nature of the event, and their minds jump to any conclusion necessary in order not to remember the Nagah for what she truly is. A Garou might remember encountering a snakelike Wyrm-beast or a serpentine spirit, even a vampire with the ability to change into a serpent instead of a bat, but it would never cross his mind that his encounter was actually with a wereserpent.

System: The player spends two Gnosis and rolls Manipulation + Subterfuge against a difficulty equal to the target's Perception +2. While only one success is needed, with three or more successes the target forgets the encounter entirely. The memory isn't blurred or faded—it's completely removed from the target's mind.

• **Blessings of Kali (Level Three)** — This Gift causes the wereserpent to develop natural armor and weaponry. Ridges and sharp barbs of bone extend from the Nagah's bony surfaces (skull, knuckles, elbows, knees, spine), as well as her shoulders, making her blows in hand-to-hand combat all the more lethal. Furthermore, a series of heavy, bonelike plates forms over the wereserpent's scaly hide, enhancing her natural defenses against most attacks.

System: The player spends one point of Gnosis and one point of Rage, then rolls Stamina + Primal-Urge to create the armor. The bony plates form over the wereserpent's torso, arms and underbelly, adding two dice to her soak pools. If the Nagah is in Azhi Dahaka, Kali Dahaka or Vasuki form, the plates of bone cover the entirety of the Nagah's hood as well. The hooks and barbs extending from the bony surfaces are extremely sharp, increasing the damage rating of claw attacks to Strength +2. As with Garou claws, this damage is aggravated. This armor doesn't affect the Nagah's mobility. Nagah hoods run from the crown of the head down to the middle of the back, so when armored in this manner, wereserpents' vital organs are granted the protection bonus from front and back, but not from the sides. The Gift's effects last for a scene.

• **Combat Healing (Level Three)** — As the Ahroun Gift.

• **Pure Venom (Level Three)** — In some cases, the Nagah find themselves up against foes that are particularly resistant to their venom. To ensure their ability to adequately dispense justice to such foes, some Nagah use this Gift, which adds an extra level of supernatural potency to their venom.

System: The player simply spends a point of Gnosis before making the attack roll to bite or spit venom. If the next bite or spit attack hits, the Nagah's venom bypasses ordinary resistances, among them the Gift: Resist Toxin. (If the victim has no other defenses against the poison, the difficulty to soak the venom's damage is increased by 1.) Vampires take full damage from Pure Venom, and even other walking dead take half damage from the venom's supernaturally corrosive effects.

• **Shield of the Dragon (Level Three)** — This Gift protects the Nagah from harsh environments. The wereserpent's body adjusts to heat, cold, radiation, disease and pressure. Electricity and fire still cause damage if they are intense enough, but affecting the Nagah with even these weapons is much harder.

System: The player expends one Gnosis point and rolls Stamina + Survival against a difficulty of 7. With even one success, all but the most inhospitable environments inflict no damage on the Nagah (though they're still unpleasant), and fire and lightning do only bashing damage. The effects last for the duration of the scene.

• **Darting Fangs (Level Four)** — Upon invoking this Gift, the Nagah grows long, sharp barbs on her arms. These barbs bear the same venom as the Nagah's fangs and can be launched from her body. Only two of these barbs grow, and the wereserpent may throw them at opponents separately or simultaneously. This Gift is normally reserved for any member of the Changing Breeds that the wereserpents feel has earned the right to a quick, painful death.

System: The character spends two Gnosis points to generate the deadly barbs. Each poisoned dart has a vicious hook at the end, making it almost impossible to remove without causing additional damage (it takes a full action to remove the dart without inflicting an additional unsoakable level of aggravated damage). Each dart causes the Nagah's Strength in aggravated damage upon impact and, if the attack wounds the Nagah's opponent, the barb injects enough venom to cause 7 dice of aggravated damage. The venom of the barbs does not count against the Nagah's usual reservoir.

• **Gaze of the Serpent (Level Four)** — The Nagah can lock gazes with an opponent, petrifying her with the intensity of her glare. An enemy under the influence of this Gift is unable to take any actions save to regenerate.

System: The player rolls Manipulation + Intimidation against the target's Willpower. Even one success freezes the target with fear. The target could spend hours or days frozen in this way, experiencing the equivalent of a *petit mal* epileptic seizure. However, the effects of this Gift last only until the target is distracted (by, say, an attack). Once the target is disturbed physically, he is freed from Gaze of the Serpent. This Gift works against only one opponent at a time. Once a target is struck by the Gift's power, he can't be affected by it again until the next scene. Nagah often use this Gift to aid in escaping from powerful foes; few use it as a means of gaining advantage in combat.

• **Swimming the Spirit River (Level Four)** — This Gift allows the Nagah to enter the spirit world freely, regardless of the presence of his Ananta.

System: Upon learning this Gift, the Nagah may step sideways as easily as Garou do. The effects of the Gift are permanent.

• **Breath of the Dragon Lords (Level Five)** — The wereserpent exhales huge gouts of scalding gases when making use of this Gift. This deadly exhalation resembles flames and causes aggravated damage to opponents, but can't actually cause materials to combust.

System: The player must make a successful Dexterity + Firearms roll for the Nagah to strike an opponent. The number of damage dice rolled is equal to the wereserpent's Gnosis + 2. This damage is aggravated and has an effective range of 20 feet. The Nagah can breathe these mystical "flames" without restriction.

• **Destroyer's Blessing (Level Five)** — When using this Gift, the Nagah sacrifices the use of her arms to combat multiple opponents. The arms of the wereserpent each split into three, each section becoming the body and head of a king cobra. Each head is autonomous and can attack of its own accord, though all are under the will of the Nagah at all times.

System: The Nagah expends three Gnosis to make the shift. Each head comes complete with enough venom to inject one target, and each cobra must make a separate attack roll in combat. Cutting away even one of these serpents leaves a very serious wound on the Nagah when the Gift wears off. This Gift lasts for two turns plus one turn per additional point of Gnosis the Nagah spends to trigger the Gift.

• **Evading the Watchers (Level Five)** — It does not serve an assassin well to be announced. This Gift cancels out the wereserpent's scent and allows him to evade detection spells, danger sense and similar Gifts, Disciplines and abilities. Nagah using this Gift can neither be tracked nor anticipated. Time itself becomes cloudy where they're concerned, preventing any sort of precognitive detection.

System: The player rolls Charisma + Stealth. Even one success allows the Nagah to evade detection for the remainder of the scene. Note that those checking the Nagah will not get any kind of strong reading of any sort and will default to whatever passes for "not dangerous."

Opponents have no chance of detecting the wereserpent unless they have a higher Gnosis (or Arete or level 5 or above Auspex, etc.), in which case the Nagah rolls his Gnosis (difficulty 10 - successes on the initial roll) and the opponent rolls Gnosis (or its equivalent) against a target number of (10 - the difference in Gnosis scores). For example, if the Nagah has a Gnosis of 7 and his opponent has a Gnosis of 9, the opponent's target number is 8 (10 - 2). If the Nagah takes any hostile action against an opponent, then the Gift's effects are canceled as far as the threatened person is concerned.

The Gift's effects last for one scene.

• **Dance of Shiva (Level Six)** — Lord Shiva, the Destroyer, is frequently called Shiva Nataraja: Shiva, Lord of the Dance. When the time comes for the world to end, Shiva will dance and flame will consume everything, preparing the world for the next cycle. This Gift grants the world a small taste of that destruction.

System: This Gift is usable only in Balaram form. As the Nagah begins the dance of destruction, the player rolls Dexterity + Performance; the number of

PRESCOTT

successes determines the destructive power and duration of the flames called forth by the dance. On the first turn, the flames spread out ten yards from the character in all directions (save up or down) and inflict four dice of aggravated damage on anything they touch. For each successive turn that the Nagah continues to dance (provided that he earned enough successes), the radius of the circle of flame doubles and the fire damage increases by a die. For example, if a player obtains six successes and his Nagah character is able to dance uninterrupted for six consecutive turns, on the sixth and final turn the flames would inflict 11 dice of fire damage on anything within 320 yards. If the Nagah stops the dance for any reason, the fires are immediately doused.

The flames called forth by the Dance of Shiva are, oddly enough, unable to harm anyone or anything that is "truly pure of heart." However, supernatural denizens of the World of Darkness who fit that description are rarer than hen's teeth; not even the gentlest Gurahl is likely to count as truly pure, much less the most virtuous of vampires.

Breed Gifts

Balaram

The Gifts used by balaram Nagah tend to reflect the self-discipline and cooperative abilities required to work together as a nest. Many of them are spiritual outgrowths of the meditative and body control disciplines practiced in India and Southeast Asia.

• **Cold Blood (Level One)** — Nagah use this odd Gift to make their Balaram form cold-blooded. This has several effects: the Nagah doesn't show up on infrared scanners, he more readily passes for a vampire, and he's capable of functioning in unusually hot environments without suffering from heat stroke.

System: The player spends one Gnosis point and rolls Stamina + Primal-Urge. Even one success allows the wereserpent to make the change. The effect lasts for a scene, or until the Nagah shifts form.

• **Persuasion (Level One)** — As the homid Gift.

• **Prehensile Body (Level One)** — This Gift allows the Nagah to grasp objects or with her tail (or catch them in her coils) about as easily as she could with her hands.

System: Once the Nagah learns this Gift, its effects are permanent. Simple acts (holding a staff, turning a doorknob) are automatic. If there's any question whether the wereserpent could perform a particularly difficult task (loading a gun, tying a cherry stem in a knot), the player rolls Dexterity + Athletics (difficulty 7).

• **Self-Mastery (Level One)** — As all effective assassins must, the Nagah cultivate a profound degree of self-discipline. This Gift lets them use that discipline to defend against mental attacks.

System: The player spends a Gnosis point and rolls Perception + Leadership, difficulty 8. For the rest of the scene, the Nagah's Willpower — for the purposes of defending against mental attacks or mind-influencing powers only — increases by the number of successes (to a maximum of 10). If the mental challenge requires a resisted roll, the wereserpent adds a number of dice to his pool equal to the number of his successes. The Gift's effects last for one scene.

• **Master the Body (Level Two)** — Before the yogi can master the world outside of himself, he must first master his own body. This Gift allows the Nagah to regulate bodily functions that are typically involuntary: heartbeat, metabolic rate, urine formation and others. In addition to allowing the Nagah to ignore wound penalties, this Gift also grants him the ability to enter a form of suspended animation. By taking control of his metabolic rate, for example, the wereserpent can survive without air several times longer than would otherwise be possible. By consciously controlling the rate of sweat and urine production, the Nagah can prevent himself from dehydrating if he doesn't have access to water.

System: The player spends one Willpower point for the Nagah to take control of his body's involuntary systems for a scene. By spending a Gnosis point in addition to the Willpower, the Nagah has control for twenty-four hours.

• **Subtle Serpent (Level Two)** — This Gift makes the Balaram's voice beautiful, easy to listen to and strangely compelling, allowing her to be extremely convincing.

System: The player spends a Gnosis point and rolls Manipulation + Expression, difficulty of the target's Willpower. Even one success means the wereserpent's voice has taken on a soothing, hypnotic quality. For the rest of the scene, the Balaram may ask "favors" of her target. These requests must be reasonable things that the target can do in one turn without endangering his health or security. "Cover your eyes," "Try a bite of this apple," and "May I see your gun?" are all permissible requests, but "Help me rebuild this engine," and "Come to Pakistan with me," are not. Extreme requests ("Slash your wrists.") will jar the target out of the trance, as will the threat of real and present danger. The target may spend Willpower to cancel out successes on a one for one basis.

• **Unexpected Venom (Level Two)** — Nagah generally don't have fangs or access to their venom in Balaram form, but this Gift allows the wereserpent both. Not only do the fangs give him a secret advantage, they also allow the Nagah to masquerade somewhat effectively as a vampire.

System: The player spends one Rage point and rolls Stamina + Primal-Urge (difficulty 8). The first success gives the character fangs and additional successes each give the character one dose of venom, up to the maximum of 3. At the Storyteller's discretion, use of this Gift may only allow the Nagah one dose of venom in Balaram form, simply because there's not a lot of room in the human head for venom sacs and associated structures. The Gift lasts until the Nagah shapeshifts again.

• **Fluid Grace (Level Three)** — As the lupus Gift: Catfeet.

• **Pierce Illusion (Level Three)** — The first step in seeing through the Veil of Maya — the illusion of the world in which all creatures are trapped — is learning to discern the simpler illusions woven by mere mortals (or mere vampires, as the case may be). This Gift allows the Nagah to determine what is real and what is illusory, as well as what the illusion is hiding, if anything.

System: The player spends a Gnosis point. For the rest of the scene, any time the Nagah comes into the presence of an illusion (mental or visual) the Storyteller rolls his Perception + Alertness against a difficulty of 6. Even one success reveals that an illusion is present. Three successes indicate the rough location of an illusion, although the Nagah is still unable to see precisely what it is the illusion conceals. Five or more successes give the Nagah some insight into the nature of the illusion (whether it's a Gift, a mage's sorcery, a vampiric power, etc.) and the illusion's creator. Only one roll per illusion is permitted; the Storyteller doesn't roll every turn that the Nagah is in the presence of a mind trick.

Once the Nagah is aware of the illusion and its general location, the player may spend a second Gnosis point and make a Gnosis roll against a difficulty of the creator's Manipulation + Expression. If the Nagah gets a success, he may see through the illusion; three or more successes allow the Nagah to extend the ability to pierce the falsehood to his nestmates.

• **Sang Froid (Level Three)** — Nagah aren't the most emotional individuals to begin with, but this Gift grants them an extra measure of discipline. While this Gift is in effect, the Nagah is practically immune to powers of emotional control or any form of mind control that works through the emotions.

System: The player spends one Gnosis point, and for the rest of the scene the Nagah's enemies lose five dice from any dice pools used for the purposes of using emotion-affecting Gifts, Disciplines or other powers on the Nagah. Those powers that work through direct control still function normally. For the duration of this Gift, the Nagah cannot regain Rage.

• **Being One (Level Four)** — Members of a nest have extremely close ties to one another; they share their lives together. This Gift allows them to share everything, including thoughts, perceptions and physical abilities. It also allows two or three Nagah to share perceptions, thereby effectively functioning in multiple places at once. Balaram often use this Gift to establish perfect communication during a hunt.

System: The player spends 1 Gnosis point and rolls Stamina + Enigmas. A telepathic connection is immediately made to the Nagah's chosen nestmate regardless of the distance between them, and each can sense what the other senses. Each success allows the wereserpent to lend one dot of a Mental or Physical Attribute, one dot of a Knowledge or one health level. (The lender loses access to any lent traits while the Gift is in effect.) Two nestmates may aid a third if both know this Gift, or if one of them opts to channel points from himself *and* a willing lender to the receiver. If one Nagah is doing all the work, his player must spend 3 Gnosis points before making the roll.

The Gift's effects last for one scene, or until the Gift user decides to terminate the connection. Nagah cannot use this Gift to contact or assist anyone but an actual nestmate, not even other Nagah.

• **Spirit Ward (Level Four)** — As the homid Gift. Balaram learn this Gift from the Wani in order to help deter unwanted attention from outside spirits.

• **Kundalini (Level Five)** — The Tantric mystics of India allude to a serpent of energy called the Kundalini that resides at the base of the spine. By raising the body's energy, the Kundalini rises through seven places of power in the body called *chakras*. By raising the Kundalini to a particular chakra, the Nagah may channel his body's energy is a variety of powerful ways.

System: The player spends one Gnosis point per chakra level and rolls Intelligence + Enigmas (difficulty 6). The Nagah spends one turn *per chakra* performing breathing exercises to raise the Kundalini to the chosen chakra. Raising the Kundalini to the Muladhara requires only 1 turn of controlled breathing while raising it to the Sahasrara requires 7 turns of meditation and breath control.

The Muladhara, or root chakra controls the will to survive. Raising energy to the Muladhara grants the Nagah a number of additional Bruised health levels equal to his successes.

The Swadhishthana or hara chakra controls vitality. By raising energy to the Swadhishthana, the wereserpent purges his body of all disease, all unwelcome spirits and all foreign poisons and simultaneously

heals a number of health levels (including aggravated ones) equal to the number of successes received on the Kundalini roll.

The Manipura or solar plexus chakra controls raw emotional energy. Raising energy to the Manipura grants the Nagah a number of Rage points equal to his successes on the Kundalini roll.

The Anahata or heart chakra controls love and compassion for humanity. Energy raised to the Anahata chakra causes the wereserpent to radiate a strong sense of love and tranquility. Those within line-of-sight of the Nagah must roll their Willpower against a target of 8 and get more successes than the Nagah got on his Kundalini roll to think or act in any hostile manner toward him.

The Vishuddha or throat chakra controls creativity and clairaudience. Raising the Kundalini to the Vishuddha allows the wereserpent to hear and understand all thoughts and words within a ten-foot radius. Others do not know they are being heard and the Nagah may probe minds for more deeply hidden information if he so desires.

The Ajna or brow chakra controls intuition and clairvoyance. Bringing the Kundalini up to the Ajna allows the Nagah to know everything that pertains to him (and by extension his nest) within his line of sight. Secrets are revealed, illusions fall away and clarity triumphs. Sweet-talking enemies are exposed for what they are, and the true forms and natures of all around are made manifest to the wereserpent.

The Sahasrara or crown chakra controls transcendence, superconsciousness and the spiritual will to be. Raising the Kundalini to this chakra allows the Nagah to briefly attain a state of cosmic consciousness during which he can get the answer to any one question he may have (subject to Storyteller's discretion).

This Gift's effects last for one scene. Regardless of the level of chakra reached, the Nagah may perform this Gift no more than once per week.

• **There Is No Body (Level Five)** — By seeing through the illusion of causality, the Balaram is able to free himself from its concomitant limitations. Specifically, this Gift renders the Nagah incorporeal. For the duration of this Gift, the body of the Balaram (and any dedicated items) is not affected by the physical world in any way he does not choose to be affected. Bullets, claws and fire pass right through him; likewise, his body passes through walls and other physical items as though they weren't there.

System: The player spends three Gnosis points and makes a Perception + Enigmas roll against a difficulty of 7. Each success allows the wereserpent to remain intangible for two turns. This Gift does not protect against powers that can affect the immaterial, such as spirit magic.

Ahi

Ahi, the offspring of two Nagah, do not suffer from either discrimination or from physical deformities as Garou metis do. They do tend to have a pronounced spiritual nature, however, that links them more strongly than the other two breeds to water and the chaos of storms. They also have seem to have insights into the larger picture, especially as it concerns the Triat.

• **Bones as Coils (Level One)** — As the Black Spiral Dancer Gift: Rathead (**Werewolf**, pg. 273). This Gift effectively makes the Nagah a master escape artist.

• **Weaver Sense (Level One)** — Through careful examination of a person or a place, the ahi may detect the ordering hand of the Weaver at work. The character mystically discerns whether there are patterns where there should be randomness, order where there should be chaos and if the degree of order suggests some form of actionable imbalance. In particular, this Gift allows the ahi to see Weaver-spirits on the other side of the Gauntlet.

System: The player rolls Perception + Enigmas, difficulty of (12 - the local Gauntlet). Success indicates that the ahi is able to detect emanations of the Weaver and their relative strength; she may also "peek" into the Umbra at will, although the only things she can see clearly on the other side are the constructs and spirits of the Weaver. Truly overwhelming Weaver-energies may disorient the Nagah, at the Storyteller's discretion. The Gift's effects last as long as the ahi is willing to concentrate on her perceptions.

• **Wyld Sense (Level One)** — By carefully focusing on a scene or a person, the wereserpent may detect the presence of the Wyld and things or places that are unbalanced toward chaos, creation or primordial energies, including magic and spiritual forces such as raw Gnosis. It also reveals powerful passions like love, anger and hatred in mortals.

System: The player rolls Perception + Enigmas (difficulty of the local Gauntlet). Success indicates that the ahi can detect the presence and strength of Wyld emanations; enough successes may, at the Storyteller's discretion, permit the ahi to "see" high amounts of Wyld-related energies in other beings (such as mental instability, high levels of Gnosis, and so on). The ahi may also "peek" into the Umbra for the purposes of seeing Wyld-spirits and energies. As with Weaver Sense, this Gift can be highly distracting, even overwhelming, in areas of powerful Wyld energy such as Wyldings. The perceptions last for as long as the ahi concentrates.

• **Wyrm Sense (Level One)** — This Gift attunes the ahi to the presence of the Wyrm in all its forms, corrupt and otherwise. Banes, fomori, vampires and other creatures of supernatural Wyrm-taint become glaringly obvious to the ahi.

System: The player rolls Perception + Enigmas (difficulty of the local Gauntlet). The Gift reveals the presence of obvious Wyrm energies, although enough successes can reveal much more subtle traces of corruption and decay, such as structural weaknesses in a building or a tumor in a person. The character may choose to observe the other side of the Gauntlet, where Wyrmish spirits and constructs become painfully obvious. The Gift lasts for as long as the ahi is willing to concentrate.

• **Face of Surya (Level Two)** — Surya, the face of the sun, is revered among the Nagah for the warmth he brings to their cold blood. The ahi may call upon Surya to show his face, bringing his light where it is needed most. The Nagah are said to have originally learned this Gift from the Mokolé, although their lack of connection to Helios makes it less effective in Nagah hands.

System: The player spends a Gnosis point and rolls Intelligence + Occult against difficulty 6. The effects last for one turn plus one additional turn for each additional Gnosis point spent.

Successes	Effects
1	Illuminate dark area with ambient light
2	Sun pierces clouds or trees with enough brightness to illuminate targets and injure vampires.
3	Sun's rays are as strong through water, glass, clouds or tree cover as through perfectly clear sky.
4	Sun's rays can light fires or bring heat when it is cold or appear inside windowless building or underground during the daytime
5+	Sun shines even at night

• **Indra's Cloak (Level Two)** — As the Black Furies Gift: Curse of Aeolus.

• **Venom Blood (Level Two)** — As the Get of Fenris Gift.

• **Call the Tides (Level Three)** — In Indian myth, the snake-shifters were credited with the ability to cause floods or droughts. This Gift grants the wereserpent control over the rise and fall of the tides.

System: The Nagah must be in sight of a tidal body of water (ocean, sea, river estuary). The player then makes a Gnosis roll, difficulty 8. The number of successes determines the result:

Successes	Effects
1	Tides come in or go out twice as fast as usual
2	Tides can be reversed, coming in when they should be going out and vice versa.
3	High or low tide can be brought in one scene
4	Unusual tides (spring tide or neap tide) can be brought in one scene
5+	Freakish tides (heavy waves, for example) can occur in one scene.

• **Command Water Spirit (Level Three)** — As the Uktena Gift: Call Elemental, save that only water-spirits may be called. The Nagah must have a natural water source such as a river or a lake. The water-spirit (invariably a servant of the Wani) will move water, dampen a foe or short out a power system at the wereserpent's command.

• **Rapture of the Deep (Level Three)** — This Gift combines the Nagah's connection to water with their skills at illusion. With but a stare, a Nagah can instill a strong desire in a target to enter any large body of water nearby and swim as far out and down as possible.

System: The player spends a Gnosis point and makes a contested Willpower roll with the target. If the player wins, the target runs to the nearest large body of water (at least the size of a small pond) and tries to swim to the bottom. If the body of water is less than twenty feet deep, the target will, in all likelihood, make it to the bottom at which point he comes to his senses. If this Gift is used near very deep water, it can very easily result in the target drowning, but if others can stop him (or if he possesses some means to breathe water) he may survive. The effect lasts for 10 turns plus one turn for every net success on the contested Willpower roll.

• **Throat Snake (Level Four)** — Through the use of this Gift, the Nagah may transform his tongue into a delicate foot-long pink-scaled snake that resides in his throat. The Nagah senses everything the smaller snake senses, so the throatsnake can perform reconnaissance work for the Nagah by crawling through tight spaces where the wereserpent cannot go. Alternatively, the throat snake can be the bearer of the wereserpent's venom, biting an enemy who was much too concerned with larger threats.

So long as the throat snake is extant, the Nagah is incapable of speech. When the throatsnake has done its work, it crawls back into the Nagah's mouth and becomes his tongue once more.

System: The player spends 2 Rage points and rolls Dexterity + Primal-Urge. If the roll is successful, the throat snake detaches, possessing one health level for each success. For purposes of combat, the throat snake has Strength 1, Stamina 2, Dexterity 5, Brawl 2, Dodge

5 and Stealth 5. The throat snake possesses one dose of the Nagah's venom, which is taken from the Nagah's own reserves; if the Nagah has used all his venom before invoking this Gift, the throat snake has no venom of its own. If the throat snake is killed, the Nagah immediately takes two levels of aggravated damage and cannot speak until that damage is healed.

• **Whirlpool (Level Four)** — This Gift allows the Nagah to cause a whirlpool in any body of water larger than a small swimming pool. Depending on the size of the whirlpool, it can suck down anything from people to boats.

System: The player spends a Gnosis point and then rolls her permanent Gnosis (difficulty 7).

Successes	Effect
1	5' diameter, large enough to suck down a human.
3	10' diameter, large enough to suck down a Garou in Crinos form.
5	20' diameter, large enough to suck down dinghies and similar craft.
6+	50' diameter, large enough to suck down medium boats.

• **Force Balance (Level Five)** — Use of this powerful Gift brings the members of the Triat into harmonious balance in a place. This Gift summons powerful spirits representing the healthiest aspects of the Triat who then work in unison to place the site back into balance. Note that balance does not indicate a state of affairs that people, shapeshifters or even the user of the Gift will necessarily prefer — it simply means that the Triat is in healthy balance in a place. Usually, this means that whoever had control of the space prior to this Gift being used will be very angry as years (if not decades) of proprietary work are undone.

System: The player spends three Gnosis points and rolls Intelligence + Enigmas against a difficulty of the Gauntlet or (12 - Gauntlet), whichever is higher. Wyrm, Weaver and Wyld spirits converge to put the site into balance. The number of successes determines the speed of the transformation as well as how strong the "gyroscope" effect is in preventing the place from becoming unbalanced again. This Gift can be used no more than once a week.

Successes	Effect
1	The process begins and is somewhat weak. Complete balance of the site will take nearly six months, and mundane forces that try to stop the balance could do so. Returning the site to an unbalanced condition will not require much effort.
2	The effects of the Gift proceed far faster than they would otherwise. Balance returns to the site within three months. Gafflings don't have the power to stop or reverse the process, although Jagglings or greater spirits could do so.
3	The site effectively has a new spirit. The place is imbued with a sense of balance that would require the attention of several strong Jagglings, shapeshifters or similarly powerful creatures to undo. Under mundane conditions, the place will remain balanced for at least ten years.
4	Change wreaks havoc on the place for a week, at the end of which the place is balanced. Powerful outside influence (an Incarna avatar, a horde of Jagglings, the efforts of shapeshifter elders) can still prevent the process, but otherwise, the place attains balance and will remain in balance for at least fifty years.
5	Everything old is new again, and it takes less than twenty-four hours. Any creature (including random spirits not part of the balancing effort) caught in the unfolding storm of order takes one health level of aggravated damage every hour as the primordial forces at work try to use her as raw materials for the new harmonious state. Only creatures of Incarna or similar level can actually stop the process of restoring the balance, and without actual interference, the site remains balanced for at least one hundred years.
6	It's like watching time-lapse photography. In the space of ten minutes, the site transforms from a nightmare into a balanced and sustainable system. Any creature caught in the transformation storm takes five levels of aggravated damage *every turn* as the balancing process incorporates him into the new system. Only the direct intervention of an Incarna or the like can stop the Gift's effects before completion. Under mundane condition, the site would require a thousand years for it to slip again so far out of balance.

• **Child of Storms (Level Five)** — Through this powerful Gift, the Nagah reclaims his place as the spiritual child of the Wani. The wereserpent surrenders his physical form and becomes the storm itself, directing the wind and waters where he chooses.

System: The player spends three points each of Gnosis, Rage and Willpower to effect the transformation. In this form, the Nagah has no physical body; he effectively becomes a force of wind and rain. While in his weather-form, the ahi can direct winds of up to 50 mph, rain, hail or snow. The Nagah may also lash out with lightning once every three turns; he requires a

Gnosis roll to hit a target, who takes 10 dice of aggravated damage. Only weather-controlling powers can avert the Nagah-turned-storm, and they may in fact damage him depending on their strength. The Gift's effects last for five turns per point of the ahi's permanent Rage, Gnosis or Willpower, whichever is lower.

Vasuki

The serpent-breed Nagah have powers that derive from their heritage, replicating or enhancing the natural powers of serpents — or the powers attributed to snakes by legend.

• **Death Rattle (Level One)** — The sound of a rattlesnake's rattle is disturbing on a subconscious level, and wereserpents can capitalize on that fact. The Nagah using this Gift grows a rattle (if she doesn't already have one), and may mystically charge the sound it makes to unnerve and distract opponents who cannot see her.

System: The player spends a Gnosis point and rolls Manipulation + Intimidation. For every success on that roll, the Nagah can assign a -1 modifier to one of her target's actions sometime before the end of the scene. The wereserpent shakes her rattle prior to the action she wants to disrupt and the player informs the Storyteller how many of the successes she wants to assign to disrupting her target's next action. The Nagah need not use up all her successes at once; she can parcel out -1 modifiers as she chooses.

For example, a Nagah who gets four successes on the Manipulation + Intimidation roll can rattle four times over the course of the scene to assign 4 separate -1 modifiers. She could also rattle twice to assign 2 -2 modifiers, rattle once vigorously to give her chosen target a -4 modifier on one action, or any other combination. Unused successes are lost at the end of the scene. This Gift ceases to work once the target knows where the wereserpent is; however, the vasuki could choose to affect a different opponent who still didn't know her whereabouts.

• **River's Gift (Level One)** — This Gift allows a Nagah in Balaram, Silkaram, Azhi Dahaka or Vasuki form to breathe water and air interchangeably.

System: The player spends one Rage point and rolls Stamina + Primal-Urge. In Silkaram, Azhi Dahaka and Vasuki form, the change requires only 1 success; in Balaram it requires 2. The Gift lasts for a scene.

• **Sense Vibration (Level One)** — Snakes do not have ears, but they do have a very keen vibrational sense that allows them to sense the approach of potential prey (or predators). This Gift enhances that sense, allowing the vasuki to detect even tiny changes in air pressure.

System: The player spends one Gnosis point and rolls Perception + Alertness; the effects last for a scene.

The serpent can discern ground vibration and miniscule changes in air pressure at a distance of one hundred feet per success, both horizontally and vertically (so a Nagah using this Gift and getting two successes could sense digging two hundred feet beneath her). This Gift lets the Nagah know such things as the size of an object, how many there are, which way it's going and how fast it's traveling. This Gift is not affected by any manner of invisibility or inaudibility; an invisible, inaudible three hundred pound Garou still makes the earth shake a bit with every step, and that is what this Gift allows the Nagah to sense.

This Gift is usable only in relatively quiet areas. Cities and most modern buildings contain too much random noise and vibration. While the wereserpent can still use this Gift in such locales, doing so quarters the Gift's effective range. Any sort of concussion (gun shots, fireworks, concussion grenades) will cause intense pain to a wereserpent using this Gift, effectively "deafening" her to vibration for the rest of the scene and inflicting one level of bashing damage to the snake's pressure sensitive membranes.

• **Treesnake's Blessing (Level One)** — Many species of snakes are excellent climbers. This Gift allows the Nagah to take advantage of that heritage to climb trees, cliffs and even walls.

System: The player spends one Gnosis point and rolls Dexterity + Athletics. For the rest of the scene, the wereserpent's climbing speed is equal to his crawling speed multiplied by the number of successes on the roll.

• **Command Snakes (Level Two)** — Vasuki use this Gift to summon the aid of their serpent cousins. The type of snakes that answer the call varies from region to region. Most are not venomous, although there are certain places — notably India, Australia, the tropical oceans and the American West and Southwest — where a large number of venomous snakes will respond. Obviously, this Gift does not work in places where there are no active snakes, including Ireland.

The vasuki cannot communicate with the summoned serpents, although they will react aggressively to any target that the Nagah is threatening. Most snakes cover ground relatively slowly, so unless the wereserpent knows that he's near a nest of snakes, he'd do well to do his summoning a little ahead of when he needs assistance.

System: The player spends a point of Gnosis and rolls Charisma + Animal Ken. One success indicates that only a few animals show up. With three successes the Nagah has summoned around thirty snakes of different varieties. With five successes, the Nagah has summoned a slithering swarm of snakes, many of

PRESCOTT

which are probably venomous. The snakes remain for the scene, or until the vasuki wills the Gift to end, at which point they return to their own territories.

• **Herpetophobia (Level Two)** — Nagah using this Gift afflict victims with a powerful irrational fear of snakes. The victim reacts with extreme fear and revulsion toward the snake, and will attack or flee from any snake he encounters while under the Gift's influence. Naturally, the size and behavior of the snake will have some influence on his reaction.

System: The player spends one Rage point and rolls Manipulation + Intimidation, difficulty 7; the target resists with Willpower, difficulty 7. The duration of the fear is one day per success for mortals, one hour per success for "mostly human" supernaturals such as mages, or one turn per success in the case of shapeshifters, vampires or other inhuman creatures. Victims may spend Willpower to fight the fear, but only for a turn at a time. Affected characters flee the presence of snakes if they can, and lose two dice on any actions involving the snakes themselves. Targets who are already herpetophobic may go catatonic with fear.

• **Lightning Strike (Level Two)** — As the Ahroun Gift: Spirit of the Fray.

• **Kitesnake (Level Three)** — With this Gift, the snake may shift around his body mass such that he is mostly hood, with only a very thin bit of tail hanging below. Any strong breeze is enough to sweep the Nagah into the air, allowing, if not exactly flight, then at least the ability to become airborne. This Gift has its obvious dangers, but it may be the only means of maintaining tabs on a target.

System: The player rolls Dexterity + Primal-Urge to manipulate the Nagah's body mass. One success will make this Gift effective in the presence of a strong wind while two or more let the snake take to the air in the presence of even a minimal breeze.

Under calm weather conditions, the wereserpent may exercise some small degree of control over which direction she goes by angling her body this way or that, but in the face of a strong wind, control is out of the question. Should the wind give out altogether, the snake may fold forward into something like a living parachute to minimize landing damage. This Gift lasts for one scene.

• **Long Strike (Level Three)** — Venomous snakes can typically strike from a distance half their body length away; thus, a six-foot rattlesnake can effectively strike a target three feet away. This Gift greatly increases that distance, allowing the vasuki to launch his entire body to strike an enemy who believes himself to be out of harm's way.

System: The player spends a Rage point and rolls Dexterity + Brawl. Each success doubles the distance from which the Nagah can strike. So, a six-foot Vasuki with a single success could strike a target six feet away. Two successes would allow him to strike an enemy twelve feet away, and five successes would allow the Nagah to come seemingly out of nowhere to strike an opponent forty-eight feet away.

• **Sidewind (Level Three)** — The sidewinder rattlesnake can move at amazing speed and with great stealth. With this Gift, vasuki gain the ability to move with a similar quiet rapidity.

System: The player spends one Gnosis point and rolls Stamina + Athletics (difficulty 7) to activate this Gift. While Sidewinding, the Nagah moves at ten times her normal land speed. The effects last for up to eight hours, during which the wereserpent can do nothing else. This Gift can only be used in Azhi Dahaka, Kali Dahaka or Vasuki form.

• **Belly Ride (Level Four)** — This bizarre gift allows a Nagah in Vasuki form to wriggle down the throat of an unconscious human-sized or larger creature and hide in its stomach. Even a twenty-foot cobra can fit into a child's stomach by use of this Gift. While coiled in the gut of her host, the Nagah perceives what her "host" perceives.

Having a snake coiled in one's stomach completely rids the host of any appetite and may nauseate her slightly. The host will be in complete denial about the situation and will grasp at any excuse to explain away the discomfort ("It must be a touch of the flu," or "Maybe I'm pregnant.").

System: The player spends a Gnosis point and rolls Dexterity + Stealth. The target must be unconscious; even a willing target will gag if the Nagah starts crawling down his throat, preventing the Gift from taking effect.

Once the wereserpent is in the host's stomach, he may stay there for as many days as he received successes on the roll, after which the stomach becomes too irritated to hold the Nagah any longer, causing the host to vomit him up. The Nagah may also choose to activate the vomit reflex at any time to escape, or leave while the host is asleep or unconscious without waking her. Nagah using this Gift are unaffected by acid or any other unpleasant elements of being in the host's stomach.

• **Storm Surge (Level Four)** — This Gift allows the Nagah to summon a powerful storm surge to batter a small patch of coastline. The target area must abut a large body of water like an ocean, a sea or a very large lake. Once the wereserpent summons the storm surge, he has only minimal control over it, although he can specify a particular building to be the focal point for the water's wrath.

System: The player spends two Gnosis points and rolls Manipulation + Occult. The size of the resulting storm surge is six feet times successes. A six foot storm surge will drag away the unwary, break windows in beach houses, pound boats to splinters and strand vehicles while a thirty foot storm surge will flood streets, knock out electricity and communications lines, batter even sturdy buildings to rubble and wash vehicles out to sea.

Once the wereserpent summons the surge, it takes about twenty minutes for the full fury of the water to build, after that it lasts about an hour, after which the water subsides. Injudicious (i.e., gratuitously destructive) use of this Gift is punished by the Sesha.

• **Assassin's Well (Level Five)** — Nagah are typically able to inject only three doses of venom before their venom glands run dry. This Gift allows the vasuki to transcend that limitation, giving the wereserpent unlimited venom for the duration of a scene.

System: No roll is necessary. The player need only expend two Gnosis points; for the remainder of the scene, the Nagah gains an unlimited supply of venom.

• **Song of Takshaka (Level Five)** — Takshaka was the greatest shapechanger of the Nagah, and his skills extended beyond his own body. This Gift functions as the Red Talons Gift: Curse of Lycaon, but transforms humans into serpents. The Gift can also force any Khurah into their animal form, not just Garou or Nagah — Ananasi must take on Crawlerling, Nuwisha are forced into Latrani, and so on.

Auspice Gifts

As noted earlier, the auspice of a Nagah does not determine their social role, merely their spiritual affinities. Thus, the Gifts peculiar to each auspice have less to do with specific tasks and more to do simply with the season's influence.

Kamakshi

The Kamakshi are in tune with spring's energies of renewal and rebirth, and thus gain powers of peace and healing — and reversing the path of healing.

• **Ganga's Caress (Level One)** — As the Theurge Gift: Mother's Touch.

• **Kind Death (Level One)** — Nagah are assassins, but they rarely harbor ill will toward those they kill. This Gift allows a Nagah to ease the shock of dying and send the spirit or soul of a dying or very recently dead foe on to the best of whatever fates might await it. In the case of a human, it prevents the target from becoming a wraith or a vampire. In the case of Khurah, it may negate any curses preventing the deceased from rejoining Gaia. This Gift also prevents dying curses and bad karma from affecting the Nagah.

System: The Nagah must be within a stone's throw of the victim and in line of sight. The player rolls Charisma + Empathy, difficulty of the dying or deceased's Willpower. One success quells the pain of dying and allows the target's soul to untangle itself from its body. Three successes prevent the Embrace from taking effect. The difficulty to lay any dying curses, hexes or similar unpleasantness is increased by one for every success gained by the Kamakshi.

• **Resist Pain (Level One)** — As the Philodox Gift.

• **Bask (Level Two)** — The heat and warmth of the sun are deeply soothing to the Nagah, and this Gift allows the wereserpent to transform that warmth into confidence and a powerful sense of purpose.

System: The player spends a Gnosis point. For the rest of the day, the Nagah regains one point of Willpower for every uninterrupted hour he spends relaxing quietly in the sun (preferably on a warm rock or on a beach). This Gift works only on warm days and in direct sunlight.

• **Calm (Level Two)** — As the Children of Gaia Gift.

• **Serpent's Sting (Level Two)** — There is no better teacher than pain, and this Gift allows the wereserpent to teach some very harsh lessons. By raising one target's sensitivity to pain a thousandfold, the Kamakshi is able to debilitate an opponent without resorting to more lethal means. It also does quite a number on fleeing prey. This Gift is considered potentially corrupting, and those who use it casually are watched very closely for Wyrmish sympathies.

System: The Nagah must touch her target; the player spends one Rage point and rolls Perception + Medicine, difficulty 7. Success indicates that for the rest of the scene, the target suffers double wound penalties: The target loses two dice from his dice pools at Hurt and Injured, four at Wounded and Mauled and ten at Crippled.

• **Assassin's Insistence (Level Three)** — As natural assassins who study the healing arts, the Kamakshi are doubly dangerous, not only for the harm they can inflict, but for their knowledge of — and ability to undermine — healing magics. This Gift prevents healing magic from working, and may even cause the healer to inadvertently harm her recipient. This Gift only affects magic that heals wounds; it does not prevent regeneration or magics that cure disease or counteract poison. Kamakshi typically use this Gift to counter the effects of Mother's Touch, Resist Pain, mages' sorcery and, most recently, the healing magics of wayward Imbued hunters. Kamakshi use this Gift only in their role as Gaia's assassins or in direst self-defense; in other circumstances is it considered to have great potential to corrupt.

System: The player spends one Gnosis point and rolls Intelligence + Medicine; the Nagah must touch the target. Every success cancels out one success on the next roll used to try healing the target. If the Nagah gets *more* successes than the healer, then the healer's target suffers the difference in health levels of bashing damage. The Gift's effects last for the scene, or until invoked by a healing attempt. After the first attempt at healing the target, the Gift's effects are spent.

• **Prevent Adharma (Level Three)** — Adharma means "wrong action" or "misstep." By use of this Gift, the Nagah prevents a being from going against its nature or its role in the universe. A Corax, therefore, could not withhold information; a vampire could not refrain from acting in accordance with its Beast, and a fellow Nagah could not spare the life of a legitimate target.

System: The player spends a Gnosis point and makes a contested Manipulation + Enigmas roll against the target's Willpower. If the wereserpent succeeds, the target is incapable of going against his dharma. A being that is clearly acting against its nature immediately "comes to its senses" and stops doing whatever it was doing. Likewise, beings that actively refrain from following their dharma (e.g., a Garou who refuses to shift from its breed form or an artist trying to be an accountant), once more begin acting in accordance with their place in the world.

There was a time when all beings had relatively obvious dharmic paths and strove to follow them. That is no longer the case. Most individuals in the modern age have no idea what their role is in the grand scheme of things, and they may not actually have one, in which case this Gift has no effect. On the other hand, this Gift is extremely effective with creatures that have a clear path to follow (e.g., Kuei-jin, Risen, mummies).

Ideally, the Nagah should at least have a vague idea of the target's dharma, otherwise it's impossible to know what the effects of this Gift might be — and the Wani and Sesha both look askance at such irresponsible use of Gifts.

If the target of this Gift is a Storyteller character, the Storyteller should decide just what the target's dharma is. If the target is another character, the Storyteller and the character should discuss what the player thinks his character's dharma really is (though the Storyteller retains final say).

• **Dazzle (Level Three)** — As the Children of Gaia Gift.

• **Denial of Wellbeing (Level Four)** — Greater understanding of the way bodies mend using magic grants insight into how an assassin might stop them from doing so. Following up on the insights taught by Assassin's Insistence, Nagah may learn to prevent even inherent healing. With a touch, this Gift prevents another creature from regenerating or resisting poison or disease.

System: The Nagah must first touch the intended target. The player spends two Gnosis points and makes a resisted Intelligence + Medicine roll against the target's Gnosis (or Willpower -2 for creatures with no Gnosis). Success halts the target's healing process completely, and the victim also suffers a two-die difficulty to resist diseases or poison (including Nagah venom). Each success stops regeneration and other healing (including Gifts) for one hour or until the Gift is somehow nullified.

The Nagah must learn Assassin's Insistence before she can learn Denial of Wellbeing.

• **Suspend (Level Four)** — A Nagah in Azhi Dahaka and Kali Dahaka form can use this gift to unhinge his jaw and swallow creatures up to the size of a Crinos werewolf. Only quiescent creatures may be so swallowed. As the creature is swallowed, it is covered with a thick anaesthetic slime that paralyzes the creature. Once swallowed, the creature enters a form of suspended animation. Fire, physical force and even the ravages of time are kept out so long as the creature remains encased in the preservative slime within the Nagah.

When the wereserpent chooses, it reverses peristalsis and disgorges the creature. The preservative slime dries out and sloughs away in a few turns and the creature returns to consciousness.

System: The character expends one Gnosis point and rolls Stamina + Enigmas. The character needs at least two successes: one to successfully swallow the creature and one to suspend the creature's life properly.

Storing a man-sized creature in one's digestive tract is extremely uncomfortable and precludes fighting; consequently, Nagah are unlikely to use this Gift except in extreme circumstances (saving a badly wounded nest-mate until she can be healed, for example). While suspending a target, the Nagah is down three dice on all Physical and Social rolls.

• **Shed the Years (Level Five)** — Snakes were often considered to be manifestations of time. The Nagah with this Gift is rather more like an incarnation of the reversal of time. Once a year, when the Nagah (or a nestmate) is undergoing the Samskara of Shedding the Past (see page 93), this Gift may be performed upon her, and along with her old skin, the wereserpent sheds a number of years of physical aging as well. A determined Nagah could return from senescence to the prime of life in the space of a decade.

System: The player sacrifices one permanent Gnosis point and rolls Stamina + Enigmas against a target number of 7 (Stamina bonuses for form do not add to

this roll). Each success counteracts one month of aging. The Nagah's knowledge and memory are unaffected, but the body loses any wrinkles, scars, long-term illnesses and the like gained during that period of time.

This Gift is usable only once a year when the target is molting.

• **Surya's Radiance (Level Five)** — As the Children of Gaia Gift: Halo of the Sun.

Kartikeya

The summer auspice grants an affinity with fire, warmth, vigor, inspiration and even some trickery.

• **Brief Sensation (Level One)** — This Gift allows the Kartikeya to project an illusory sensation into the mind of her target. The illusion lasts only for a moment, can affect only one sense at a time, and cannot be very complicated. Still, the ability to invoke any small sensation from the smell of baking bread to a hot flash to a brief shimmer of blue light is no small trick. Creative Nagah have used this Gift to evoke everything from the sound of a lover's voice to the smell of the Wyrm.

System: The player spends a Gnosis point and rolls Wits + Subterfuge. The number of successes indicates how many different brief hallucinations the Nagah can cause over the course of the next scene. Certain sensations, like the feeling of the hairs standing up on the back of one's neck, the shine of gold or the smell of rotting meat can very effectively lead people to or from a location.

• **Eyes of the War God (Level One)** — The Kartikeya draw their name from the god of war and the son of Shiva, who had six faces and could never be surprised. This Gift grants the Nagah an emulation of the war god's legendary perception.

System: The player must spend one Gnosis point and roll Wits + Alertness. If successful, the wereserpent gains full vision extending 360 degrees for the scene's duration. Furthermore, each success adds one die to any dice pool the Nagah uses to perceive enemies for the remainder of the scene.

• **Scent of the True Form (Level One)** — As the Philodox Gift.

• **Secret Serpent (Level Two)** — As the Ragabash Gift: Blissful Ignorance.

• **Forked Tongue (Level Two)** — As the Ragabash Gift: Obscure the Truth.

• **The Serpent's Voice (Level Two)** — The Kartikeya, more than any other Nagah, have a great love for song and euphonious sound. This Gift allows the Kartikeya to imitate any sound he has heard with perfect accuracy — sirens, gunshots, musical instruments, even conversations.

System: Once the Kartikeya has learned this Gift, he may reproduce any sound he hears. This is not the same thing as voice imitation; the Nagah cannot improvise in another's voice, only repeat the things he's heard the imitated person say. If the Nagah is clever, he can create new combinations to form new sentences, but this tends to be choppy. The player must roll Charisma + Performance if the intended audience knows the voice very well or suspects a ruse.

• **Lance of the Summer Sun (Level Three)** — This Gift allows the Nagah to project a brilliant and searing bolt of concentrated sunlight from his palm. This bolt is extremely bright and hot enough to burn through fabric, sheetrock and wood.

System: The player spends one Gnosis and rolls Charisma + Leadership, difficulty 7. The bolt of light flashes out from the Nagah's extended hand. Creatures that take damage from fire will take a number of aggravated health levels of damage equal to the wereserpent's successes. Vampires take twice that amount.

• **Might of the Mountain (Level Three)** — As the Get of Fenris Gift: Might of Thor.

• **Blood Running Hot (Level Four)** — As the Ahroun Gift: Stoking Fury's Furnace.

• **Veil of Maya (Level Four)** — As the Fianna Gift: Phantasm.

• **Hydra Warrior (Level Five)** — This terrible Gift allows the members of a nest to fuse into one enormous and devastating snake monster. The resulting hydra has one tail and as many arms as the members

had separately, but beyond that, the shape of the hydra is determined by the wills of those comprising it. Some may have three separate trunks joined by a massive prehensile tail, other hydras have taken the form of an enormous Azhi Dahaka with six arms and three faces on one head. Lethality is the only common denominator.

System: The player spends one point of Gnosis and one point of Rage for each nestmate. When the Nagah touch, they fuse together into an enormous multi-armed destroyer with health levels equal to the sum of the health levels of the nestmates plus one additional health level for each success. The nestmate's Rage, Strength, Dexterity and Stamina are all pooled while individual members retain their separate Gnosis pools.

While in hydra form, members automatically benefit from shared thoughts. Each Nagah may still act as usual, although the form must move together. The nest members must all be in Azhi Dahaka form and all members must be willing to join the Hydra Warrior or the Gift will not work.

• **Jungle Snake's Hoodoo (Level Five)** — This Gift sends the target's mind into a waking dream controlled by the Nagah. The wereserpent can use this gift for purposes that are kind (letting a man see his dead lover one last time), cruel (making a woman believe she's covered with bugs that are burrowing into her skin) or utilitarian (getting the target to reenact important conversations while talking aloud). While the Nagah sets the tone and nudges the

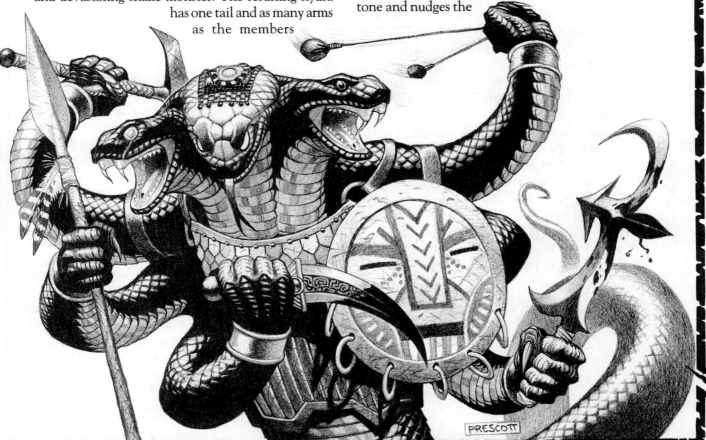

PRESCOTT

hallucination as he chooses, the setting and "players" of this psychodrama are pulled from the target's unconscious. Bad hallucinations make use of the target's worst fears, while pleasant hallucinations draw on the target's desires and pleasant memories. The Nagah may even be able to watch the visions unfold.

System: The player spends two Gnosis points and rolls Manipulation + Occult against a target number equal to the victim's Willpower. Even a single success sucks the target into delirium, but the wereserpent can't see what's going on in the target's head. Two successes allow the Nagah to see about a quarter of what's happening. With three successes, the Kartikeya perceives about half of the hallucination, while five successes show the Nagah everything the target sees. Six or more successes pull the wereserpent into the hallucination with the target, allowing full participation, unless the player spends a Willpower point to avoid doing so. Wise old snakes generally recommend against entering the hallucination directly because the target's "psychic immune system" can do ugly things to a Nagah who trespasses where he's not wanted. This Gift lasts for one scene.

Kamsa Gifts

The autumn-born Kamsa's Gifts focus on psychological warfare and insight into a target's weaknesses.

• **Executioner's Edge (Level One)** — As the Shadow Lord Gift: Seizing the Edge.

• **Predator's Patience (Level One)** — Good assassins must be able to wait for hours for their prey, and sometimes in uncomfortable positions. This Gift allows the Kamsa to remain absolutely still for extended periods without cramping or growing tired. The Nagah does not even appear to breathe, and may easily be overlooked (or mistaken for a mannequin) due to the total lack of motion.

System: The player spends a Willpower point and rolls Stamina + Stealth. For each success the Nagah is able to remain absolutely motionless for one hour. Until he moves, attempts to see him in any but the best lighting conditions are at +1 difficulty.

• **Slayer's Eye (Level One)** — As the Shadow Lord Gift: Fatal Flaw.

• **Forked Tongue (Level Two)** — As the Ragabash Gift: Obscure the Truth.

• **Inattention to Detail (Level Two)** — Targets of this Gift lose focus, become preoccupied with daydreams and are largely oblivious to just about everything. The target still notices glaringly obvious goings-on, but even token stealth is enough to allow a small army to slip past unnoticed.

System: The player spends a Gnosis point and rolls Manipulation + Subterfuge against the target's Willpower. Each success allows the Nagah to drop the target's Perception or Alertness by one dot for the duration of the scene; the target cannot fall below Perception 1 or Alertness 0.

• **Staredown (Level Two)** — As the homid Gift.

• **Eye of the Cobra (Level Three)** — As the Galliard Gift.

• **Smothering Question (Level Three)** — There are times when the Nagah need information and don't have time to acquire it subtly. This Gift allows the Kamsa to pose one very carefully phrased question to a target and have the target answer the question with the utmost honesty and thoroughness.

System: The player spends a Willpower point, and rolls Manipulation + Intimidation in a contested roll against the target's Willpower. The Nagah locks eyes with his target and asks the question. If the wereserpent succeeds, the target can do *nothing* but answer the question, starting with the most salient points and gradually telling everything he knows that's connected to the topic at hand.

Being the recipient of this Gift is not a pleasant experience. The target feels as though he's drowning in the question and the only way to save himself is to answer as completely and in as much detail as possible. For the duration of the Nagah's concentration, nothing exists for the target of this Gift but the question, and his complete and honest answer. If the target knows nothing, he'll babble and cry and lapse into a debilitating anxiety attack for the duration of the interrogation. The question must be asked in a language the target understands.

• **Summon the Accused (Level Three)** — To the Kamsa, it's a bad hunter who stalks her prey. A good hunter simply waits for the prey to come to her. This Gift summons the Nagah's prey to her. By hissing quietly and swaying hypnotically, the Kamsa sets up a sort of beacon that calls her prey to her. As long as the wereserpent maintains the hissing and alluring movement, the target will wander, somewhat dazed, right into to presence of his summoner. Once the Nagah stops moving and hissing, however, the spell is broken, the target comes to his senses and probably flees. The Nagah must know the target's name for this Gift to work.

System: The player rolls Manipulation + Primal-Urge (difficulty 7) to command her target to approach. The target defends by rolling Willpower (difficulty 8). Unless he gains more successes, the target enters a fugue-like state and begins seeking out the Nagah, though all he's consciously aware of is some deep-seated urge to follow a faint hissing sound (that others cannot hear) to its source. This Gift will not work if the target is aware of the wereserpent's presence, nor does it work in combat. The Gift's effects last only for a scene.

• **Doppleganger (Level Four)** — As the Glass Walker Gift.

• **Open Wounds (Level Four)** — As the Shadow Lord Gift.

• **Heartstrings (Level Five)** — As the Galliard Gift: Head Games.

• **Undying Serpent (Level Five)** — Nagah master assassins can not only negate their foe's attacks but undermine them by appearing to take the blow, only to become stronger than before. A wereserpent using this Gift is not wounded by his enemies' blows, but rather strengthened.

System: The player spends a Gnosis point and rolls Dexterity + Enigmas. All damage delivered to the Nagah for the rest of the turn, up to the number of successes, is added to his health levels instead of subtracted from it. Bashing damage heals bashing damage; lethal damage heals lethal and bashing damage; aggravated damage heals all damage types. Any health levels above the Nagah's normal maximum fade at the end of the combat.

Kali

Nagah born to the winter auspice are particularly driven to the tasks at hand, and their Gifts reflect their determination.

• **Guided Strike (Level One)** — Some enemies are more difficult to hit than others. This Gift increases the wereserpent's accuracy for one strike.

System: The player spends a Willpower point and rolls the Nagah's Gnosis, difficulty 8. For each success, the Nagah gains one additional die on his next roll to hit his target.

• **Iron Coils (Level One)** — As the Silver Fang Gift: Grasp of the Falcon, except this Gift affects the Nagah's ability to catch an opponent in her coils rather than her jaws. This Gift inflicts no extra damage, but escaping the Nagah's constriction is all the more difficult.

• **Wyrm Sense (Level One)** — As the ahi Gift.

• **Discern Weakness (Level Two)** — As the Philodox Gift: Weak Arm.

• **Executioner's Privilege (Level Two)** — As the Get of Fenris Gift: Halt the Coward's Flight.

• **Solidify Water (Level Two)** — By touching a body of water, the Nagah can make large portions of it solidify. The water doesn't freeze or change temperature — it simply becomes solid, allowing the Nagah to walk across it or take cover beneath it to escape pursuers. Fish or other animals trapped in the solidified water do not die, but rather enter a brief hibernation until the Gift wears off.

System: The player spends a Gnosis point and rolls Intelligence + Occult; she may affect an area up to 10 feet in radius for every success. Solidified water possesses the hardness of glass and bullets will ricochet from a large volume of the newly rigid material.

• **Assassin's Strike (Level Three)** — This Gift allows the Nagah to disappear into the Umbra and instantly reappear behind her opponent. The wereserpent then attacks her victim from behind, coolly exploiting the advantage of surprise.

System: No roll is necessary, but the character must spend one Gnosis and one Rage. This Umbral "leap" can be up to 50 feet as long as the victim is within line of sight. If the Nagah chooses to attack immediately, the strike is rolled at -2 difficulty; the difficulty cannot be reduced below 4. This attack cannot be dodged unless the victim is using a supernatural ability to heighten his perceptions.

• **Destroying Blow (Level Three)** — As the Black Furies Gift: Coup de Grace.

• **Indirect Strike (Level Three)** — By means of this Gift, the Nagah concentrates and converts his venom into an odorless, colorless and nearly undetectable poison with which he can coat blades, needles, shards of glass or other sharp objects or insinuate into food or drink. If a victim is damaged by the coated object or consumes the poisoned food, she suffers the full effects of the Nagah's venom.

System: The wereserpent milks his venom glands and spends one Gnosis to distill the deadly essence of his venom and one Gnosis for every day (beyond the first) that he wants the venom to remain potent. If the venom is introduced into the victim's bloodstream or eaten by the victim, the venom takes effect just as if the Nagah had just bitten the victim.

The Nagah are hesitant to use this Gift because the time delay increases the chances of the venom affecting someone other than the target. Needless to say, killing an innocent victim is considered the work of an incompetent assassin, and the Sesha frowns on such mishaps.

• **Mindblock (Level Four)** — As the Silver Fangs Gift.

• **Song of Winter (Level Four)** — As the Wendigo Gift: Chill of Early Frost.

• **Magistrate's Icy Judgement (Level Five)** — As the Wendigo Gift: Heart of Ice.

• **Mahanaga (Level Five)** — While the Nagah prefer to carry out their duties as stealthily and as indirectly as possible, direct conflict is sometimes unavoidable. It occasionally comes to pass that the Nagah must judge and punish offenders who are more powerful than they can deal with even in Azhi Dahaka form. The Wani teach wise and responsible Kali to take a form that is again as powerful relative to the Azhi Dahaka form as that form is to the Nagah's breed form.

When Mahanaga takes effect, the Nagah's battle form becomes even more enormous and lethal; her hood becomes wider, her natural armor becomes harder and her scales take on the appearance of highly burnished copper, gold and obsidian.

System: The Nagah must be in battle form. The player spends one Gnosis and one Rage and rolls Stamina + Primal Urge against a difficulty of 7. With a successful roll, the player may increase Physical Attributes above those of the Azhi Dahaka form by spending Rage to increase Strength, Willpower to increase Stamina and Gnosis to increase Dexterity. The player may increase each Physical Attribute by up to four points. The Attribute gains last for one scene.

Samskara (Rites)

The Samskara (or rites) of the Nagah are notably different from those of the Garou. The most dramatic difference, of course, is that Nagah keep no caerns of their own, and therefore have no rites that might affect a caern's disposition or fortunes. While the wereserpents recognize the value of caerns and their necessity to both Gaia and the Changing Breeds, and while the wereserpents occasionally act to punish those whose incompetence results in the loss of a caern, they do not believe that it is their place to create or use caerns. Nagah move around too much to protect a single caern, and their Samskara may be performed at a variety of places that, while not charged like caerns, are sacred to the wereserpents.

Without the need for caerns in the observance of Samskara, Nagah are free to hold their rituals wherever they choose. By far the most common setting for a Nagah Samskara is near a river. An island in the river is considered particularly auspicious, but Samskara may be held on the banks of a river or, in some cases, in the river itself. Other common sites for Nagah rituals are deep in tropical jungle, surrounded by their snake Kin, or in the heart of a desert, surrounded by great sand dunes and little else. Nagah prefer to perform Samskara at night by the light of the moon.

While rites, to the Garou, are often a time of social interaction, due to the nest structure most wereserpents organize themselves into, the Nagah concern themselves much, much less with the social elements of Samskara. The nest itself is the Nagah's social life, and performing Samskara together is an important element of nest life. Samskara are considered private, and performing them with anyone but one's own nestmates is awkward and embarrassing at best. With the exception of the Sesha conducting certain important rituals for a

nest, it is a rare and somewhat uncomfortable thing for more than one nest to perform Samskara together.

Proper performance of the Samskara are an important element of virtuous living among the Nagah. There is very little emotion shown during Samskara, and they are exceedingly formal. Proper protocol and spirit etiquette are valued highly. Each movement or phrasing must be crisp and to the point. The core demands of Nagah Samskara are elegance and parsimony. Even if there is great emotion behind a rite, it always remains seething beneath the surface. Allowing raw emotion to flow out into a Samskara is considered an embarrassing breach of etiquette, though it is not commented on beyond that.

Repetition of mystically resonant phrases called mantras makes up a great deal of Nagah ritual. The ritemaster repeats the mantras of a given ritual until the words themselves lose meaning and hang in the minds of the nest like ungrounded aural objects.

Since there are four auspices, and given that very few nests have more than three members, no particular auspice has the responsibility of being the ritemaster of their nest. By frequency, Kamakshi fulfill the role of ritemaster in their nest relatively more frequently than the other auspices, followed by Kamsa, Kartikeya and, lastly, Kali, who only rarely take the responsibility of seeing to their nest's ritual needs.

Atonement Samskara

Level One

Nagah are very cognizant of the spiritual dangers of killing other beings. Not only is corruption a possibility should the Nagah grow blind to the gravity of taking life, but the Nagah is also more likely to suffer from the personal spiritual consequences of killing. This Samskara reminds the wereserpent of the significance of death while granting the opportunity to apologize to the victim and his quondam spirit allies.

The nest gathers and speaks a mantra enumerating both the dangers and the necessity of killing. They then make honest apologies to any spirits (including wraiths) their actions may have offended. They take special care to seek the forgiveness of the spirit allies of their recent victims including spirits that were bound to the victim, the victim's totem spirit and so on.

System: The player rolls Charisma + Rituals, difficulty 7. Each success decreases by one die the efficacy of any attack made by a victim's ghost or spirit allies for the rest of the month.

Celebration of First Venom

Level One

While vasuki Nagah are almost always poisonous from birth, balaram and ahi rarely have access to

venom until their first change. This coming of age ritual reaffirms the young wereserpent's new maturity while acknowledging her nascent lethality.

Her sponsor, the Nagah responsible for bringing her into Nagah society, brings the Nagah before the Sesha. The sponsor brings along a trussed food animal, generally a lamb, but possibly a calf or a young elk or deer. While the sponsor talks her through it, the new Nagah changes to Azhi Dahaka form (sometimes Silkaram or Kali Dahaka, but the easier battle form is the most common) and the young Nagah bites the bound animal, injecting it with venom. Once the animal is dead, all present assume Azhi Dahaka form and help devour the animal to celebrate the efficacy of the young wereserpent's venom.

There is also another, subtler reason for this Samskara: to make sure the young Nagah is capable of killing. A Nagah that cannot kill even a clear prey animal will likely have serious difficulties carrying out her duties to Gaia. She is not considered to have successfully fulfilled this Samskara if she is unable to kill when called to do so. If she is not capable of killing the animal at the time of this Samskara, her sponsor will coach her until she is capable of making an appropriate kill without a second thought.

System: Before the Celebration of First Venom, Nagah are not yet Rank 1. The Wani will not teach any Gifts until the young wereserpent has undergone the Celebration of First Venom.

Invocation of the Spirit Messenger

Level One

Communication between nests is no easy matter; the Nagah must be certain that their messages travel quickly and in utmost secrecy. This rite bypasses the usual difficulty by summoning a spirit messenger in service to the Wani (who may take any appropriate form), who will bear a message to the nest of the ritemaster's choice. This rite can even be used to deliver messages to the Sesha, although the Sesha are obviously not to be trifled with minor matters.

System: The roll is Charisma + Rituals, difficulty 7. The messenger arrives within ten minutes, and can carry a short message to another nest anywhere on Earth within the hour.

Rite of Bearing

Level One

When a Nagah becomes pregnant by another Nagah, she intuitively knows if her child will be ahi or not. If her child is not destined to be ahi, however, she must determine which form she will take for the pregnancy. This, in turn, determines whether she will give birth to a human child (or children; twins are more common than single births in these instances) or lay eggs that

91

hatch cobras (although the clutch tends to be smaller than it would be if she had mated with a non-Nagah). To ensure that her pregnancy will proceed in a healthy fashion, the Nagah must perform the Rite of Bearing Samskara within a week of conception. If she waits any longer, the growing child will not have a true form of its own, and is absorbed back into the Nagah's body.

In the company of her nest, under the light of the moon, the pregnant Nagah chants a mantra that lists all the strengths of the breed form she has chosen. Once she has spoken the mantra enough that the words themselves have lost their meaning, she enters the river while taking the form in which she intends to remain. The river and the moon bless the mother's choice, and she will not change form again until after she has laid her eggs or given birth. In accordance with the Nagah laws requiring balance, Nagah tend to choose human and cobra forms equally (barring extenuating circumstances).

System: The Nagah's nestmate or nestmates are the ones to actually perform this Samskara. If there are two, one invokes a Lune while the other invokes a spirit of the river, and both attempt to get their spirit to bless the mother. If only one, the nestmate may invoke both spirits, but the difficulty rises by one. If the mother must perform the rite herself, the difficulty rises by two.

Those enacting the rite must roll Charisma + Rituals, difficulty 6 (or 7 or 8, as denoted above). One success indicates that the spirit(s) has been coaxed into blessing the mother while further successes indicate the relative strength of the blessings. The more successes, the more likely the pregnancy and birth proceed smoothly and easily.

Naginah who take human or cobra mates bear children according to their breed form as usual, but may also use this rite within a week of conception to change their children's nature as if the father were also Nagah. The difficulty, however, rises by one in addition to any other modifiers.

Birthing the Ananta

Level Two

Upon his release into the world, a young Nagah is likely to receive his Ananta as a gift. This Samskara takes a portion of the recipient's spirit energy and binds it with portions of the spirit world's energy, shaping the Ananta. Most nests have at least one member who knows this rite, in case the Ananta of one of their own is damaged or destroyed. The rite is a lengthy one, often lasting hours, but is also relatively safe.

System: This rite can be performed only in the Umbra. The ritemaster rolls Wits + Rituals; the difficulty is 8, or 7 if the Ananta to be gained is the ritemaster's own. The ritemaster needs at least as many

successes as the number of Background points invested in the Ananta. If the ritemaster gains fewer successes, the Ananta is simply smaller than planned, and the excess Background or experience points are not lost.

First Glory

Level Two

The completion of a Nagah's first assassination is a glorious moment, and this Samskara is a celebration of the Nagah's new station in life as a high-functioning agent of Gaia's will. Typically, the nestmates of young Nagah watch a first-time assassin very closely, monitoring her for signs of unease, hesitation, poor judgement, sadism or excessive enjoyment of killing. Provided the mission went smoothly, the nest assembles and the new killer's nestmates list the things their celebrated nestmate did properly and all the lessons she learned from her first kill. Afterward, the nest chants a mantra of celebration and thanks.

System: If the neophyte spent any Willpower during the course of the assassination, she gets it all back during the observance of this Samskara.

Nestbinding

Level Two

Among the most serious Samskara observed by Nagah, the nestbinding ritual binds two or three wereserpents together into nestmates for life. The three Nagah to be joined assemble before the local Crown and exchange vows of friendship, protection, mutual support and rigorous honesty. For the duration of the nest's existence, the wereserpents bound by this Samskara interact as close friends, as family, as teammates, as lovers, as reciprocal caretakers during molting, and as a highly skilled strike force of assassins.

The bond between the wereserpents of a nest runs deep as it must in order to keep the nest together through all it will go through over its organizational lifespan. It is assumed that the members of a nest will, over time, experience for each other every possible permutation of friendship, love and respect. It is also assumed that the members of a nest will experience every possible permutation of frustration, anger and resentment towards one another, as anyone in an intimate relationship does. The nestbinding Samskara helps assure that the bond between the Nagah is stronger than the forces that may challenge the integrity of the nest.

Nestbindings must be performed by the Crown of an area, or in rare cases, by the Sesha.

Rite of Auspicious Beginning

Level Two

When a nest begins a new assignment, the ritemaster leads them in a powerful rhythmic mantra that boosts the nest's morale. While the exact contents of the mantra vary from place to place, it always emphasizes the Nagah's strength, discretion and cunning.

System: The ritemaster rolls Charisma + Rituals. If the nest's morale is generally good, difficulty is 5. If the nest seems largely neutral, the target number is 6, and if the nest's morale is not good (if the last mission turned out badly, for example), then the target number is 8. So long as the ritemaster gains even a single success, each member of the nest gains one extra temporary Willpower point (even if this would take him above his normal Willpower rating) for use sometime during the course of the new mission. Should the ritemaster get 5 or more successes, each member gets 2 Willpower points. If the excess Willpower is not spent in the course of duty, it fades away on the assignment's completion.

Shedding the Past

Level One

Snakes molt, or shed their skins, once a year; Nagah, even those who mostly remain in Balaram form, do the same thing. Most Nagah prefer to molt in Vasuki form, as molting in human form is particularly uncomfortable. The molting process takes several days, during which time the molting wereserpent is seriously compromised; he is mostly deaf and blind as the skin over his eyes and "ears" begins to come loose. During this time, one of the Nagah's nestmates functions as a caretaker, providing food for the molting wereserpent. The other functions as the ritemaster, performing a prayer of purification over the molting Nagah four times a day: dawn, noon, dusk and midnight. The caretaker attends to the molting nestmate's needs, bringing food, water and anything else he may require. The caregiver is prohibited from touching the molting Nagah, however. That task belongs to the ritemaster and consists mainly of helping the molting snake off with his old skin and holding the molting serpent when he wakes from sleep confused and unable to see or hear.

Molting is one of the sources of the Nagah's highly developed skills of cooperation and interdependence; each wereserpent takes his turn being helpless and taking care of his nestmates when the situation is reversed. It teaches the members of a nest both responsibility and trust.

Considered among the most important of the Nagah's Samskara, Shedding the Past fulfils many functions. Most importantly, it helps prevent the Nagah from becoming beholden to any one member of the Triat. This Samskara acts as a personal Rite of Cleansing. Any excessive degree of allegiance to any one member of the Triat is sloughed off with the skin, presuming the Nagah is willing to let go of the affiliated energy.

Furthermore, by examining the sloughed skin, the Nagah's nestmates can determine which of the Triat, if any, the wereserpent was becoming overbalanced toward. If the Nagah was secretly beholden to the Wyld, his skin reveals random chaotic markings instead of the usually beautiful symmetrical markings. The shed skin of a wereserpent with excessive loyalty to the Weaver, on the other hand, is overly precise and symmetrical, having a sterile, cold and almost technological appearance. The skin of a Nagah who sympathized with the Wyrm is both darker and more fragile than usual and somewhat slimy. By looking closely at a nestmate's shed skin, the other two can gain insight into what kinds of imbalance they should be attentive to over the course of the next year. A Nagah who becomes imbalanced toward the same member of the Triat two consecutive years is generally watched very carefully by his nestmates and prevented from having further dealings with that member of the Triat.

Shedding the Ppast has notable effects when the Nagah shifts back to Balaram form as well. Tattoos, brands, sun tans, piercings and most scars disappear, leaving the Nagah's skin smooth and unblemished.

System: The ritemaster invokes spirits of protection at dawn and dusk and spirits of purification at noon and midnight for the several days of the molting process. Players who want an intense roleplaying experience can roleplay the whole molting experience; alternatively the players can simply make two rolls to determine the outcome of the Samskara.

To help the molting Nagah rid himself of negative elements that have built up during the past year, the ritemaster rolls Charisma + Rituals to summon a spirit to unweave or cut any negative threads connected to the molting snake. Each success cancels out one success earned by any enemy casting long-term non-beneficial magics (curses, possession, emotion or thought control, ghouling or blood bonds, spirit markings and similar effects). Any opponents' remaining successes will be the first to be unwoven the next time the Nagah molts.

The second roll is to determine any Triat imbalance in the wereserpent. The ritemaster rolls Perception + Rituals to determine how capable he is of carefully collecting and reading the sloughed skin of his nestmate.

Thanks to River Mother

Level Two

By any of her names — Apsa, or her lesser names of Euphrates, Tigris, Ganga, Congo, Nile, Amazonas, Mississippi — the River Mother is the serpent folk's kindest benefactor. Not only does she give succor to the wereserpents, but she is also the Nagah's link to the Wani. For these things and more, the wereserpents frequently gather to thank her. This Samskara is also performed before setting up an Ananta in a new river.

System: The nest assembles on the banks of a river and speaks mantras of praise, thanks and love to the River Mother.

Naming the Target

Level Three

Among the more mystic Samskara, Naming the Target is performed when the nest is ready to perform its next assassination. Once all the business from the last mission has been put behind them, the Nagah gather near a river or in a dark room, join hands and speak an extended mantra of invocation to the Wani. When properly summoned, the Wani are able to grant information, visions and flashes of insight into the nest's next target. Ideally, this Samskara also discloses the target's transgression against Gaia, his whereabouts and possibly other facts relevant to the Nagah's inquiry.

System: The nest gathers and all members roll Perception + Rituals, difficulty 7, adding all successes gained. Five successes reveal the target's name and a quick vision of her face. With seven successes, the Wani also grant insight into the target's whereabouts. Nine successes also reveal the nature of the target's transgression. If the nest gets twelve or more successes, the Wani may add particularly juicy tidbits of information — the target's exact whereabouts, full identity, the precise nature of her transgression, frequent travel routes, common allies or other random bits of information that will help the Nagah successfully complete the assignment.

Punishing the Improper Strike

Level Three

The wereserpents take their calling extremely seriously. They have been given a remarkable amount of power to kill, and the Wani expect the Nagah to use that power responsibly. Misuse of the Nagah's power, particularly assassinating the wrong individual, is considered serious incompetence and a grave offense to the Wani. Wereserpents have a certain latitude in the execution of their duties, but any Nagah who kills the wrong target while allowing the real target escape more than once will be punished.

The Sesha waits until the nest returns, at which point they make their accusations. The offending wereserpent is given the opportunity to introduce mitigating circumstances. The nest of the accused is expected to defend their nestmate — given the close-knit nature of Nagah nests, it would be odd for them to do otherwise. If the accused is acquitted, he is free to go, though his future performance will be scrutinized.

If the defendant is found guilty of two or more improper assassinations, a circle is branded over his heart, indicative of where the spear will go should he repeat his mistake. The circle brand is an emblem of incompetence and marks the one who wears it as a figure of pity and disgrace. The most difficult aspect of coping with the brand is the disgrace it brings to a wereserpent's nest.

System: Nagah having no formal Renown system, there are no real game effects of this punishment. However, everyone the Nagah associates with, from the Wani's brood to his own nest, will treat him as the disgrace he is until he makes amends. Gaining Rank is also all but impossible under such a brand of shame.

Sati

Level Three

Nothing matters to a wereserpent more than his nest. Should it come to pass that a Nagah loses both nestmates in the performance of Gaia's work, many say there is nothing to be done but follow them out of this cycle in hopes that the nest may be reunited by the next turn of the wheel. Sati is a ritualized suicide that can only be performed by a Nagah who has, firstly, lost both the other members of his nest while carrying out their primary function and, secondly, completed the assassination the nest was involved in at the time of the deaths. This rite is frowned upon in the modern day, as there are really no Nagah to be spared, but it still survives.

Unlike most Samskara, this ritual does not use mantras, but is performed in complete silence. The surviving Nagah first performs Shraddha for his dead nestmates. Once those rites are finished, the survivor builds a funeral pyre for himself. Some build pyre-rafts, so their ashes may join their dead nestmates in the river once the pyre has finished burning. The wereserpent lights the pyre and while it is catching, he climbs to the top of the pyre and enters a deep state of meditation wherein he focuses on seeking out the souls of his lost nestmates. The Nagah's soul is believed to leave his body before the flames even get near.

System: The Nagah rolls Perception + Rituals as he enters a trance focusing on rejoining his nestmates. So long as the wereserpent gains at least one success, he is able to transcend his flesh before he even feels the warmth of the flames. Barring unusual circumstances, three successes are generally enough to allow the Nagah to discern where the souls of his nestmates have gone, and five successes, while no guarantee, facilitate his spirit returning as near to those of his nestmates as fate can manage.

Shraddha (Rites for the Dead)

Level Three

The close-knit nature of Nagah nests makes losing a member almost unbearably painful. It is as if the surviving nestmates have lost a lover, a sibling and a best friend in one individual. For that reason, it happens more often than not that if one member of a nest dies in the line of duty, the other two will fight all the more relentlessly, hoping to avenge their nestmate or die in the attempt. The Shraddha, or Nagah rite for the dead, is one of the more emotionally charged of all the Nagah Samskara. An outsider, however, would never know that.

The Shraddha is ideally performed by the two surviving members of a nest, although it can be done by one, if both of the other nestmates have been killed, though in such cases the Shraddha is almost always followed immediately by the survivor's Sati. One survivor sits at the head of the deceased in Balaram form while the other is coiled in Vasuki form at the deceased's feet. The human-skin Nagah quietly chants the mantra of loss while the Vasuki softly hisses along. The mantra translates loosely, as "The best part of us is gone."

Once the mantra has been repeated until the words have lost their meaning, the two deliver the body to the embrace of the river and immediately turn their backs so as not to prolong what is thereby formally ended. This is the one Samskara where Nagah are not only allowed to show emotion, but are encouraged to do so, up to the moment the body is placed in the river.

Nagah residing in desert climes may take the body instead to a canyon and drop it in or build a *dakhma* or "tower of silence" upon which the body is left exposed for the elements and carrion birds. In other places, the body may be placed on a pyre and burned. The specifics vary, but the essence of the Samskara does not.

System: The intent of Shraddha is to experience all of the grief, sadness and loss over the deceased nestmate in one powerful moment of catharsis. By experiencing the grief as fully as possible in the moment, the Nagah believe that they are more easily capable of letting go of it while ushering out the soul of the departed on a wave of emotion that will both honor and sustain her until her next incarnation. As with the Garou's Gathering for the Departed, Shraddha is likely to make it easier to contact the spirit through the Ancestors Background. Barring extraordinary circumstances, however, doing so is considered problematic, as it suggests that the survivors maintain an unhealthy connection to the deceased.

Conclusion

Level Four

The conclusion Samskara is held after completing an assassination as a means of reviewing why the death was a necessary one, thereby reaffirming the rightness of the Nagah's actions. The ritemaster distills the essence of the victim's crimes against Gaia or Dharma down to a relatively simple mantra that the nestmembers repeat until meaning has left the words, at which point the ritemaster interrupts the mantra and intones the final phrase, which translates as "Punishment was necessary. Punishment was delivered. Punishment is now concluded. May his (or her) next life be better spent."

Investiture

Level Four

Before her first kill in Gaia's name, the young Nagah must be gauged suitably judicious to mete out death or other forms of severe justice. In effect, this Samskara invests the Nagah with the right to assassinate (or punish by lesser means) the enemies of Gaia by any means necessary.

This Samskara may be performed by any suitably high-ranking member of the inexperienced wereserpent's nest, though it is occasionally performed by the Sesha, particularly in cases where the young Nagah exhibits extraordinary potential and judgement or when a new nest of young Nagah has just come together.

The ritemaster, in metered verse, praises the postulant's good judgement, her discretion and her talents in the arts of assassination, making an argument for why she is a suitable choice for Gaia's punisher. If possible, the ritemaster recounts instances of extraordinary judgement or right action from the postulant's past lives.

While it almost never happens that a postulant is *not* found worthy of Gaia's confidence (after all, it's what the Nagah are all about), certain candidates may be refused investiture due to instances of poor judgement, insufficient discretion or subtlety, inappropriate killing or a particularly dishonorable past life. In such instances, the only course open to the postulant (assuming she wants the legitimacy of Gaia's backing) is to wait one full year, during which she must show exemplary judgement, character and good sense, and then offer herself for consideration again.

System: The ritemaster rolls Charisma + Rituals to summon a spirit representative of Gaia. Four or more successes indicate that an avatar of Gaia herself answers the call. The spirit assesses the wereserpent's judgement, dedication and responsibility and, based on that estimation, invests the Nagah with the right and freedom to take life without consequence. Only the most unbalanced or irresponsible wereserpents are denied investiture, and they may petition for investiture once every year after molting.

Those wereserpents who defy Gaia and try to act as assassins without investiture suffer a -2 dice penalty to *all* rolls until they cease attempting to function in that capacity or successfully receive investiture.

River Mother's Eyes

Level Four

Very similar to the Garou Rite: The Badger's Burrow, River Mother's Eyes allows the Nagah to see what's happening along the banks of a river (and in the water itself) for a great distance. The Nagah perform this Samskara to hunt for their targets, to reconnoiter unfamiliar territory and to sense if a river is being defiled.

The ritemaster chants a mantra of enlightenment and must be in contact with the river through which he's extending his senses; a significant portion of a tail, hand, foot or other part of the wereserpent must be immersed. Some Nagah prefer to perform this Samskara as they're actually swimming in the river, staring up at the water's silvery surface.

System: The player rolls Perception + Rituals against the given difficulty level. Each success enables the Nagah to ask one question regarding a length of the river. The difficulty increases the more of the river the Nagah wants to see. Failure indicates that the wereserpent sees nothing, while a botch shows him what he hopes to see, regardless of the truth.

Area	Difficulty
Thirty feet	5
Quarter-mile length	6
Half-mile length	7
One mile length	8
Ten mile length	9

Sannyasa

Level Five

When a Nagah has reached an age when she no longer feels she can effectively carry out Gaia's work — and a surprising number of wereserpents are clever and subtle enough to do so — she may undergo the ritual of Sannyasa (renunciation) and forego service to Gaia for the remainder of her existence.

During the course of the Samskara, the wereserpent recounts to her nestmates (and possibly the Sesha as well) precisely how she served Gaia. She delivers a chronological list of the enemies of Gaia who died by her hand and recounts all the stories that accumulate during a long life as an assassin. Subsequently, the wereserpent sequesters herself away at some deserted place alongside the river and speaks with the Wani and generally an avatar of Gaia herself. The spirit representatives of Gaia accept the Nagah's "resignation" and bless her with health and wellbeing. In return, the wereserpent vows to return to Gaia's service if called or if her former vitality should return.

The wereserpent performs her own funeral rites, dives into the river (or just walks off into the desert, jungle or whatever wilderness is available and departs society to live as an ascetic — wearing ashes, living under trees and eating only what she can scrounge or what she is given. Sannyasin often opt to live out the rest of their lives in vasuki form, a life of asceticism being somewhat easier as a snake. Sannyasin rarely settle in civilized areas, though certain old Nagah may have a fondness for a particular village and watch over it in their dotage. Any who expect an old Nagah to be an easy target, however, are painfully — and generally lethally — surprised; underestimating the deadly cleverness of an experienced assassin, even one moments from dying of old age, is a good way to get killed.

Many nests comprise wereserpents of largely the same age, so it's not uncommon for an entire nest of Nagah to perform the Sannyasa Samskara at the same time.

System: Only Nagah who are notably impaired by age or infirmity (i.e., suffer a permanent loss of one or more points of a Physical Attributes due to age or sickness) may honorably undergo Sannyasa. Once the wereserpent has told all of her stories (which may literally take days if hers was a particularly interesting life), she says her farewells to her nest (unless they're becoming renunciates as well). She then finds a quiet place by the river (or far from others, in any case) and calls the spirits she needs to talk with. The player spends one Gnosis point and rolls Charisma + Rituals. One or more successes summons the Wani while 3 or more successes allow the wereserpent to attract the attention of Gaia herself. In essence, the Nagah formally requests to be freed from her duty to Gaia. Provided the wereserpent is in good standing with the Sesha, the Wani and Gaia and provided she vows to return to Gaia's service if things change or if she is needed, she is generally freed of her duties to Gaia. The spirits bless her with good health and, when the time comes, a painless death.

Once the spirits depart, the Nagah performs her own Shraddha to indicate her break with her old life and wanders off into legend.

Should the Nagah regain her former vigor, either through the Gift: Shedding the Years or any other means, the Wani *will* know and they'll expect her to resume her former role as Gaia's assassin, with a new nest if necessary.

Traitor's Torment

Level Five

While assassinating the enemies of Gaia causes them no distress, Nagah do not like torture. It reeks to them of mishandled power and offends their surprisingly serene sensibilities. However, the wereserpents have no tolerance for betrayal. Deliberate perfidy is a far graver sin than murder to the serpent people, and one that demands the gravest punishment. This Samskara summons pain spirits to torment, madden, and finally kill a traitor.

The ritemaster begins by reading a precise description of the traitor's deeds. He then looks the traitor in the eyes, explains to her what is about to happen to her, explains why *again*, wishes her a wiser and better life in her next incarnation and then summons the spirits of pain with an ugly, guttural mantra. Once the pain spirits have executed their duty, the ritemaster performs atonement Samskara to free him of the bad karma brought on by such cruelty.

While it is used almost exclusively on other Nagah (and extremely rarely at that), Traitor's Torment may be used on any target whose violation of trust was so grave as to warrant such punishment.

System: The ritemaster's player spends a point of permanent Gnosis and rolls Charisma + Rituals. Each success indicates one full day of the most perfect torture an unleashed pain spirit can provide. Within seconds of the ritemaster finishing the last syllable of the mantra, the punishment begins as the victim's gastrointestinal tract violently and uncontrollably empties itself at both ends. The target is subsequently overwhelmed by physical, mental and emotional pain so excruciating that coherent thought becomes impossible, and the target must spend a Willpower point every turn just to keep from curling into fetal position. The target gains a derangement for each day of such torment. Even if the pain-spirits are somehow driven off (by exorcism, banishing, Sanctuary Chimes, etc.) before the target's death, the derangements are permanent unless supernatural means are used to remove them. The would-be healer must get more successes than the ritemaster did to remove one derangement, and each derangement must be healed separately.

In the agony and madness caused by this punishment, victims have been known to eat their own arms nearly to the elbow, bite off their own tongues, and scratch their own skin and muscles from their bones with their claws. The victim's muscles may clench so hard that they snap her own bones like matchsticks. Physical damage accrues at whatever rate the ritemaster chooses, though the default is two levels of bashing damage per day. The process can be sped up so as to inflict three levels of aggravated damage an hour, or slowed down so that the victim takes only one level of bashing damage a week. If a target's treachery warrants it, this Samskara can be performed as an extended ritual, allowing for weeks upon weeks of pain and horror.

The pain-spirits that execute this rite are relatively powerful and far from stupid. If the victim is completely and utterly free of all the wrongdoing she is accused of, this Samskara does absolutely nothing. Furthermore, if the target is completely innocent *and* the ritemaster botches, the pain-spirits take him as their victim instead.

Merits & Flaws

Merits and Flaws are an optional system introduced in the **Werewolf Players Guide**. They are not suitable for all chronicles, and players should be sure to check with their Storyteller whether or not they are permissible for the game in question.

Spirit Acquaintance (2 or 4-pt Merit)

For some reason, a spirit outside the courts of the Wani has taken a great liking to you. Perhaps it has taken you for another Khurah; perhaps one of your ancestors was important to it in another life. Whatever the reason, your spirit friend has agreed to assist you as if you and it shared the bonds of the Pact. If you offer it the proper chiminage, it will answer your rites of summoning, teach you non-Nagah Gifts (though not at reduced cost, as learning Gifts through sources other than the Wani is still difficult for you) and other such favors. You should discuss the actual spirit type with your Storyteller. The 2-point Merit indicates your acquaintance is a Gaffling; the 4-point Merit indicates a friendly Jaggling. Your acquaintance will not deliberately spill your secrets, although it might be forced into doing so. At no point will it defy its superiors on your behalf — your friendship goes only so far.

Infrared Vision (4-pt Merit)

You are capable of detecting heat sources in your immediate area by sensing the infrared radiation they give off. The range of this sense is relatively short (about 50 feet or so), and you cannot access this sense in Balaram form. However, this sense may give you an edge in night operations (so long as your target isn't cold-blooded or undead).

This Merit is appropriate only for Nagah with relatives in the Crotalinae subfamily (pit vipers, rattlesnakes, fers-del-lance and moccasins); other venomous snakes don't have this sense.

Step Sideways (6-pt Merit)

Your connection with the Umbra is closer than that of most Nagah. You are able to step sideways as Garou do, crossing the Gauntlet without need of your Ananta.

Mnesis (7-pt Merit)

The Mokolé insist that a special bond exists between Dragon's Children and the Nagah; in fact, several Mokolé legends claim that the Nagah were once Mokolé themselves. The Nagah dismiss such stories, but are not so quick to downplay the connections between the Wani dragon-spirits and the spirit of Dragon. Your existence muddies the water further, as for some inexplicable reason, you are able to tap into the tiniest trickle of Mnesis, the racial memory of the Dragon Breed.

To properly access these memories, the Nagah must enter a memory trance and the player must roll Willpower, difficulty 8. Each success extends the trance by a minute, revealing more information. The events depicted may or may not have anything to do with the current assignment, though they almost always have some relevance to *something* important to the Nagah. The Nagah may remember events taking place up to a century ago, and then only events as they occurred to an ancestor; anything else is the province of the Mokolé. Even so, this ability can prove remarkably useful in unearthing knowledge that would be otherwise lost.

Largely Deaf (1-pt Flaw)

The poor hearing of your snake heritage has extended into most of your forms. You are completely deaf in Kali Dahaka, Azhi Dahaka and Vasuki, your hearing Perception rolls in Silkaram are at +3 difficulty, and even in Homid form you make auditory-related rolls at +1 difficulty.

Inauspicious (1 or 3-pt Flaw)

You were unfortunate enough to shed your First Skin in a season other than the one of your birth. For most Nagah, this is simply unlucky, but you have it rather worse. You cannot purchase auspice Gifts at reduced cost; all auspice Gifts count as "outside auspice" for purposes of spending experience to learn them.

If you take the 3-pt. version of this Flaw, not only do you suffer the above penalties, but you are also harried by conflicting urges and desires. The difficulty of all Willpower rolls is increased by 1, and you have trouble regaining Willpower as well. You do not regain all your Willpower at the end of a story as usual; you always begin the next story one Willpower point down.

Weak Venom (2 or 3-pt. Flaw)

Much to your undying shame, your venom lacks the spiritual potency that should be your birthright. Although the dosage is still enough to severely hinder an opponent, your bite lacks the power to put down potent targets. Your nest may find you a liability in combat and assign other tasks unless you're somehow able to make up for this defect.

The 2-pt version of this Flaw indicates that your venom does lethal damage, and no damage to vampires or other unliving things. The 3-pt. version means that your venom does bashing damage (only to living opponents), and, truth be told, isn't much good for anything other than knocking a target out for a short period of time.

Defanged (4-pt. Flaw)

Before you shed your First Skin, you were captured and your fangs pulled from your head, most likely to make you an unwilling accomplice to a snake charmer or other performer. Although such an injury often brings on a premature shedding of the First Skin, in your case you did not learn to change forms until after the wounds had already healed. As a result, you have no fangs in any form, and cannot use bite attacks or inject venom. In Vasuki form, you are effectively helpless, and probably have a hard time catching food. No Gifts will heal this injury — you must rely on your claws, weapons or guile to carry out your mission.

This Flaw is appropriate only for vasuki, although the Storyteller may allow a character of other breed to take it as long as the player offers a valid reason for why his Nagah is permanently fangless.

Fetishes

For obvious reasons, Nagah are at a slight disadvantage when it comes to crafting fetishes. Only a very limited number of spirits will respond to the Nagah's rites of binding — to create a fetish, the Nagah must either call on one of the Wani's brood, or an elemental affiliated with his auspice. Even so, the Nagah, with their love of crafting beautiful objects, have devised their fair share of fetishes over the millennia.

Yantra

Level 1, Gnosis 6

A yantra is a complex, radially symmetrical diagram, also called a mandala, that symbolically represents the entire universe. The yantra is meant to serve as a focus of meditation that draws the mind toward the center point, called the bindu. By activating the fetish and meditating on the bindu for three turns, the owner of the yantra may ascertain exactly where he is in the universe. If he is in the distant Umbra, he may need to meditate for up to ten turns, but at the end of that time he'll know how to get back to more familiar territory (though the yantra does not empower him to get there).

To create a yantra, one must first inscribe a complex mandala onto an animal hide of some sort and bind into the design a spirit of knowledge.

Spirit Rattler

Level 2, Gnosis 6

This simple item is just a snake's rattle tied with sinew to a long bone of any medium-sized animal. When activated and shaken, the spirit rattler causes all spirits in a 30-foot radius to freeze in place with fear for one turn per success on the activation roll. Spirits with Gnosis of 7 or higher may make a contested Gnosis roll against the rattle's wielder to flee.

To create a spirit rattler, one finds a rattle from an old rattlesnake, preferably 7 years or older. If a snake is harmed or killed to get the rattle, the fetish will not work. The rattle is tied to the bone so that it can shake freely. The Nagah then binds an appropriate spirit of the Wani's brood into the rattle.

Jewel of the River Spirit

Level 3, Gnosis 7

When the owner tosses this jewel into a natural body of water and speaks the name of the spirit within, the elemental shows itself and may be asked to provide some service for the owner of the jewel, including towing a boat, splashing an enemy or chasing away dangerous fish. The elemental will not endanger itself for the owner of the fetish. The elemental remains for one scene or long enough to complete a single task, whichever is shorter. When the task is done, the elemental returns to the jewel, which shoots out of the water and back into the hands of the owner.

Treating the elemental poorly will probably result in losing its service as it refuses to place the jewel back in the hands of its previous possessor.

Creating one of these fetishes requires binding a water elemental into a precious transparent stone of some sort, preferably sapphire, though aquamarine or even a smooth lump of cobalt glass will work.

Strangler's Scarves

Level 3, Gnosis 7

The most famous of India's assassins were the Thuggee, known for strangling their victims with beautiful silk scarves. The Nagah observed the Thugs (as they were called), assimilated their better tactics, and improved upon them. This fetish is a skillfully woven and generally attractive silk scarf that wraps itself tightly around the wearer's neck, strangling her. Each turn the scarf strangles its victim, it inflicts a number of health levels of bashing damage equal to the owner's Gnosis. When activated, the scarf has an effective Strength (to keep from being unwrapped) of 5, a Stamina of 3 and six health levels.

To create a scarf of the Thuggee, the Nagah himself weaves the scarf from silk threads, requiring an Intelligence + Crafts roll against a difficulty of 9. This is best done as an extended action; the wereserpent may make one roll for every full day he works on the item. Binding a spirit into a scarf that the wereserpent did not weave is possible, but increases the difficulty by 2. When he reaches 7 successes, the scarf is done. The Nagah must bind an appropriate spirit servant of the Wani into the scarf.

Danbhalah's Drum

Level 4, Gnosis 6

Nagah from Africa, the Caribbean and the Southeast United States learned to make these fetishes to summon their targets to them. While they involve more work and are *far* less subtle than the Gift: Summon the Accused, they have their advantages as well.

The drummer keeps his target in mind while pounding out a primal rhythm on the drum. If he stops drumming before the target arrives, the drum loses control over that target permanently. As soon as the drum starts pounding, the target, no matter how far away, does everything she can to get to the location of the drumming without knowing (or caring) why. While the target's main impulse is to find the site of the drums, she doesn't neglect her own well-being. Answering the call of the drum does not cause her to ignore her own survival instincts. She may risk a little violence to answer the drum, but she won't behave stupidly.

Though Danbhalah's drum can call a subject from anywhere, it's most efficient when calling someone in the same general region; it can take a long time for a target in Syracuse, New York to arrange for travel to Bahia, Brazil (especially if she doesn't have a passport). The target's finances obviously play a part as well.

If the summoner has no idea where the target might be, he had better be prepared to drum continually for weeks. Luckily, a nest of Nagah looking for the same target can alternate drumming so long as the rhythm isn't interrupted (roll Dexterity + Performance to check). Each time a new player takes over, he has to make an activation roll. Failing the activation roll frees the target from the drum's control permanently. Botching the activation roll rips the drum pad.

Danbhalah's drums are loud. There is no way to quietly play a drum of Danbhalah. If the drummer is in a building, the rhythm will resonate through the entire infrastructure, quickly making enemies of the neighbors. If the drummer is in the wilderness, the target may not be the only one trying to find the drummer....

Garland of Skulls

Level 4, Gnosis 7

Rare in the extreme, garlands of skulls are very powerful fetishes to wear during combat. When activated, the wearer gains 5 temporary Rage points and grows two additional arms just under his normal ones.

While a garland of skulls is pretty easy to get away with in the depths of the jungle or desert, getting them through customs can be extremely difficult, and much more trouble than they're worth. Necklaces of skulls (or shrunken heads) are precisely the kind of thing authorities frown upon, particularly in a country like India that's trying to portray itself as a first world nation.

To create a garland of skulls, one must first gather at least 8 skulls (shrunken heads will work in a pinch) from enemies and string them together on a thick piece of sinew. Into this grisly garland one must bind one of the Wani's spirits of war.

Dart of Nullity

Level 5, Gnosis 7

This dreaded weapon is a dart made from a bird bone, weighted with gold dust and fletched with peacock feathers. When the dart leaves the thrower's hand, it immediately becomes invisible to anyone but the individual to whom it's dedicated. When it strikes, the target neither sees nor feels anything. However, so long as the dart is stuck in the target, he is unable to use Gnosis or Rage (nor is a vampire capable of using its blood pool).

Sensing the dart is tricky, requiring a Perception + Enigmas roll against a difficulty of 8.

Worse still, while pulling out the dart causes no damage, all the pain the target would have felt all along from having a dart stuck in his hide hits at once. The longer the dart has been in, the more pain the target will feel. Though the dart does hardly any damage (Strength bashing damage), the target will suffer wound penalties as though he were wounded for a number of turns equal to the number of turns the dart was lodged in his skin.

Talens

Ascetic's Ashes

Gnosis 6

Hindu folklore is full of tales of wise men, gurus and ascetics wandering the wilds wearing nothing but ashes. This talen reflects the spiritual potency of such a practice. When rubbed over the naked body of the wearer, Ascetic's Ashes grant a potent degree

of protection from damage and turns the wearer's skin a dark shade of gray.

Any part of the wearer covered by the ashes is protected. When striking against a protected area of the wearer's body with weapons, enemies roll damage against a target number of 7 instead of 6. The ashes don't last especially long, generally no more than one intense combat, but a pouch of ascetic's ashes generally contain enough to cover the entire body three or four times.

Creating Ascetic's Ashes requires gathering ashes from a recently burned funeral pyre and binding into them an elemental spirit.

Cloud Popper

Gnosis 6

Shooting one of these arrows into a rain or storm cloud causes the cloud to burst and drop its contents in a relatively short period of time. Such storms are generally intense and likely to result in flooding in flat or low lying areas. Any outdoor fires in the affected area must be sheltered immediately or they'll be extinguished by the storm. Provided there are any clouds at all overhead, these arrows are useful for relieving droughts. Storms caused by these arrows typically last between one and four hours depending on the size of the cloud.

Making a cloud popper requires the creation of an arrow with a turquoise or quartz arrowhead and binding one of the Wani's rain spirits (or a water elemental) within.

Flood Dust

Gnosis 4

A pinch of flood dust causes the water in a 30-foot radius of the user to rise by five feet per pinch. The dust typically takes effect within five minutes of hitting the water. Flood dust can be used to cause a river to burst its banks or to overwhelm a dam on a large river. Flood dust works in any natural body of water (within reason; an entire sea or Great Lake is unlikely to flood, although a local beach might). A bag of flood dust generally contains between five to ten pinches. Needless to say, accidentally dropping a bag of flood dust into a body of water is a recipe for disaster.

To create flood dust one must take dust from a dried-out riverbed and bind a water elemental into it.

Lightning Arrow

Gnosis 6

When a user shoots the lightning arrow directly up at a storm cloud (wispy cirrus clouds will not work) and specifies some general striking point within his range of vision; a bolt of lightning immediately blasts down somewhere in the vicinity specified by the user. These arrows do not come back down. These items aren't accurate enough to be of much use in combat, but they have their uses.

The individual shooting the arrow has some small degree of control over where the lightning strikes (Commands like "Strike the lake" or "Strike somewhere on the other side of the river" are fine, but "Strike that Garou" is a bit too specific. If the Garou is in the lake, however, or on the other side of the river, and happens to be the tallest thing around, it's entirely possible that the lightning might strike him anyway. The lightning can generally be relied on to strike a place within twenty feet of the point the user assigns as the strike point. Any creature struck by lightning takes from one to ten health levels of aggravated damage.

To create one of these talens, the creator makes an arrow with an iron arrowhead and binds one of the Wani's storm spirits (or an air elemental) into the arrow.

Snake Oil

Gnosis 5

Snake oil is a mild restorative or tonic for creatures with either Gnosis or Arete. The creature drinking the snake oil (which tastes terrible and has a texture somewhere between that of phlegm and raw egg yolks) rolls his Gnosis and adds health levels equal to half the successes (rounded up, minimum of 1). The drinker gets no benefit if he is not wounded and snake oil isn't strong enough to heal aggravated wounds.

Curiously, creatures *without* Gnosis also believe that they receive the healing benefits from snake oil (and therefore suffer fewer wound penalties), but no health levels are actually restored.

Brewing a batch of snake oil requires pressing oil from castor beans or flax or pumpkin seeds and binding an appropriate spirit into the potion. Snake oil, oddly enough, doesn't actually contain fat or oil from snakes or any other kind of animal.

Venom Arrows

Gnosis 6

These arrows are popular among the Nagah who use them to great effect without needing to worry about poisoning themselves. When the arrow damages a creature, the target must roll Stamina + Survival, difficulty 8. If the target does not get at least one success, the arrow does an additional 4 health levels of lethal damage from the venom of the snake spirit.

If any non-Nagah user of these arrows botches, he has cut himself and must make the Stamina roll or be poisoned by his own arrow.

To create a venom arrow, one fashions an arrow with two separate points (or "fangs"). A crescent moon-shaped arrowhead is the most common type for these kinds of arrows. The creator then binds one of the Wani's snake-spirits into the arrow.

Bindhi

A bindhi is a small jewel worn on the brow over the *ajna*, or third eye chakra. When properly worn and activated, these brow-jewels typically enhance thought or perception. Mystic bindhi simply need to be pressed to the third eye (about an inch above the bridge of the nose) where they remain in place of their own accord. Since there is only one third eye, only one bindhi may be worn at a time.

Indian iconography features many of the great gods and heroes wearing brow-jewels, which are among the most common fetishes in India and throughout the Middle Kingdom of Asia. Nagah are particularly fond of bindhi because they evoke the wereserpents' royal patronage in India. Only three bindhi are listed here as examples, but all manner of thought- and perception-enhancing brow-jewels may be created, discovered or won. The duration of any bindhi's effects is equal to one turn per success on the activation roll.

Bindhi of Surya

Level 1, Gnosis 6

This brow-jewel is commonly made from topaz or diamond. When worn over the *ajna* and properly triggered, the bindhi shines with the pure golden light of the sun, illuminating any dark place with the light of full day. Vampires caught in the light of the Bindhi of Surya take damage as from full sunlight.

Bindhi of Disillusion

Level 3, Gnosis 8

Commonly made from moonstone or onyx, these brow-jewels (when activated) reveal illusions to their wearer for what they are. While those around the wearer may still see a convincing illusion, the wearer of this fetish will see only the vaguest hint of the image and will know it for what it is.

Indomitable Eye

Level 5, Gnosis 9

This bindhi may be made from any deep red gem; the most common is garnet.

Indian myths speak of Kama, the god of love, trying to make Shiva fall in love with a young woman to distract him from his meditative and yogic practices. Shiva instead disintegrated Kama with one shining ray from his bindhi and returned to his meditations.

Among the most powerful of the legendary brow-jewels of India, the Indomitable Eye, when activated, renders its wearer immune to all thought and emotion manipulating attacks while punishing those who would attempt such tactics.

All difficulties for affecting the wearer of the Indomitable Eye with emotion control or thought control Gifts, Disciplines, magic or the like are raised to 10. Furthermore, the individual trying to use such magic suffers an agonizing headache and one level of bashing damage for every point of Gnosis, Arete or the like that she has. Thus, a Garou with a Gnosis of 6 trying to affect a Nagah wearing the Indomitable Eye with the Shadow Lords Gift: Obedience would make her roll against a difficulty of 10 and suffer 6 levels of bashing damage for her trouble.

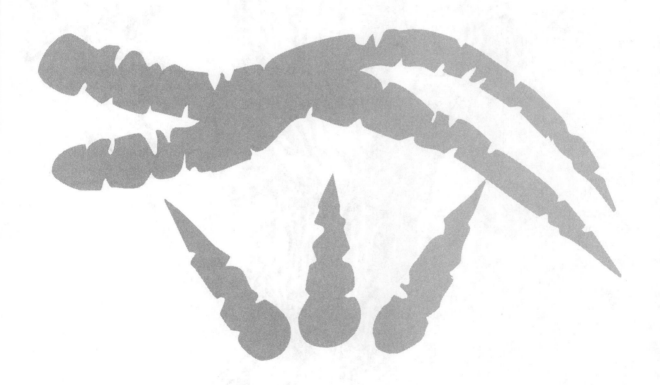

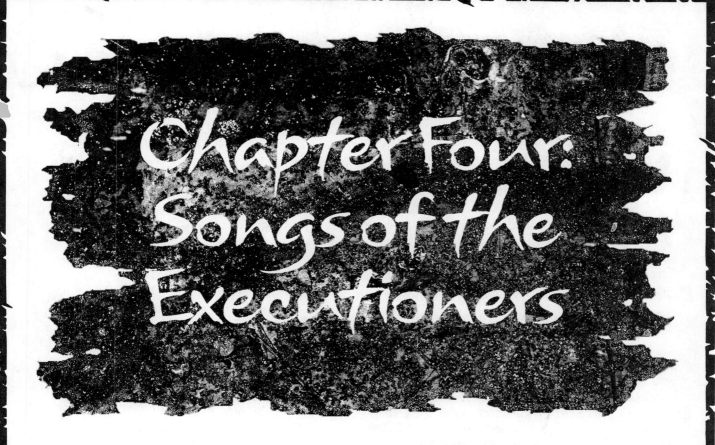

Chapter Four: Songs of the Executioners

"Such a trial, dear sir," said the mouse to the cur,
"Without jury or judge, would be wasting our breath."
"I'll be judge, I'll be jury," said cunning old Fury,
"I'll try the whole cause, and condemn you to death."
— Lewis Carroll, *Alice's Adventures in Wonderland*

Essence of Storytelling

Regardless of the subject or genre, every good story you hear adheres to a time-honored formula. Every story has a somewhat sympathetic protagonist. Every protagonist pursues some goal. Every goal lies just on the other side of some obstacle that the protagonist must overcome. Stories you tell your friends about what happened to you during the day follow this simple pattern, and even the most intricately layered tale of intrigue and deception does the same.

Stories of the Nagah are no different, whether they are historical tales of Gaia's glorious and terrible judges, or grim urban legends of embittered assassins who have all but lost hope. But although the main thrust of the story may be familiar, the devil's in the details, as they say. A properly spun game session involving a Nagah nest shouldn't have the same feel as a standard Werewolf game, or a game centering on a different Changing Breed such as the Bastet. If you can capture the cold-blooded but still emotionally charged feel of the Nagah story, your players won't forget the experience.

The Quintessential Nagah Story

As is the case for any Changing Breed, the simplest Nagah story you can tell is that of the Nagah pursuing their duty to Gaia. Before Gaia and her servants, the Wani, the Nagah judge their fellow shapeshifters and punish them when they forsake their timeless responsibilities. Since the forms of evil, corruption and sloth are manifold in the World of Darkness, you can create and run an infinite number of stories about how the wereserpents excise those forms from Gaia's creation.

The basics of that quintessential story follow, and they provide a sturdy foundation on which to construct one-shot or short-lived Nagah games. They also serve as the building blocks that combine to form an ongoing chronicle.

Discover the Target and Observe the Target

The first and most important part of any Nagah story is that of setting the stage and motivating your characters. Doing so is fairly straightforward in a one-story game. When you pitch the idea to your players, you simply tell them who their characters' target is as well as the way in which he is suspected of failing in his duty. You give them the information that the characters are assumed to have amassed on the target's habits and whereabouts and start the action with the characters following it up.

For a more in-depth story or a long-running chronicle, you should start the characters farther back along the plot arc. Begin the game with one of the characters uncovering a story on television or a newspaper about a suspiciously mysterious crime that sounds to your characters like a Khurah's frenzy or some other abuse of power committed by one of Gaia's servants. You could also establish a story mechanism of Kinfolk servants in local police departments, nationwide newspaper offices or even the FBI's Special Affairs Division who direct the Nagah's attention to potential targets. If nothing else, you can begin every story in your chronicle with the Nagah of the Sesha assigning your players' characters to specific cases of interest and charging them to go out and do Gaia's good work. (This last tends to lend itself to *Mission: Impossible* and *Charlie's Angels* jokes, though, so don't say you weren't warned.)

Once the characters have begun the hunt, you can pace the narrative like modern detective fiction. The Nagah investigate the scene that caught their attention for clues, trying to reconstruct what happened and determine whether they should be involved. If they have a better grasp of who their target is, they follow him around and watch him as he goes about his duty. The action of this stage of the story revolves around maintaining their secrecy and keeping their target from realizing that he is under surveillance.

The purpose of this part of the story or chronicle is to set the stage and provide the necessary exposition. It is primarily upon you to establish the mood of the story, characterize the antagonists through the actions the nest witnesses and give them enough information to form an opinion on whether they should suffer their target to live. You should also provide examples of how powerful the main antagonist is, what defenses he may have in place and the impact his death will have on the world around him. After all, no character exists in a vacuum, and every piece of information you give your players will affect the decisions they make throughout the rest of the story.

Pass Judgment and Make Ready

While the preceding portion of the story is largely your domain, this section shines the spotlight on your players. It will also likely be the most strictly roleplaying-intensive part of the game. The characters regroup and examine the implications of the data they have gathered. They reflect on the nature of the antagonist's Breed's duty and discuss whether he's fallen short of it or if he is merely fulfilling it in an unusual or heretofore unrevealed way. They may see that their target is trying to do the right thing, but he is doomed to fail because of the way he is going about it.

Once they have made up their mind about the target's intentions, it's time for the nest to decide what they're going to do about it. Are the antagonist's actions so heinous that he must be destroyed post-haste? Is his "crime" merely the result of an oversight for which he is unlikely to ever forgive himself? Will a poignant reminder of his guilt and laxity of duty suffice to correct his behavior in the future? Would it perhaps be easier and more fulfilling to subtly reform the antagonist, or do the Nagah even allow their victims that leeway? The Nagah consider each of these possibilities before every fateful decision to end a victim's life, and it is in that consideration that Nagah stories and chronicles play up the themes of justice and duty. If you want to explore these aspects of the Nagah experience in depth, don't rush your players through this portion of the story. Let their characters talk the subject out to their satisfaction, leaving no doubt unaccounted for and answered. Just be sure to encourage them not to vacillate for too long. While the Nagah are thorough and thoughtful, they don't waste their time in drawn-out, maundering philosophical explorations of the oft-heavy and soul-wearying burden of exacting Gaia's dolorous vengeance upon her wayward and overzealous children.

Once the nest has decided on a course of action, finish out this part of the story by planning how exactly they will carry out their goal. This is the time

Complications

The outline for the classic hunt story provided tends to assume that everything goes as planned. But that doesn't mean it should — quite the opposite. The players should face complications now and again in just about every stage of the mission — this keeps them from simply performing their duties by rote, and actually gives them things to sweat about.

Complicate the observation process by having a "copycat" duplicating the target's crimes, so that the nest must sift the red herrings from the true evidence (and possibly have to pass judgement twice). If you want to make the nest's judgement more difficult, balance the target's crimes with deeds that make his neighborhood a better place. Have an unexpected visitor drop by the target's home at precisely the wrong time. Give the target someone else that's been keeping tabs on him, such as a reporter, detective or private investigator — that will make the "disappear" stage all the trickier. These complications are what make a hunt memorable rather than routine.

Remember, though, that you don't want to frustrate your players too severely. If they aren't ever allowed to execute a mission flawlessly — or even a stage of a mission — then they're going to feel thwarted or even incompetent. Spread out your monkeywrenches; don't add too many complications to any one mission unless you want it to be the classic "what *else* could go wrong?" botched hit story — and even then, realize that such a story can affect your chronicle in unforeseen ways.

to examine the data they collected previously for patterns of their target's behavior and evidence of where he is weak. How well protected is he from mundane and supernatural threats? Is he part of a pack? Perhaps his packmates can be alerted to his sins and turned against him, assuming that they aren't already part of the problem. Does he live in a high-rise apartment building that is monitored electronically? Perhaps the Nagah can examine the building plans and find a safe way to break in. Is he surrounded at all times by a staff of attendants and well-armed bodyguards? Perhaps the Nagah can infiltrate that organization in order to get close to him.

Be sure to either have this information ready at the beginning of the story (so that the nest can find it during their surveillance and plan around it) or make it available to them as they ask for it. Have them plan their operation thoroughly in advance so that you can mold the next phase of the story around their plans.

Strike

This part of the story is usually the most tense and exciting, and it's the most dice-reliant as well. It is during this phase that the Nagah physically track their victim down, isolate him from his friends and associates, confront him with his sins and kill him — all without getting caught. You can pack all of these actions together into one story session and end it with your characters standing over their victim's body, or you can stretch the narrative out over several sessions. If the Nagah decide to infiltrate their victim's lair in order to get close to him, you can spend several sessions telling the story of how they gain the victim's confidence and the lengths to which they must go to maintain their cover. You can also reveal further information as the Nagah close in on their prey that casts his actions in a new light and forces them to back off and reconsider their intended course of action. If the antagonist in your story is actually a group of shapechangers who have *all* fallen short of their duty, you can even extend this storytelling phase to show your players' nest hunting each of them down individually.

Regardless of its duration, though, this phase culminates in combat or distanced assassination, and it represents the climax of the story. Just be warned that general elements of the Nagah's style typically preclude running gun battles on crowded streets, helicopter dogfights in winding canyons and other such over-the-top action sequences. The Nagah act with subtlety in all things. However, multi-angle melee battles on the high steel of partially constructed buildings, frenetic chases up (or down) treacherous cliff faces and harried rooftop pursuits through squalid tenement cities in the dead of night are not entirely out of the question. After all, nearly anything can happen when a victim realizes that he is about to die, and no Nagah can plan for every desperate contingency that might arise.

Disappear

What truly separates the average Nagah story from that of the other Changing Breeds is the secrecy that the Nagah's work ethic demands. No matter how messy the climax of the story turns out to be, the Nagah must disappear and leave no trace of their passing. Regardless of how villainous the antagonist was and how much he needed to die, the Nagah cannot announce their victory over him and expect a ticker-tape parade for their efforts. No sign or clue may give rise to the suspicion that Gaia's judges even exist, much less

that they take an active role in shapechanger affairs on Earth. Once the story's climax has come and gone, and the characters have demonstrated their martial prowess, let them exercise their cleverness and creativity by vanishing without a trace.

Poetic or outraged nests of Nagah may also take this time to arrange the forensic evidence of a victim's death scene in such a way that the scene tells its own story. Rather than revealing that the victim has fallen prey to ghostlike assassins despite his security precautions, the scene often suggests that he died as a result of whatever crime the Nagah judged him guilty of originally. If your players appreciate this kind of irony, encourage them to think about it as early on as during the planning phase of the story and prepare for it ahead of time. If they do a particularly good job dressing the stage of their characters' actions, give them a fourth-wall glimpse of the reactions of the supporting characters who find the antagonist's body, in order to show them that their efforts have been successful.

Going Before the Sesha

You can end a one-story Nagah game at this point if you want to, but an extended Nagah chronicle requires a final bit of resolution. When all is said and done, the ruling elite of Nagah society will require a report concerning the Nagah characters' actions. A passageway opens through the Umbra from the nest's Ananta to the Nandana, and the characters are summoned to relay the news of what they have done since the last time they were summoned.

If your players feel the need to have their characters expostulate at length about the conduct of their nestmates, dress up and aggrandize their characters' actions, actually lie to the Sesha outright or just listen to the sound of their voices, let them roleplay this encounter with you one at a time. You can use it to tie loose ends of the plot together in their minds, and you can also use the one-on-one time to interview each player about how he liked the game itself. And while you chat with each player individually, the other characters can roleplay among themselves in order to develop the side of their characters' personalities that are not dedicated strictly to the hunt.

The primary purpose of this phase of the story, however, is to determine each player's experience-point award as well as his standing in the esteem of the Sesha. (Both of those factors will determine what Gifts the Wani will teach the characters once the Sesha has deemed them worthy to enter the Wani's Realm.) Should you so desire, you can simply establish that the characters are allowed some much-needed rest and downtime at the Nandana and assume that the individual interviews with the Sesha take place off-stage.

Frankly, neither you nor any of your players may see any need to go *back* over the events you've all just spent so many sessions roleplaying through together anyway.

At this point, you're back where you started, and you can decide whether to continue the chronicle in the same way through multiple iterations or change the nature of the story to make it more complicated.

Theme

Incorporating thematic elements doesn't change the way a story plays out, but it does affect the way your players think about the story and relate to it. As you lay the story before them, the themes you emphasize lend greater import to the decisions the characters make and help them understand the context in which the story evolves.

The following themes are particularly appropriate to Nagah stories:

Justice

More than anything else, the Nagah serve the concept of justice. In a manner of speaking, they are the very embodiment of that concept. But who defines justice? What standard should the Nagah uphold as they go forth and do their good works? Is dispassionate, efficient punitive action the only just recourse against a wayward shapechanger's sins? Is the idea of mercy a facet of justice, or is it merely an apologetic disguise for one's weakness of conviction? If the Nagah are responsible for judging their Khurah cousins, who is qualified to judge them when they fail?

By showing examples of alternative responses to each of these questions throughout the course of your story, you can keep the theme of justice foremost in your players' minds.

Redemption

Is every shapechanger who fails in his duty doomed to be the Nagah's prey? Some Nagah would say so, but others would not agree. After all, no shapechanger is a paragon of responsible conduct for every second of his life. Many fail at some time in their lives, but most of them realize that they have done so and strive to make amends.

How then do the Nagah react when one of their victims seeks to atone for his crimes? Do they watch him for signs of hypocrisy and strike when they notice even one? Do they help him subtly as he does what he can to put right what he caused to go wrong? Do they take the stand that he should never have failed in the first place? It can be said that a man who fails to accomplish something may yet accomplish an even greater thing as he makes up for his failure, but it is up

to the Nagah to decide whether he even gets the chance. And if they judge that he does not deserve that chance, they must then decide whether they will put right his error themselves.

Isolation

The Nagah are few, and they have no one but their own kind to rely upon. Normal snakes are independent by nature, but a Nagah's humanlike side craves companionship. Humans throng and mill all around the Nagah, but people can tell on an instinctive level that even human-breed shapechangers are intrinsically different from them. The Nagah's duty demands that they isolate themselves from the rest of the world's shapechangers. When all is said and done, no one truly understands the Nagah but other Nagah, and their numbers are few and scattered all around the world.

When you tell Nagah stories, play up the distance between the Nagah characters and everyone else. Make sure they understand that they have only their fellow nestmates to turn to when they need a deep and spiritual connection. Side-stories of the lengths the Nagah will go to in order to break their isolation can add romantic, brooding or tragic touches to any chronicle.

Storytelling Concerns

Before you actually tell a Nagah story — be it a version of the quintessential tale or a variation thereof that explores a particular theme in greater depth — certain concerns arise that you will probably want to address. Telling a Nagah story shouldn't come off as a chore or an overly stressful undertaking, but portraying the Nagah in the spirit in which they were created does beg certain questions. For instance, how do you fit Nagah characters into a story that isn't about them specifically? How do you track the rank and Renown advancement of the Nagah when no actual system appears in these books? How do you portray the Wani?

Fitting the Nagah into a Story

Attaching Nagah to a chronicle in which they are not the main characters is no easy task. Most Nagah stories revolve around a particular nest as that nest does its work, and most nests are composed of only three Nagah. However, if you have more than three players who don't all want to play wereserpents, you have to make some adjustments and allowances.

Nagah and the Khurah

One of the most difficult types of stories into which you can insert the Nagah is a story that centers on one of the other Changing Breeds — especially a standard werewolf story. Most of the other Khurah assume that the Nagah are long extinct, and those who might know or remember otherwise are few and far between. You could, conceivably scrap the Nagah's reliance on secrecy for ease of play in your chronicle and hope that your players' characters are more understanding that the typical shapeshifters. If you prefer to inspire a more challenging roleplaying experience, though, force your players' Nagah characters to keep up the secrecy. Whether the characters are ringers under your discreet command from the beginning or simply constructs of adventurous and clever players, encourage them to downplay their supernatural powers, to assume their alternative skins infrequently (and never in sight of the other characters) and to mislead their fellow characters at every opportunity.

You can even help these players out by bending the rules in a couple of places. The first change you can make is to increase the scope of the Veil of the Wani Gift. One success on a die roll with this Gift normally causes a target to remember a Nagah's activity incorrectly, and gaining multiple successes erases the memory entirely. In order to allow your Nagah characters to disguise their activities more easily, you can say that each success on the Veil of the Wani die roll erases damning evidence from a separate target's mind and fills in the gaps subconsciously with information that the target would be more likely to accept. Therefore, using this Gift and rolling four successes after a Nagah has frenzied on an enemy in front of four werewolves will edit out the image of the Nagah's Azhi Dahaka skin in each of the four werewolves' minds and replace it with that of the Crinos form they subconsciously expect to see. If that mechanic is too cumbersome or unreliable in your chronicle, you could also make a variation of the Nuwisha Gift: Sheep's Clothing available to your Nagah characters.

The big question, of course, is why the Nagah characters are mixed in with the other Khurah in the first place? Is one of the other players' characters the Nagah's target? Are the other characters hunting down the Nagah's target on their own, only to cross paths with the Nagah in the course of the hunt? Have the Nagah characters been excommunicated from Nagah society and the grace of the Wani? Ordinarily, only extremely desperate circumstances would force a Nagah to seek out the help of any other shapeshifter, regardless of how subtly and furtively he does so. That being the case, such cross-Breed cooperation rarely ever happens. The Wyrm itself would practically have to be loose on Earth before the Nagah reveal their existence, and even then, such an action might prove disastrous in the end.

Hengeyokai Stories

The Far East setting is actually the easiest one in which to run a multi-Breed game that involves the Nagah. The hengeyokai of the Beast Courts know that the Nagah are still alive, and they understand the wereserpents' role on Earth. While the Nagah are reclusive and rare in the Beast Courts, the arrival of one at an important caern is not going to be the spark that ignites a new War of Shame. Even in the Far East, though, the Nagah must remain subtle and secretive as they go about doing their duty. Acting with too much cavalier abandon will cause the secret to leak out to the Sunset People eventually, and the westerners are far less understanding than the Nagah's hengeyokai allies.

The Grace of the Wani

The Wani and their servants teach the Nagah their Gifts and remind the Nagah always of their duty. But as the Wani give, so also can they take away.

Awarding Renown

No formal system exists to track a Nagah's rank or Renown, because the Nagah see no need for such distinctions. However, they understand that only the most wise and responsible among them should have access to the most powerful Gifts. Therefore, they leave it up to the Sesha to determine when individual wereserpents are ready to be granted such access.

What that means for you the Storyteller is that you get to judge your players' characters approximate rank and Renown independently of their experience points. In fact, you can relieve your players of the costs of new Gifts altogether and let them spend their experience points entirely on Attributes, Abilities and other game Traits. Doing so allows your characters to become quite powerful even before you add in the powers of their Gifts or their increased form statistics, but there isn't anything wrong with that in an all-Nagah chronicle, where the characters are measured against other Nagah. Gaia's judges and executioners are supposed to be fearsome and terrible, after all.

In doing so, you must be careful to make sure that your players' characters are acting in line with their duty, rather than just going mad with unstoppable killing power. The Nagah learn no Gifts at all without the express permission of the Sesha, and the Sesha does not suffer irresponsible fools to disgrace the Wani. Make it clear to your players — either throughout the course of play or in an out-of-game discussion before the story begins — what type of behavior the Sesha expects from the players' characters. Lay down your ground rules of conduct, and judge the characters on how well they follow it up.

Also remember that although most Nagah visit the Sesha only once or twice a year, they need not be allowed new Gifts or advances in rank every time. It could take a young Nagah years to mature sufficiently in the Sesha's eyes to be allowed high-level Gifts. Your players will not want to wait around forever, though, while you withhold the more entertaining special effects. If they are progressing through your chronicle handily and everyone is enjoying himself, don't hesitate to reward the characters with more power. Just be sure to increase the power level and challenge of the antagonists they face as well so as not to upset the pace and balance of the game.

The specific criteria on which to judge the characters is largely up to you, but a general set of guidelines is not entirely out of the question. Even though they do not keep a running tally on a scorecard, the Sesha does expect all Nagah to mind two aspects of conduct universally. The first such aspect is that of wisdom, for an unwise Nagah is not fit to judge or take life in Gaia's name. The second aspect is that of cunning. The way in which a Nagah does his duty is equal in importance to the reasons why he does it. If the Nagah does not proceed with guile and cleverness, he will fail. His prey might escape, his nestmates could die, and the Khurah might find out what he is. Honor is too subjective to make an adequate criterion (a Nagah who is the picture of honor to his people would be considered highly dishonorable to others), and Glory is the antithesis of proper secrecy.

If you prefer a proper system of rank and experience, award the Nagah Renown from Wisdom and Cunning categories out of game. Keep a list of each Nagah character's temporary and permanent Renown Traits among your other chronicle notes. Award Renown Traits equal to the characters' experience point awards for each session or story, but divided in a way that reflects which aspect of conduct the character focused on up until that point. When the character gains 10 temporary Traits, he may exchange it for a new permanent Trait. Then, after every fourth permanent Renown Trait he earns, he is allowed access to the next highest level of Gifts. (That is, each character starts with 0 Renown Traits and access to only Level One Gifts. When he has earned four permanent Renown Traits in any combination, he may have access to Level Two Gifts, and the progression continues thus.) To keep in line with the spirit of the typical Nagah experience, make sure to adhere to this system *entirely* out of game.

Portraying the Wani

Once the Nagah have spoken to the Sesha and been granted permission to learn new Gifts, they travel to Xi Wang Chi through a gate leading from Nandana. In Xi Wang Chi, they commune with the Dragon Kings who then teach the Nagah their Gifts. The characters need not specifically *do* anything to convince the Wani to teach these Gifts once they arrive, but you may still narrate the proceedings if you wish. Describe the Wani's Umbral home as the Nagah enter it. Is it a vast cave through which a river of pure water runs? Is it an ever-changing landscape in which each Wani's dreams of a perfect world struggles to assert itself over the others? Is it a Realm of non-space in which the only things that are real are the immense bodies of the Dragon Kings themselves? Xi Wang Chi might be any one of these things or any combination of them, but it should become clear to your players that it is like no place else on Earth or in the Umbra.

The way the Wani teach Gifts should be unique and fantastic as well. Do spirit servants of the Dragon Kings re-form the characters' bodies physically to reflect their new capabilities? Do the Wani appear in the form of Nagah themselves in order to teach by example? Do the Wani consume a character whole, merge its consciousness with his and demonstrate the new Gift's power as one of the many mundane abilities that the Dragon Kings share with the wereserpents? However you portray the lesson, be sure to get across the point that the Gifts come only by the grace of the Wani, and that the Wani can take those Gifts away should the characters fail in their duty.

Other Tales

The following are just a few of the many ways in which you can tell Nagah stories on your own.

The Hunt in Passing

In this type of story, distance your characters from the hunt, but keep it always in view. Set your scenes to occur just after the Nagah have completed some task in relation to their current mission or just before they must make ready, and let them tell a story about how they live their lives. What do the Nagah do when they aren't hunting? Do they pursue artistic endeavors? Do they spend time looking for suitable mates? Do they just shut themselves away and try to escape their terrible duty for a while? Let your characters show how they spend the moments between the times they must devote to aspects of the hunt. Do they help each other to achieve their individual goals? Do they find ways to compete with each other after being forced to cooperate all the rest of the time? Do they resent each other, even though their nestmates are the closest comrades and family they really have?

You can use these sessions on their own or as tangential side-stories scattered throughout a longer chronicle. They allow your players the chance to flesh out the sensual, beautiful aspects of their characters and explore the lonely hearts behind the Nagah's 100-yard stares. You can also foreshadow and drop hints about upcoming missions your characters will undertake, leaving the characters to wonder just how much distance they can truly put between themselves and the burden of meting out justice in Gaia's name.

The Judgment of the Sesha

This game takes the unique tack of putting your characters in positions of supreme authority right at its outset. The characters portray several of the wereserpents of the Sesha in the ananta at the mouth of Xi Wang Chi.

You can run this type of game largely dice and character-sheet free, but it is not a particularly action-intensive game. The way it works is you act as the members of various nests who have come to Nandana to make reports on what they have done recently. You portray one nestmate after another in succession, giving your players the opportunity to ask questions as the characters speak, then deliberate between hearings. When each member of the nest has spoken and evaluated his peers, you allow your players to discuss among themselves what they have heard and give their judgment. They decide if the nestmates acted rightly, and they decide if the nestmates are worthy to learn new Gifts from the Wani.

Variations on this type of story abound. You can set the scene such that the Nagah who are addressing your players each have incomplete pieces of a puzzle after their last mission. They have come to the Sesha for guidance, which means that it's up to your players to listen to all the characters' disparate clues and try to figure out exactly what happened to the Nagah that has them so confused. Another option is to tell the point of view story, in which each nestmate understands a slightly different version of the same story. It's then up to your players to glean the most likely (and empirically precise) course of events and judge the nestmates based on it. You can also present the story as a Nero Wolfe style mystery in which one of the three nestmates who speaks before them has been corrupted by the Wyrm and caused a great injustice to be committed. It is up to the Sesha (i.e., your players) to figure out which nestmate is corrupt and see that he or she is punished suitably.

When Enough Is Enough

The Nagah are not overflowing with the human failing of compassion. Compassion is the bane of objectivity, and Gaia would not build such a self-defeating flaw into her perfect judges. However, the Nagah *do* possess compassion to some extent, and even a Nagah can have his fill of killing if he convinces himself that his efforts are worthless and that nothing is ever going to change. If he and his nestmates are emotionally close enough to one another, his discontent may even rub off on them.

You can run this type of story in one of two ways. Your players can take the roles of these disaffected Nagah who must try to cope with a world that no longer has a place for them. Conversely, they could play the nest of Nagah that the Sesha must necessarily command to put the disaffected ones to death. After all, Nagah who will not do their duty are almost worse than traitors.

As the traitors try to live peaceful lives that don't require them to commit cold-blooded murder, they must wrestle with the moral dilemmas that making such a decision gives rise to. If they will take no action, what right have they to complain about the declining health of the world around them? To what lengths should they go to defend themselves from their brothers and sisters sent by the Sesha? By what outlet can they release their Rage as they are confronted by signs that the Khurah are just not doing their jobs? Is what the Nagah are doing even right in the first place? If not, are they still required to keep the secret of the Nagah's existence?

Telling the story from the opposite perspective is less introspective, but it's a lot more action-oriented. The Wani may well revoke the traitors' Gifts, but a desperate Nagah outcast still has plenty of advantages to draw from. How will your players' nest catch a fugitive or group with the same background training in the hunt as they have had? Can any of the nestmates be baited out of hiding to turn over the others? Can any of them be reformed rather than executed? And if the desperate, disaffected Nagah do decide to endanger Nagah secrecy, how will your players' nest stop them?

Manyskins

The ancient Nuwisha has done and seen more in his lifetime than many shapeshifters can imagine ever doing in their own. He has spied on members of every Changing Breed and learned secrets about them that they would kill their own for revealing. Now his trespass and his audacity have exceeded all expectations, for the Old Man has infiltrated even the Lengthening Shadows themselves. The Sesha has been alerted to this egregious breach of secrecy, but how will it decide to deal with him? Can Manyskins be trusted to keep the Nagah's secret, or do tears fill up his footprints as he runs away laughing at the very thought? When the Sesha makes its decision, will your characters' nest abide by it? Will your players' Nagah hunt the Old Man down if they are so ordered? If so, how will they find him? How will they kill someone who has escaped Malfeas and cheated death more times than they have seen the sun rise over the mouth of a river?

And if the Sesha decrees that Manyskins be left alone, how will your characters' nest take that news? Will the characters agree and cower in their hoods hoping that the Old Man dies before he can do too much damage, or will they take the matter into their own hands and eliminate this dangerous, unpredictable liability once and for all?

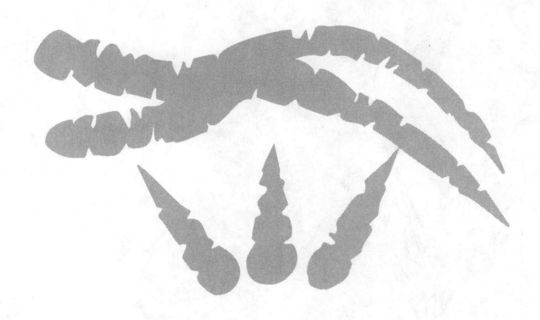

Appendix One: Judges

All Nagah are individuals who are fully capable of carrying out their responsibilities independently. With the proper training, any Nagah could act as judge and executioner over his wayward Khurah cousins. Such was the Nagah's way before the War of Rage, and before Vinata.

Today, Nagah operate in nests in order to make sure that no individual abuses the privileges of his responsibility as Vinata did. This cooperation allows each nestmate to develop skills that complement his nestmates' skills and make up for his nestmates' weaknesses. Working together also helps abate the loneliness that the solemn, self-reliant Nagah are heir to.

Above all, however, every Nagah character is an individual.

Seductress

Quote: *I wouldn't have let you buy me that drink if I didn't know exactly how this night was going to end.*

Prelude: The first sensations you remember specifically are those of the stench of human sweat, the warmth of human flesh and the sad, graceless gyrations of a pitiful human woman. You clung to her shoulders and hung from her neck; lights and smoke blinded you, and you were forced to endure her careless, loveless manhandling as she draped you across her knobby limbs and jerk-weaved around in soulless paroxysms. No matter how fervently you tried to crawl away or escape, she held you close, smearing your skin with her sweat.

When you finally discovered the nature of your torture, you were too horrified to remain complacent any longer. For the first time in the life you remember, you looked around for some respite in the world beyond the human woman's ungentle ministrations. You prayed for release, but you saw only the eyes of human men capering behind the many veils of smoke all around you. They slavered over you and the woman who held you. They drank impure water and pressed as close as they dared to the stage on which the human woman stood. Some reached out their hands to touch her, but she kicked their hands away. Some fought with each other over who would come closest to the both of you. Every move the woman made (and forced you to make across her sweat-slick body) filled the men's eyes with an unholy fire.

But as you watched them, something coiled on the floor. A serpent greater than yourself twisted over and among them, sometimes sliding right through them, touching them as you were forced to touch the woman. The men did not see it or feel its touch, but you could see it — its path followed the woman's hateful, hollow eyes, infecting everyone it touched. Its jaws snapped and its fangs flashed, clamping each of the men in turn and laying clutches of tumescent, writhing eggs in their hearts. The men did not cry out in pain when this happened — they yowled for joy and pressed ever closer to the woman who held you. You could *hear* them — it was the sound that brought you out of your First Skin. Feeling Rage for the first time, you turned on your "handler." Panic reigned supreme as the lusting, thronging men beheld your terrible wrath, but their panic and flight trampled the spirit serpent into dust and oily smoke.

Years have passed, and you have found your nest, but you remember every move and motion of the woman who had enslaved you. You remember how she lured and teased. You remember the effect it had. Sometimes, you can still smell her stench.

Concept: You understand the effect that the anticipation and promise of sex has on the members of other species. You understand how it makes them weak and robs them of their will. Be it in sinuous dance, subtle conversation or magnetic eye contact across a crowded room, your every move pulses with a heat that melts your victims' better judgment and leaves no question in their minds about what you want from them. Whether you seduce your victims merely to gain information or you set out to lure them to your waiting nestmates, you know how to tease and tantalize and promise just enough to turn a victim into a biddable, willing slave.

Roleplaying Hints: The more often you do your duty — as your nestmates call it — the more revolted you become by the thought of having sex in your Balaram skin. You can see the lust in the way others' pupils dilate and crawl over every contour of your body. You can tell it in the way they try to touch you as they speak to you. You try to act cold and unwelcoming when you are not specifically doing your job, but so many people see that subtle resistance as a challenge to overcome. Only your nestmates respect you when you need your distance, and you love them more than any pathetic victim of yours has ever claimed to love you.

Equipment: Classy clothing that shows off your figure, cigarettes (no lighter), synthetic pheromone roll-on, stun gun

NAGAH

Name: Breed: Vasuki   Nest:
Player: Auspice: Kali   Crown:
Chronicle: Kin Species: Cobra   Concept: Seductress

Attributes

Physical
Strength ●●○○○
Dexterity ●●●○○
Stamina ●●●○○

Social
Charisma ●●○○○
Manipulation ●●●●○
Appearance ●●●●○

Mental
Perception ●●○○○
Intelligence ●●○○○
Wits ●●○○○

Abilities

Talents
Alertness ●●○○○
Athletics ●○○○○
Brawl ●○○○○
Dodge ●○○○○
Empathy ○○○○○
Expression ●●●○○
Intimidation ●●●○○
Primal-Urge ●○○○○
Streetwise ○○○○○
Subterfuge ●●○○○

Skills
Animal Ken ●●○○○
Crafts ○○○○○
Drive ○○○○○
Etiquette ○○○○○
Firearms ○○○○○
Leadership ○○○○○
Melee ○○○○○
Performance ●●●○○
Stealth ●●●○○
Survival ●●○○○

Knowledges
Computer ○○○○○
Enigmas ●●○○○
Investigation ●●○○○
Law ○○○○○
Linguistics ●○○○○
Medicine ○○○○○
Occult ○○○○○
Politics ○○○○○
Rituals ●●○○○
Science ○○○○○

Advantages

Gifts
Sting of Sleep
Sense Vibration
Iron Coils

Gifts

Gifts

Backgrounds
Ananta ●●○○○
Contacts ●●○○○
Pure Breed ●●○○○
Rites ●●○○○
___ ○○○○○
___ ○○○○○
___ ○○○○○

Rank

Rage
●●●●○○○○○○
□□□□□□□□□□

Gnosis
●●●●○○○○○○
□□□□□□□□□□

Willpower
●●●●○○○○○○
□□□□□□□□□□

Health
Bruised		□
Hurt	-1	□
Injured	-1	□
Wounded	-2	□
Mauled	-2	□
Crippled	-5	□
Incapacitated		□

Experience

Stalker

Quote: *She's so beautiful when she's sleeping. And her skin is so soft.*

Prelude: You were a lonely child. You were too skinny to play sports, too easily distracted for serious study and too strange to make many friends. Instead, you watched the other children as they played and imagined yourself among them. In your fancy, you lifted the toys they dropped and caught them when they tripped to save them skinned knees and bruised elbows. You imagined long conversations with them that you never actually had. In your mind, you kept them from making mistakes by telling them what was right and wrong.

In high school, you did much the same, but you were more active. You picked the most beautiful and popular student in your school — Samantha, whom you knew from your grade school and junior high — and you became a silent part of her life. When she went to movies, you sat behind her. When she went home to her parents, you saw her off to sleep from just outside her window. You knew her better than everyone else put together. And you watched her ruin her life.

She drank too much, your Samantha, and she had too many boyfriends. Her grades slipped because her parents pressured her too often about choosing the right college. The potential and beauty that made her so special to you drained away before your eyes. She stopped taking care of herself, and her friends stopped calling on her one-by-one. All except you. When she had fallen to her lowest point — just after finding out that her last unofficial boyfriend had gotten her pregnant — you visited her. You wrote a note in her own hand-writing and left it on her nightstand. You weighed the note down with her mother's prescription head-ache medication. You opened a bottle of single-malt scotch from her father's liquor cabinet and left it there beside the note. You locked her door from the inside and waited for her to wake up the next morning. When she did, you explained to her what she had to do. Although terrified of you, she knew that you were right. An hour later, you laid her down in her bed and left the way you had come in. And you found that someone had been watching you just as you had been watching your sweet Samantha.

Concept: Ninety percent of a Nagah's duty relies on monitoring one's victim for signs of weakness, and surveillance is your specialty. You monitor your nest's tar-get in search of weaknesses of character or lapses in his responsibility, and the nest's judgment often relies solely on the information you uncover. But you are not a dispassionate observer. As you learn about and absorb the daily routine of a prospective victim, you get to know the person as well as she knows herself. Even if your judgment of her is not ultimately in her favor, you can't help but love her a little. When a mission comes to an end, you can't help but weep silently at the loss of something that's become such an intimate part of your own life. Your nestmates may consider you selfish, but they have learned not to gainsay your judgment.

Roleplaying Hints: Always be polite and deferential when you speak. You don't want word to get back to your target somehow that you are a boorish lout. When one of your nestmates performs some small action or utters a turn of phrase in a way that reminds you of your target, point it out to him. When you meet your nestmates in a place that your target frequents, try to sit where your target would sit and order what your target would order.

If your judgment demands that your target be put to death, don't waver in your devotion to your duty. Remain impartial, and carry out Gaia's will. Just be certain that your face is the last your target sees so that he or she will know that what you've done had to be done for his or her own good. When your mission is over, don't dwell on it. Remember your target fondly for the fleeting joy it brought you, and move on.

Equipment: Digital camera; notepad; shotgun microphone; tape recorder; small, easily replaced souvenir from your victim's home

NAGAH

Name: _____ Breed: Balaram Nest: _____
Player: _____ Auspice: Kamsa Crown: _____
Chronicle: _____ Kin Species: Copperhead Concept: Stalker

Attributes

Physical
Strength_____ ●●○○○
Dexterity_____ ●●●●○
Stamina_____ ●●○○○

Social
Charisma_____ ●●○○○
Manipulation_____ ●●●○○
Appearance_____ ●●○○○

Mental
Perception_____ ●●●●●
Intelligence_____ ●●●●○
Wits_____ ●●○○○

Abilities

Talents
Alertness_____ ●●●○○
Athletics_____ ○○○○○
Brawl_____ ○○○○○
Dodge_____ ●●○○○
Empathy_____ ●○○○○
Expression_____ ○○○○○
Intimidation_____ ●●●○○
Primal-Urge_____ ○○○○○
Streetwise_____ ●●○○○
Subterfuge_____ ●●●○○

Skills
Animal Ken_____ ○○○○○
Crafts_____ ○○○○○
Drive_____ ●●●○○
Etiquette_____ ○○○○○
Firearms_____ ●●○○○
Leadership_____ ○○○○○
Melee_____ ○○○○○
Performance_____ ○○○○○
Stealth_____ ●●●●○
Survival_____ ○○○○○

Knowledges
Computer_____ ●○○○○
Enigmas_____ ●●○○○
Investigation_____ ●●●●○
Law_____ ○○○○○
Linguistics_____ ●○○○○
Medicine_____ ●●○○○
Occult_____ ○○○○○
Politics_____ ●○○○○
Rituals_____ ○○○○○
Science_____ ●○○○○

Advantages

Gifts
Eyes of the Dragon Kings
Persuasion
Predator's Patience
_____
_____

Gifts
_____
_____
_____
_____
_____

Gifts
_____
_____
_____
_____
_____

Backgrounds
Ananta ●○○○○
Contacts ●●●○○
Resources ●●●○○
_____ ○○○○○
_____ ○○○○○
_____ ○○○○○
_____ ○○○○○

Rage
●●●○○○○○○○
☐☐☐☐☐☐☐☐☐☐

Gnosis
●●○○○○○○○○
☐☐☐☐☐☐☐☐☐☐

Health
Bruised		☐
Hurt	-1	☐
Injured	-1	☐
Wounded	-2	☐
Mauled	-2	☐
Crippled	-5	☐
Incapacitated		☐

Rank
_____

Willpower
●●●●○○○○○○
☐☐☐☐☐☐☐☐☐☐

Experience
_____

Cleaner

Quote: *I see. No, don't explain. I'll be right over.*

Prelude: You shed your First Skin in a horrible mess that came late in your life and for no reason. You and your wife were arguing about who would care for your aging parents, and your anger just exploded. You remember her face as your claws picked her apart with cruel, vicious precision. You remember stopping up her screams by spraying bile and venom into her mouth. You coiled around her over and over, crushing her into submission as your fangs rent her flesh once, twice and again. Your argument was ridiculous, far out of proportion to the ferocity with which you destroyed her.

When you came to your senses very shortly thereafter, she lay in your arms, and her blood soaked the tatters of your clothing. As you stirred, you became aware of two men standing above you. You tried to speak, but one pinned you with his eyes as the other lifted you roughly to your feet. They called you family and said that they had been watching and waiting. They said this all without speaking to you or to each other, and an unknown but familiar coldness beneath your skin convinced you that they did not lie. They commanded that you trust them, and you did.

Immediately, one of them left and returned shortly with the fresh and much-abused corpse of a man roughly of a height with you. He wore your clothes, and his hair had been cut the same way. One of the two men knocked this dead man's teeth out with the butt of a knife — likely the one that had ravaged the unfortunate's body — and collected the pieces as they fell. The other turned on the gas vent in your fireplace. When all was done, they helped you fold down into your smallest shape and stuffed you into a bag one of them carried.

Three nights later, before they turned you over to the Sesha and disappeared, they showed you a newspaper. It ran a story on page three about the brutal double-murder that had taken place in his former home. It told about how the vicious attackers who had done the crime had set the house on fire to cover their trail. Witnesses had seen a vehicle leaving the scene as the fire began, but they could not identify the driver or passenger. The van had been found abandoned nine miles away. The two Nagah, as they called themselves and you, commanded that you learn from what they had done and never forget. Thus far, you have not.

Concept: The Sesha has charged you with one of the most important duties possible: You help maintain the myth that the Nagah are extinct. Rather than rely on Gifts, you specialize in doctoring forensic evidence and dressing the scene of a disaster to tell a false but believable story. Your nestmates mislead human authorities and shelter indiscreet Nagah who need to lie low, but you handle potentially damning messes directly. When time is of the essence, you can dress the site of a Nagah's vicious frenzy so that it looks like nothing so much as desperate robbery that got out of hand, but you prefer to simply make a corpse disappear without a trace. Regardless of how you clean up such a problem, though, you always make a note of who caused it. And you always report it back to the Sesha.

Roleplaying Hints: Let your experience and reputation speak for itself, rather than letting young fools second-guess what you're doing. Don't let your clients explain what they did wrong; don't let them try to justify their actions or lay blame for their mistakes. Remain professionally distant both from your work and from the careless ones who called you, so that you can get your job done faster.

Give orders that leave no room for discussion. Don't explain what you're doing or listen to suggestions. Be thorough and precise so that those who are watching can learn from you. Never scold, never patronize, and never offer suggestions that your actions can teach just as effectively. Make your calm command of the situation plain for your clients to see, and let their shame teach them to be more careful in the future.

Equipment: Five-year-old gardening truck; tarp; assorted mops, brooms and household cleansers; drum of sulfuric acid

NAGAH ™

Name: | **Breed:** Balaram | **Nest:**
Player: | **Auspice:** Kamakshi | **Crown:**
Chronicle: | **Kin Species:** Common Adder | **Concept:** Cleaner

Attributes

Physical
Strength ●●●○○
Dexterity ●●○○○
Stamina ●●●○○

Social
Charisma ●●○○○
Manipulation ●●●○○
Appearance ●●○○○

Mental
Perception ●●●●○
Intelligence ●●●●○
Wits ●●●●○

Abilities

Talents
Alertness ●●○○○
Athletics ○○○○○
Brawl ●●○○○
Dodge ●○○○○
Empathy ○○○○○
Expression ○○○○○
Intimidation ●●○○○
Primal-Urge ○○○○○
Streetwise ●●●○○
Subterfuge ●○○○○

Skills
Animal Ken ○○○○○
Crafts ●○○○○
Drive ●●○○○
Etiquette ○○○○○
Firearms ●○○○○
Leadership ○○○○○
Melee ●●○○○
Performance ○○○○○
Stealth ●●●○○
Survival ○○○○○

Knowledges
Computer ●○○○○
Enigmas ○○○○○
Investigation ●●●●●
Law ●●●○○
Linguistics ●○○○○
Medicine ●●○○○
Occult ○○○○○
Politics ○○○○○
Rituals ○○○○○
Science ●●●○○

Advantages

Gifts
Self-Mastery
Resist Pain
Scent of Running Water
_____
_____

Gifts
_____
_____
_____
_____
_____

Gifts
_____
_____
_____
_____
_____

Backgrounds
Contacts ●●○○○
Kinfolk ●●○○○
Resources ●○○○○
_____ ○○○○○
_____ ○○○○○
_____ ○○○○○
_____ ○○○○○

Rank
_____

Rage
●●● ○○○○○○○○
☐☐☐☐☐☐☐☐☐☐

Gnosis
● ○○○○○○○○○○
☐☐☐☐☐☐☐☐☐☐

Willpower
●●●●●● ○○○
☐☐☐☐☐☐☐☐☐☐

Health
Bruised		☐
Hurt	-1	☐
Injured	-1	☐
Wounded	-2	☐
Mauled	-2	☐
Crippled	-5	☐
Incapacitated		☐

Experience
_____

Sensei

Quote: *Get up. Keep your feet farther apart, and don't lock your back knee when you lunge this time.*

Prelude: All that you know is war. One short year after you were born, both your mother and your father gave their lives defending your court's caern. You remember only that your mother helped free you from your shell and your father shaded you from the sun with his hood as he held you on the bank of the river that he most loved and played you beautiful music on a wooden flute. Every other memory you have of your youth is one of desperation, bloody battle or fleeting moments of rest. Your court was built around a river caern high in the mountains, and it was second in power only to the Cherry Phoenix Court. Bakemono and Akuma and villainous Kumo lusted after this power, and every hand that could hold a sword in the caern's defense could do your home a valuable service.

The caern general adopted you and trained you in the varied forms of war after your parents' deaths. He reminded you constantly that you had no home but this court. He made sure that you knew you had no family but the warriors who would stand beside you and defend it. He warned you that you would have no vengeance if you did not inscribe every lesson he taught you in the stone of your heart.

But as you grew and learned and became able to stand in your caern's defense with the other warriors at your general's command, you realized that you did not thirst for vengeance. Your parents were shadows and pleasant dreams to you. The general is your real family. You remember his lessons as you remember his name, and you have taken it upon yourself to pass those lessons on to the new generation of warriors in your court.

Concept: Where the general organizes the forces that support and protect your court's caern, it is your responsibility to train his eager young warriors in the art of war. Your general expects his warriors to act without fail or hesitation when he gives orders, and he expects you to make them able to do so. You instruct the would-be defenders of your court's caern in swordplay, unarmed combat, controlling and focusing their Rage and squad tactics. On the rare occasion in which you form part of a sentai, you assume the Pillar auspice.

Roleplaying Hints: When you train warriors, do not fill their heads with koans and esoteric shadow lessons. Do not assign them mundane tasks that will aid them only *if* they discover how to apply those tasks to the field of battle. Tell them what they need to learn, demonstrate it perfectly, and have them repeat it. If they fail to perform their lessons to your standards, demonstrate again and have them repeat again. Never shame them or make yourself their enemy, lest they waste their energy trying to defeat you. Remind them always that their general demands perfect, instant performance from each of them. Remind them always that their enemies will seize upon any weakness in their technique to destroy them.

If your general should choose you to form part of a sentai, do so without hesitation. Refrain from taking the lead, even if the other members of your war party are all former students. Support them, guide them, and teach them, but do not force them to become dependent upon you. Be confident that your tutelage has forged your students into capable warriors and leaders in their own right.

Equipment: Loose clothing, conical straw hat, katana, bokken, wooden flute

Nagah

NAGAH™

Name: _____ **Breed:** Ahi **Nest:** _____
Player: _____ **Auspice:** Kartikeya **Crown:** _____
Chronicle: _____ **Kin Species:** Cobra **Concept:** Sensei

Attributes

Physical
Strength _____ ●●●●○
Dexterity _____ ●●●●○
Stamina _____ ●●●●○

Social
Charisma _____ ●●●○○
Manipulation _____ ●○○○○
Appearance _____ ●●○○○

Mental
Perception _____ ●●●○○
Intelligence _____ ●●○○○
Wits _____ ●●○○○

Abilities

Talents
Alertness _____ ●○○○○
Athletics _____ ●○○○○
Brawl _____ ●●●○○
Dodge _____ ●●●○○
Empathy _____ ●○○○○
Expression _____ ●○○○○
Intimidation _____ ●○○○○
Primal-Urge _____ ●○○○○
Streetwise _____ ○○○○○
Subterfuge _____ ○○○○○

Skills
Animal Ken _____ ○○○○○
Crafts _____ ○○○○○
Drive _____ ○○○○○
Etiquette _____ ●●○○○
Firearms _____ ○○○○○
Leadership _____ ●●●●○
Melee _____ ●●●●○
Performance _____ ●●○○○
Stealth _____ ●○○○○
Survival _____ ●●○○○

Knowledges
Computer _____ ○○○○○
Enigmas _____ ●●○○○
Investigation _____ ○○○○○
Law _____ ●●○○○
Linguistics _____ ●○○○○
Medicine _____ ○○○○○
Occult _____ ●●○○○
Politics _____ ●●○○○
Rituals _____ ●○○○○
Science _____ ○○○○○

Advantages

Gifts
Slayer's Eye
Wyrm Sense
Eyes of the War God
_____
_____
_____

Gifts
_____
_____
_____
_____
_____
_____

Gifts
_____
_____
_____
_____
_____
_____

Backgrounds
Ananta _____ ●●○○○
Ancestors _____ ●●○○○
Pure Breed _____ ●●○○○
Rites _____ ●●○○○
_____ ○○○○○
_____ ○○○○○
_____ ○○○○○

Rank

Rage
●●●●●○○○○○
□□□□□□□□□□

Gnosis
●●●○○○○○○○
□□□□□□□□□□

Willpower
●●●●●●○○○○
□□□□□□□□□□

Health
Bruised		□
Hurt	-1	□
Injured	-1	□
Wounded	-2	□
Mauled	-2	□
Crippled	-5	□
Incapacitated		□

Experience

The Hush of the River

Stones in a river's bed shape the river and guide it, but they are also polished by it. Stones may dam a river or chop it into a turbulent rush of white diamonds, but their edges will all wear away in time. Then, when the sigh and whisper of the river has fallen silent, only the smooth-polished stones remain.

Vinata

We spare no compassion for traitors or for fools who betray. But between the two, I believe that She Whose Name is Never Spoken but is Always Remembered is among the latter. She is reviled, and rightly so, but she was not born in our contempt. There was a time when she could have been the greatest among us. Although she was young, she was a legend in every ear that heard her name. Especially her own. She heard the fearful, reverent whispers of those who witnessed her just actions, and she let them inspire her to further greatness. Never was she content with the last praise sung in her name; always did she strive to be worthy of more and greater.

Thus did the subtle Wyrm ensnare her. It played the strands of its cold, woven prison as harp-strings and praised her as the pure and unbound avatar of balance reborn on Earth. It sang her to sleep and gave her a vision of the world in harmony. It showed her the peace and balance that it had striven to achieve before the Wyld drove the Weaver insane and the Weaver's webs had ensnared more than was right and proper. The Wyrm told the One Whose Name is Not Spoken that such a world of harmony was possible in her lifetime if she but made a crucial decision.

When she smiled, it showed her the one on Earth who stood in the way of that peace. It showed her an young and vicious werewolf whose howls carried over the seas and whose fangs dripped with brother blood. The Wyrm told her that this werewolf's eyes would see the last of balance and peace on the Earth.

She awoke then and hunted the Silver Fang down, never knowing that the Wyrm had given her the most bitter of poisoned apples. After all, even the Corrupter can tell the truth when doing so suits its purposes.

I understand that the old Nagah who lived then — and who would become the first Sesha — did not let her die for a very long time. I can only hope that they let her live long enough to see how thoroughly she herself had been betrayed. I hope she was allowed to understand that no one of us can serve a single master and claim to uphold the balance that so pleases Gaia. I hope that I remember this as well for all the days of my life, just as I will remember the name that is never spoken.

Vasana

I also will return to the river this day to pay my respects. Vasana the Three-Hooded, Vasana the Emerald, Vasana the Terrible lies dead. They claim that he lies down merely to sleep, but I know death's aspect well enough. He asked only, I am told, to lie at the foot of the mountain nearest his home so that his Third Mother could judge him as he lay dying. The moment he closed his eyes — so a witness explained as I lay her stomach open — a spring swelled up beneath him where none had ever run before. He lay immersed in his Third Mother's joyous tears and disappeared from view. Those who knew him, such as the poor girl I spoke to, say that he smiled as the water surrounded him and his Third Mother took him home to her bosom.

I remember Vasana well. A generation of rakshasa cringed to hear his name in memory of what he did to their prince Jatadaka. The scrolls that hang in the Cherry Phoenix Court praise him for standing atop Fujiyama when all that court's defenders had fallen. I know of the time that he allowed an elephant to trample him flat so that he could hide between the reeds of the demon Kodomo Gunjin's sandals and destroy the giant as it led its army to war against the Temple of the Ancestors. For every soul I have taken, for every word of hatred I have given and received, Vasana has slain two bakemono and taken vengeance for three vile deeds. Of all the warriors of this bright Age, Vasana is the first among them.

Ten Steps has never spoken to me, aloud or in night's whispers, but that's the reason I miss him. He does not ask me questions, so I am never tempted to tell him the things I will soon tell the Sesha. I do not feel compelled to confess to him of my fear or my occasional uncertainty. I do not discuss with him any matter of weight or consequence because he does not ask. And what he does not ask, I need not answer.

The last time I addressed the Sesha and was denied an audience with the Long Lu, Ten Steps came and sat beside me on the rock where I had gone to sulk. He looked at me with the same open respect that had lit his eyes when my nestmates and I arrived at Nandana. He offered me no comfort, nor did he offer me advice on the ways in which I could improve my performance before the Sesha sent for me again. He did not gaze on me with his eyes wide and his head tilted in soulful pity. He only sat beside me as both of my other nestmates learned at the feet of the Dragon Kings.

This is why I love Ten Steps and miss him when I am away from Nandana. He did not demean me with pity or patronize me with useless suggestions. He did not let me brood and isolate myself from my nestmates. Although I revile it in every other member of my species, Ten Steps did not judge me. I have spoken to my nestmates of this feeling, and they have felt it too. Blessed is he who shows us that to judge is only the whole of our duty, not the whole of our being.

I will go to the site of his grave as so many have already this year. I will stare at the mouth of his grave-spring. I will try to see his eyes between his Third Mother's fingers. Like so many of my kind and his, I will shed one tear of pure water into that river to show that even such as I can respect one such as he.

Ten Steps

I do not love the Sesha or relish the time I spend with them, but I miss Ten Steps. He waits at the ananta before the Xi Wang Chi for ones like you or I. He welcomes us to the home of our judges and looks after our needs. When we are weary, he leads us to rest. When we are thirsty, he brings us pure river water in a wooden ladle that is older than he is. When the Sesha calls us to report to them of what we have done and seen, it is Ten Steps who calls on us as we relax and escorts us to their chamber.

I don't know how old he is or who his parents were. I know that he is American by the rattle on the end of his tail. I know that he is ahi by his tongue that always splits at the end. I know that he is lonely by the way his deep and yellow eyes hold my own when I look at him. I know that he loves the Sesha by the faltering reverence I see in the way he bows toward their chamber when he escorts one such as you or I into their presence.

Abraham Waverly

I know exactly who you're talking about. English guy. Looks about 70 years old on a good day. Only talks out loud when he's giving you orders or a lecture. Always cranes his neck way forward when he's looking around. You're talking about Waverly. Now don't panic, kid. I wouldn't know his name unless he wanted me to know it, and I wouldn't mention it to you if I didn't want you to know I knew the guy.

I was about your age when I met him. I'd just lost my First Skin, and I was all alone. I'd bred true from two Kinfolk, and Waverly tracked me down. He told me what I was. He told me what it was I was supposed to do. He spent years with me just like he did with you, teaching me about the others and what they're supposed to do. He taught me how to find them, how to judge them and how to kill them when they fall short. You're starting to relax, so I guess that means he did all the same for you. That's what he spends all his time doing, according to some other folks I've talked to. He finds those who are lost, he trains them, and he forms them into nests like he's done for you and me. He'll have one more coming to join us in the next year or so if I know Abraham.

Let me warn you right this minute, son, you had best remember every word that man has ever said to you. You had better not ever fall short. One of my last two nestmates fell short. Marin, the one you're replacing. She hesitated in her duty, and she got our partner Andreas killed by the piece-of-shit HK Glass Walker we were after at the time. She and I took the Walker down and cleaned up — we even got Andreas' body all the way home to fucking Mississippi — but Waverly found out. He showed up the night after we buried Andreas. He just walked right in on us while we were sleeping, dragging Andreas' body by the hair. Waverly shoved the corpse in bed between Marin and me. He looked at us and turned us into stone, and he made us do some shit I'm taking to my grave and on into whatever hell Gaia has waiting. After that, he left and took Marin with him. He made her carry Andreas' body. He didn't even let her get dressed.

Now here you are, and we're expecting another soon. I know Marin's off in another of Waverly's nests somewhere, if she's lucky. But kid, if you fall short in a big way and Waverly finds out about it, you're going to see for yourself that Andreas was really the luckiest of the three of us.

Appendix Two: Snakeskin

By Nick Esposito

First, a disclaimer: I speak from personal experience, so please remember one thing; venomous or large constricting snakes are NOT for the inexperienced handler. While snakes make wonderful pets, please leave snakes that can do you harm to people that have enough experience to handle them.

The Anatomy of a Snake

Snakes are one half of the order Squamata, falling under the sub-order of Serpentes. This sub-order is divided into a debated number of families, although only four families are important for this limited space; the Boidae (boids), Viperidae (vipers), Colubridae (colubrids), and Elapidae (elapids). The Boidae family is the larger constrictors, both boas and pythons. Then there is the Viperidae family, which includes the rattlesnakes, adders, and vipers. The largest family of snakes is the Colubridae, with everything from cornsnakes and rat snakes to boomslangs and catsnakes under its large tree. Lastly, we have the Elapidae a family that includes mambas, sea snakes, coral snakes, and the cobras.

One of the first things that must be understood about snakes is that they are not warm blooded as mammals or birds are, but control their body temperature in one of two ways. All snakes are ectothermic, or cold-blooded. Though this might lead people to assume

that a snake is cold to the touch, it simply means that a snake's body temperature is controlled by its surroundings, and not internally. It's a popular assumption that snakes are slow and sluggish, but more often than not (assuming environmental conditions are favorable), a snake's body temperature is higher than that of most mammals, and therefore they function at a much higher metabolic rate than might be assumed.

Some snakes regulate their body temperature by basking under the sun, usually on objects that absorb heat, such as rocks or streets. This method, which is called heliothermic, is demonstrated in a smaller number of snakes, and is more often used by lizards, turtles and the crocodilians.

These characteristics would seem to imply that snakes are limited to tropical locales, but that is not the case. I myself have caught everything from garter snakes to rattlesnakes near my home, in the suburbs north of Chicago. However, this does give the snake the advantage of needing to take in far less food than most other animals. Warm-blooded animals spend between seventy and eighty percent of their energy maintaining their body temperature. Thus, mammals need to eat food almost daily to remain in top health, while reptiles may go weeks without eating before they suffer any ill effects. Anacondas regularly eat only once every three months (although these meals are sometimes as large as a deer). At the extreme end of the spectrum, there are documented cases of adult ball pythons that have gone a full sixteen months without eating.

Possibly the most interesting area of a snake is its head. The snake's forked tongue, one of the most distinguishing features of a snake, is also one of the most useful. To sense its surroundings, a snake sticks its tongue out and flicks it in the air. As the snake does this, each tong, or side of the fork, picks up different scents and different information. The tongue is then pulled into the mouth and the snake slides it into the Jacobson's organ on the roof of its mouth, one fork on each side. The Jacobson's organ is a highly specialized sensory device that relays information to the brain about the snake's surroundings. The information received from this tells the snake what its surroundings are, where heat sources are, and which direction they are in. It is in this manner that snakes receive most of their information about their surroundings. To supplement this information, some snakes have pits on their lip just over the mouth to process additional information; these pits are how the pit viper received its name. Pit organs convey the ability to sense heat, in particular the body heat of prey.

Another unique development in the head of a snake is the jaw. Most people believe that a snake unhinges its jaw to eat, but this is purely myth. The snake is able to open its jaw almost 180 degrees because it has extra bones —as compared to other animals, of course. Most animals have one jawbone that connects directly to the skull. In a snake, however, there are four bones. First, the jawbone itself is split directly in the center, and connected with a stretchable tendon. Secondly, there are two extra bones, one on each side, that fall between the jawbones and the skull.

Internally, snakes are quite confusing creatures. They have pairs of most of their organs, like most animals, but one is usually under-developed. For instance, the left lung is usually quite reduced in size, while the right lung is enlarged and elongated. The walls of the heart do not fully separate in snakes, so deoxygenated and reoxygenated blood flow together.

A snake's most unusual feature is its lack of legs. This special adaptation allows the snake to go into the dens and hiding places of their prey. The snake compensates for this lack of limbs with a set of specialized scales and muscles on its stomach. While most of a snake's body is covered with a tile-like scaling, the stomach scales (or scutes) are rear-faced and overlapping, like shingles on a roof. Using these scales to provide traction, the snake then flexes its stomach muscles in waves, and glides through its surroundings. Arboreal snakes have developed this ability to such a degree that they can climb up the side of a tree. Sidewinders use a similar ability, though it looks quite different.

Snakes have developed two other ways of specialized movement as well. The sea snake, which has a flat, thin, vertical tail, swims almost like a fish, and has the capacity to swim backwards. There are also snakes who can flatten the muscles in their stomachs out and glide through the air on their now thin, flat bodies.

From Birth (or Hatching) to Death as a Snake

Snakes reproduce in one of two ways, egg laying or live birth. Those snakes that do lay eggs often incubate them until the young hatch. A reptile's eggs differ from those of other egg layers as they are flexible and leathery, not hard shelled. Snakes that give live birth incubate internally, in a way similar to other animals. Either way, the mother abandons the snakes as soon as they are born. (Incidentally, cobras are egg-layers — and king cobras are the only snakes to make nests for their eggs. The female pulls together a mound of leaves, usually bamboo, with her coils; the eggs are laid in a lower "chamber" while the female rests in an upper section of the nest.)

Once a snake is out in the world, it is on its own for survival. Fortunately, snakes come out of the egg (or womb) both ready and able to hunt on their own. Snakes eat a myriad of foods, including eggs, birds, rodents, pigs, fish, insects, even lizards and other snakes.

Snakes grow rapidly in their first year, and as they do so, they shed. As animals develop, they grow too large for their skin to accommodate them. Animals such as mammals and birds, lose and regrow the outer layers of their skin one cell at a time continuously. Reptiles, however, lose all their outer skin at one time. A few days before a shed, a snake becomes duller in color and its eyes take on a milky appearance. This is because a thin layer of fluid is between the old and new layers of skin, to help the skin glide off during the shed.

The sizes of grown snakes are some of the most varied in all of the animal world. The smallest snake, the flower pot snake of Mexico, if full grown at a mere four inches. In contrast, the largest of the snakes, the reticulated python, can exceed thirty feet in length.

Long before reaching full size, however, a snake will have reached sexual maturity. During breeding season male snakes hunt down and court the females of the species. This courtship can be anything from mock combat with other males to elaborate dances. After copulation, the male snake is on his way, possibly to breed with another female. Outside of breeding, almost all snakes are solitary creatures. While some snakes do indeed live near each other or even den together, this is not a social function as much as it is the snakes sharing prime territory.

The Venom and Constriction of Snakes

While only three of the families of snakes actually possess venom, there are many varied functions of venom, and almost as many ways to deliver it. It was once thought that only a few types of venom existed, each belonging to a certain group of snakes. However, we now know that there are almost ten different compounds of snake venom, and while the effects may look similar on the surface, each type of snake's venom is different. Depending on the venom injected, a long list of symptoms may occur. Some of these are swelling, hemorrhaging, the breaking down of the nervous system, and the necrosis, or death, of tissue. Do remember, however, that snakes only attack when they feel threatened. First and foremost, venom is for catching food. Generally speaking, there are two types of snake venom — hemotoxins, which attack the blood, and neurotoxins, which attack the nervous system. (Cobras use neurotoxin.)

All of the snakes in the Viperidae family are venomous, and have one of the most recognized means of delivery. When you see fangs extending, these are the snakes. This is because this family's fangs are by far the largest — so large, in fact, the fangs must fold back to allow the snake to close its jaws. Larger snakes in the family have fangs that measure a full two inches. They deliver their venom with a quick strike, never grasping onto their victim. As they hit, the fangs, which are hollow, inject the venom in the same manner as a hypodermic needle. This family's venom most often attacks the circulatory system and causes swelling, inflammation, and hemorrhaging. It was once believed that this type of venom was localized in its affects, but it is now known that the localization of this venom's effects was caused by tying off the area to prevent the venom from spreading. In modern times, it is believed that the best course of action is to allow the venom to spread, so that when the antivenin is delivered, no one area has suffered the full affects of the venom.

Once again with the Elapidae family, you have a family that is completely venomous. Snakes in this family do have distinct fangs in the front, but they are much shorter and do not need to be folded back when the mouth is closed. When a snake of this family wishes to inject its venom, it must actually clamp onto its victim. As this venom spreads throughout the body, it most commonly attacks and breaks down the nervous system of the victim. Some snakes in this family have specialized fangs that allow them to spit their venom from a distance. This is done as a defensive maneuver only, and is designed to target the eyes of its attacker.

This attack is highly accurate, and can cause permanent blindness in the victims.

Last of the venomous families, we come to the Colubridae family. While most of the snakes in this family are harmless, some of these snakes are indeed venomous. However, they do deliver it in a different enough manner that it deserves mention. These snakes have fangs in the rear of their mouths and must chew their venom into the wound for it to have an effect.

Snake Warning Systems

Snakes have a wide variety of ways to ward off and trick predators. Some of these defenses are common throughout the animal world, while others are specific to the snakes alone. Snakes use two types of warnings, audible and visual.

One of the most common visual ways to fool a predator is to mimic an animal that is dangerous to it. A perfect example of this lies with the eastern coral snake from the southern mid-west. This highly venomous snake's bright black-yellow-red-yellow pattern warns other animals of its toxicity. Numerous harmless snakes in the area have developed similar, yet slightly different, patterns. It's still subject to debate whether or not mimicry is the actual reason for these similarities between non-venomous and venomous snakes, but it certainly seems to work. This variance gave rise to the rhyme "Red on yellow, kill a fellow; red on black, friend of Jack" — only the coral snake has the red to yellow color connection. The hog nosed snake uses another unusual defense. When threatened, the hog nosed snake will puff up and hiss loudly. If this trick does not work, it will flop over, open its mouth, and pretend to be dead. While making itself defenseless may seem ineffective, some predators won't scavenge, so this defense actually works quite well.

The most recognized of a snake's visual defenses are known as neck displays. While this ability is often accredited to the cobra, other snakes have the capacity to do so as well. When a snake expands its neck in such a way, it is either done horizontally or vertically. However, a snake will only have the ability to do one or the other, not both. The most impressive of these displays is that of the cobra. No image is so commonly connected to snakes as the defensive display of an open cobra hood. However, most people misunderstand the full usage of a cobra's hood. While yes, a cobra does indeed use its hood to threaten attackers that it is facing, there is good reason to believe that it is used to ward off attacks from behind as well. If you look at a picture of a cobra hood from the front and then the rear, you will notice that the markings are far more distinct from behind the snake. These markings look similar to a pair of eyes or a face. This is used as a defense in other species to make predators believe the prey is far bigger than it is, or that it is even a different animal. Another often-unknown fact is that cobras often lean their heads forward, displaying their hood markings to the sky. This is believed to ward off airborne attackers.

Snakes use two audible warnings to ward off predators. The most common is the hiss, a simple defense used by exhaling. However, more distinctive is the rattle of the rattlesnake. The end of a rattlesnake's tail is made up of thick, hollow scales the snake shakes when agitated. As the scales hit each other, they produce the distinctive rattle. This noise can be heard for quite some distance, and is unmistakable. As the rattlesnake grows older and sheds, new rattles develop. It is assumed that you can count the number of sheds a rattlesnake has had my the number of rattles on its tail, but as rattles fall off and wear off through time and use, the number of rattles only reveals the minimum number of sheds the snake has had. Since this defense is so distinct and effective, some harmless snakes such as cornsnakes that live in the same area have learned to rattle their tails in the grass or leaves around them to mimic the noise of the rattle. the sound is different enough that someone with experience can tell the difference, but is convincing enough to fool most predators.

The King Cobra

Since the Nagah's original breeding stock is the king cobra, this snake deserves some specific attention. One of the most unknown facts about the king cobra is that it is an arboreal snake. This snake is commonly depicted on the ground, though in all cases, it is a tree dweller. Another virtually unknown fact about the king cobra is that its diet is almost exclusively other reptiles. Since it is often seen on nature shows fighting with mongoose, it is assumed that these snakes dine upon mammals, when, in actuality, mammals dine upon them. Surprisingly, though an arboreal snake, the king cobra is the largest venomous snake in the world, the largest ever recorded topping off at an impressive eighteen and a half feet.

No discussion about the king cobra would be complete without touching on snake charmers. Not surprisingly, what you are told is happening and what is actually happening in a snake charmers act are quite different. If you were to believe the act, the cobra falls into a trance, due to the hypnotic melodies and rhythmic movements of the snake charmer. While a snake charmer may indeed play a good tune, it is highly unlikely that the cobra is put into a trance by the music. Like all snakes, a cobra is totally deaf. In actuality, the cobra feels threatened by its "charmer," and is waiting for the right moment to strike out in defense. However, as long as the snake charmer keeps moving, the cobra holds back its strike, and the show goes on.

Rattlesnakes

One of the most recognized of all venomous snakes in the world, and the best distributed throughout the United States, is the rattlesnake. Found only in the New World, this snake, from the Viperidae family, is the most likely candidate for Nagah to breed with in the US. Rattlesnake territory extends from the far north in America, down into Central America. These snakes can be found in every environment, from the tropical, to temperate. The largest of the rattlers, the eastern diamondback, can reach up to seven feet. At the opposite end of the spectrum, some pigmy rattlers stop growing at a foot and a half. All rattlesnakes have strong enough venom to kill a human, though only the most venomous, such as the Mojave rattlesnake, are dangerous enough to kill a healthy adult quickly. These snakes are almost always heavy bodied and terrestrial, though some are slightly arboreal.

Other Unusual Snake Facts

• Snakes in the Boidae family have spurs that are possibly the remnants of back legs. These spurs are much larger in males so that they may use them in courtship.

• Venomous snakes may choose whether to inject venom or not when they bite. Bites without venom are often called "dry" bites.

• Australia is the only country that has more venomous snakes than constrictors. It is also home to some of the world's most venomous snakes, as anyone who's seen the Crocodile Hunter show already knows.

• The idea for the heat-seeking missile came from the thermoreceptive pits of vipers.

• There is a temple in Malaysia that is home to the Wagler's viper, a viper so docile, visitors feel safe enough that they handle them regularly.

• Some snakes can sense a temperature change as slight as 0.003 a degree from up to ten feet away.

Rattlesnakes Round-Ups

Rattlesnake round-ups are a common pastime and "sport" in the southern US, primarily in Texas. In these round-ups, local people go out in the wild and catch rattlesnakes by the thousands, they are then brought, *en masse*, to a central location, and placed in holding pens.

Often times, snakes die because they are piled so high in their pens, that the ones on the bottom are crushed to death. The remaining snakes are then used in games, one of which involves dumping a dozen snakes into a ring with the contestant, and seeing how fast they all can be caught. At the end of the round-up, which often lasts more than one day, they remaining snakes are either eaten or just outright killed. Do keep in mind that the count of rattlesnake bites each year includes those foolish enough to participate in the round-up.

Pets

Having said all that I have about the dangers of snakes, some of you may wonder why anyone would keep a snake as a pet. While all snakes are wild animals, and domestication is a ways off, if even possible, some breeds are quite docile, and make excellent pets. Your author recommends corn snakes or rat snakes as a beginner's snake, as they are hardy, usually docile, and stay a maintainable size. Please, please, please do some reading to learn what would be expected of you beforehand, though; no pet deserves an owner who isn't prepared to take care of it!

Bibliography

Obviously, the above information is only the basics of what there is to know about snakes. I have spent years learning about reptiles and have only just scratched the surface. There are far too many books in my reference library to name them all here, so I will only name the books I actually pulled of the shelves to do research.

Snakes, by David Badger

The Worlds Most Spectacular Reptiles and Amphibians by William W. Lamar, with contributing author William B. Love

A-Z of Keeping Snakes by Chris Mattison

Snake by Chris Mattison

The Encyclopedia of Snakes, once again by Chris Mattison

Reptiles Magazine, various

Vivarium Magazine, various

Acknowledgment

This chapter would not have been possible without the help of my friend and colleague Donnie Schladt. His reptile knowledge and experience was vital for more than one part of this chapter.

Nagah™

Name: **Breed:**   **Nest:**
Player: **Auspice:**   **Crown:**
Chronicle: **Kin Species:**   **Concept:**

Attributes

Physical
Strength ●OOOO
Dexterity ●OOOO
Stamina ●OOOO

Social
Charisma ●OOOO
Manipulation ●OOOO
Appearance ●OOOO

Mental
Perception ●OOOO
Intelligence ●OOOO
Wits ●OOOO

Abilities

Talents
Alertness OOOOO
Athletics OOOOO
Brawl OOOOO
Dodge OOOOO
Empathy OOOOO
Expression OOOOO
Intimidation OOOOO
Primal-Urge OOOOO
Streetwise OOOOO
Subterfuge OOOOO

Skills
Animal Ken OOOOO
Crafts OOOOO
Drive OOOOO
Etiquette OOOOO
Firearms OOOOO
Leadership OOOOO
Melee OOOOO
Performance OOOOO
Stealth OOOOO
Survival OOOOO

Knowledges
Computer OOOOO
Enigmas OOOOO
Investigation OOOOO
Law OOOOO
Linguistics OOOOO
Medicine OOOOO
Occult OOOOO
Politics OOOOO
Rituals OOOOO
Science OOOOO

Advantages

Gifts

_____
_____
_____
_____
_____
_____

Gifts

_____
_____
_____
_____
_____
_____

Gifts

_____
_____
_____
_____
_____
_____

Backgrounds
_____ OOOOO
_____ OOOOO
_____ OOOOO
_____ OOOOO
_____ OOOOO
_____ OOOOO
_____ OOOOO

Rank

Rage
O O O O O O O O O O
☐ ☐ ☐ ☐ ☐ ☐ ☐ ☐ ☐ ☐

Gnosis
O O O O O O O O O O
☐ ☐ ☐ ☐ ☐ ☐ ☐ ☐ ☐ ☐

Willpower
O O O O O O O O O O
☐ ☐ ☐ ☐ ☐ ☐ ☐ ☐ ☐ ☐

Health
Bruised		☐
Hurt	-1	☐
Injured	-1	☐
Wounded	-2	☐
Mauled	-2	☐
Crippled	-5	☐
Incapacitated		☐

Experience

NAGAH

Balaram
No Change

Difficulty: 6

Silkaram
Strength (+2)____
Stamina (+2)____
Appearance (-2)____
Manipulation (-2)____
Bite (Str); Claw (Str)

Difficulty: 7

Azhi Dahaka
Strength (+3)_____
Dexterity (+2)____
Stamina (+3)____
Appearance 0
Manipulation (-3)
Bite (Str+1); Claw (Str+1)
Constriction

Difficulty: 6

INCITE DELIRIUM IN HUMANS

Kali Dahaka
Strength (+2)____
Dexterity (+2)___
Stamina (+2)____
Appearance 0
Manipulation 0
Bite (Str+1); Claw (Str)
Constriction

Difficulty: 7

Vasuki
Strength (-1)____
Dexterity (+2)___
Stamina (+1)____
Manipulation 0
Bite (Str+1)

Difficulty: 6

Other Traits

_____ OOOOO
_____ OOOOO
_____ OOOOO
_____ OOOOO
_____ OOOOO
_____ OOOOO
_____ OOOOO
_____ OOOOO
_____ OOOOO
_____ OOOOO
_____ OOOOO
_____ OOOOO
_____ OOOOO
_____ OOOOO
_____ OOOOO
_____ OOOOO
_____ OOOOO
_____ OOOOO
_____ OOOOO

Fetishes

Item:_____ Level____ Gnosis____
    Power:_____
Item:_____ Level____ Gnosis____
    Power:_____
Item:_____ Level____ Gnosis____
    Power:_____
Item:_____ Level____ Gnosis____
    Power:_____

Samskara

_____
_____
_____
_____
_____
_____
_____
_____
_____
_____

Combat

Maneuver/Weapon	Roll	Difficulty	Damage	Range	Rate	Clip

Brawling Chart

Maneuver	Roll	Diff	Damage
Bite	Dex+Brawl	5	See Above/A
Body Tackle	Dex+Brawl	7	Special/B
Claw	Dex+Brawl	6	See Above/A
Grapple	Dex+Brawl	6	Strength/B
Kick	Dex+Brawl	7	Strength+1/B
Punch	Dex+Brawl	6	Strength/B

A=Aggravated Damage
B=Bashing Damage

Armor:_____

NAGAH™

Nature: _____   **Demeanor:** _____

Merits & Flaws

Merit	Type	Cost	Flaw	Type	Bonus
_____	_____	_____	_____	_____	_____
_____	_____	_____	_____	_____	_____
_____	_____	_____	_____	_____	_____
_____	_____	_____	_____	_____	_____
_____	_____	_____	_____	_____	_____
_____	_____	_____	_____	_____	_____
_____	_____	_____	_____	_____	_____

Expanded Background

Ananta
_____
_____
_____
_____

Ancestors
_____
_____
_____

Contacts
_____
_____
_____
_____

Kinfolk
_____
_____
_____
_____

Pure Breed
_____
_____
_____

Resources
_____
_____
_____
_____

Possessions

Gear (Carried):_____
_____
_____

Equipment (Owned):_____
_____
_____
_____

Experience

TOTAL:_____
Gained From:_____
_____
_____
_____
_____
_____

TOTAL SPENT:_____
Spent On:_____
_____
_____

NAGAH™

History
Prelude

_____
_____
_____
_____
_____
_____
_____
_____
_____
_____
_____
_____

Description

Age:_____   _____
Hair:_____   _____
Eyes:_____   _____
Race:_____   _____
Nationality:_____   _____
Sex:_____   _____

	Height	Weight
Balaram:		
Silkaram:		
Azhi Dahaka:		
Kali Dahaka:		
Vasuki:		

Battle Scars: _____
_____
_____

Visuals

Nest Chart   ### Character Sketch